THEN SINGS MY SOUL

Anna Christian

Dadielte Production
Moreno Valley, Ca.

LCCN: 2015905038
ISBN-978-0-9799273-2-4

Published and distributed by
Dadielte Production
P.O. Box 1266
Moreno Valley, CA. 92556-1266

First Printing,
Cover design by marcSierre' Design

This book is dedicated to Richard O. Jones, author, poet, playwright, comedian and friend who encouraged me, inspired me, and always made me laugh. Here's to you, Richard.

<u>Books by the Author</u>
Daniel's Wife
The Newcomer
Mrs. Griffin is Missing and Other Stories
The Big Table
Meet it, Greet it, and Defeat it! The Biography of
        Frances E. Williams, Actress/Activist

1

Tricia

I was standing in the center of this huge stage like at the Apollo Theater; the dark velvet curtains behind me were closed. It was just me, out there alone. The spotlight was glaring in my face so I couldn't see the audience, but I knew the place was packed. The applause almost blew me away. I felt so proud. I bowed and threw a kiss as I ran towards the wings. I felt as if I'd won a million dollars, but I was tired, so very tired. All I wanted to do was sleep.

In the distance I heard this faint sound of a bell and feet shuffling. Somebody tapped me on the shoulder; somebody was laughing as I shifted my body. Slowly, I raised my head.

Damn, I thought, not again.

The classroom was almost empty except for Mrs. Stern, my English teacher, who sat at her desk grading a stack of papers.

"Don't you get enough sleep at night, Miss Porter?" Mrs. Stern's voice sounded harsh. A short stocky woman, who wore thick sweaters and polyester pants in her always-cold room, glared at me.

"I'm sorry," I said as I picked up my books and hurried to the door. "I didn't realize how tired I was. It won't happen again, I promise."

"Just a moment. I'd like to speak to you."

I glanced at my watch. It was three o'clock and school was over for the day. I had a rehearsal in the evening and a lot to do before going.

"You'd better start staying awake. Your grades are going down," she said, staring at me like I was something she ate that didn't agree with her.

"I know, Mrs. Stern." I looked down at my long fingernails. They needed to be filed and polished. I wondered if I'd have time this evening.

"You're missing several homework assignments, and you've hardly turned in any class assignments." She flipped the pages of her grade book. "You're a senior. This is not the time to slack off unless you don't intend to graduate.

I glanced down at my watch again and then at Mrs. Stern. "I'll get everything caught up before the end of the semester."

"Just like that, huh!   Every year you students think you can goof up all year long and then, just before school ends, make it all up. Well! It doesn't work that way in my class. Either you do the work now or you fail. Is that clear?"

I nodded impatiently. I knew she was right and I did want to graduate "Is that all? Can I go now?"
She turned back to her papers dismissing me with a wave of her hand. Thank goodness. I rushed down the steps, out of the building and across the quad.

I made it to the corner just in time to catch the RTD home. The bus prodded along, stopping at every other corner to take on more and more passengers. One advantage of leaving school late was I didn't have to ride with all the other rowdy kids coming from Truman High. I couldn't stand their juvenile behavior.

"Move to the rear of the bus. Plenty of seats in the rear," the burley bus driver yelled as the people standing shifted barely an inch. One skinny lady squeezed through the wall of bodies and found a seat beside a sweating man who was asleep. His head kept bumping against the window. I stifled a laugh

Finding a window seat in the back, I watched the houses go by. My part of the song we would be rehearsing tonight jumped into my head. It was a tricky arrangement. Since I've always had a good ear, I didn't have much trouble learning it. Singing backup for a local artist was fun though I would love to sing backup for somebody like Whitney Houston or Mariah Carey. Now wouldn't that be something? Better yet, what I really wanted to do was sing solo and maybe someday I would.

The bus stopped on the corner of La Brea and 56th. I hopped off feeling free and easy. It was a beautiful spring day and if I was a little kid, I'd skip all the way home. The block was empty except for a few children riding their tricycles along the sidewalk and the man across the street who mowed his lawn like he loved his grass more than his wife who scowled at him from behind the window. Every day he mowed it. And if he wasn't doing that he was down on his knees searching for weeds or planting flowers.

When I reached our building, I climbed the steps up to our apartment. After putting the key into the lock, I pushed open the door. "Shanell, I'm home," I called as I threw my purse and backpack down and walked into the living room.

2

Tricia

My baby sister Shanell was fourteen years old trying to be twenty. All skin and bones, 5'1, shoulder length brown hair that she kept in a ponytail, light brown eyes and honey complexion. Cute. She was at that awkward stage, half way between playing Barbie dolls and playing with boys. She was smart, much smarter than I was when I was her age but she didn't half try to get good grades. But who was I to talk.

At one time, I could get Shanell to do anything I wanted her to do like give me her allowance, or do my chores, and she'd do them without question. Whatever I'd tell her, she believed. It was really funny. Now that she thinks she's grown we barely get through a day without arguing.

I stopped in my tracks, a cold feeling washing over me. Shanell leaped up quickly grabbing the front of her blouse.

A young boy about the same age smiled sheepishly up at me.

"I...," Shanell stuttered. "This is Johnny, Johnny, my sister."

A little taller than her, Johnny had a dark brown complexion and light gray eyes that seemed to sparkle. His hair was cut in the latest fashion with lines going every which a way, like Sinbad, the comedian. Johnny wore a white Fubu tee shirt, stone washed jeans and Nikes. He jumped up, not meeting my stare. "Nice to meet ya," he said and shook my hand as he picked up his backpack. At least he had manners. "Nell, I gotta go. I'll see you tomorrow in class."

He was gone before I could say a word.

I looked at Shanell, my anger rising. Then I noticed she had on one of my best blouses. Her eyes avoided mine as she gathered up her books and straightened the covers on the couch. When she moved to leave, I blocked her way.

"I know what you're thinking but we was just studying." She pushed past me brushing against my shoulder.

"I'm not gonna fight with you," I said. "But you better be careful. You know Momma said not to have anybody in this house when she's not home."

"So, I guess you gonna tell?" Shanell stood with her hands on her hips like she was ready to fight me.

I put my hands on my hips, not giving an inch. I looked down at her. "No, I'm not gonna tell. But if I come home and find him or any other boy with you alone, you're gonna wish I hadn't." My voice rose to meet Shanell's challenge. "And another thing. Take off my blouse! You got your own clothes."

Shanell unbuttoned the blouse, threw it at me, and stormed out of the room slamming her bedroom door. I sank down on the recliner, tears filling my eyes. 'I will not cry,' I told myself. My relationship with Shanell had gone down the drain since she reached her teens. We were drifting farther and farther apart. I tried to think back to when I was her age. Was I like her when I turned fourteen? Always ready to fight, always arguing? I didn't think so. I knew I needed to talk to her about boys and sex. Momma never seemed to have time. She didn't like to discuss things like that. Every time I tried to say anything to my sister, she'd get mad and start to argue.

After changing my clothes, I went into the kitchen and started dinner. Momma would be home at five and I knew she'd be tired. She had school that evening so she wouldn't have time to talk. I had rehearsal too, so Shanell would be alone again tonight. I would take her to rehearsals, but she wasn't interested in my singing career. If she did come, she'd spend the time grumbling and complaining.

Momma came home at 5:30, took off her shoes, threw her briefcase and purse on the coffee table and sank into the living room chair.

"Shanell, get me a glass of water," she yelled.

I sat on the arm of her chair. The smell of Momma's L'air Du Temps perfume filled my nostrils. "How was work?" I asked.

She shrugged. "Oh, it's okay - the same thing everyday." She looked up at me. "How was school? You keeping up your grades?"

"Yeah," I lied, hoping she wouldn't ask me more questions. I promised myself I'd do better.

"Where is that girl? Shanell, you hear me calling you?"

"I got rehearsal tonight," I said.

"Tricia, you know I don't like you going out on a school night."

"I'll be home by nine."

"You be careful. You may think you're grown, but you're still only seventeen."

Momma never discouraged me in most anything I wanted to do as long as it wouldn't harm me or anybody else. She said when she was growing up her mother always criticized her, made her feel like she couldn't do anything. She was determined not to raise her daughters that way.

Shanell came in all gloomy with a glass of water filled with ice. She handed it to Momma and turned to leave. Momma looked at her and then at me.

"What's the matter with you two? Looking so moody. You've been fighting again?"

A pleading look on her face, Shanell's eyes met mine. I could see she didn't want me to tell Momma about Johnny.

" No," I answered. "She took one of my blouses and wore it to school without telling me. That's all."

Shanell sighed. She went over to Momma and sat down at her feet. Momma stroked her hair. "How many times I got to tell you, honey. You got your own clothes. Leave you sister's alone."

"I didn't get it dirty or nothing. I just borrowed it to wear with my green skirt. Tricia, you can borrow my clothes any time you want," she said, sliding up into Momma's lap and curling up like a baby.

"That's stupid!" I said. "Now why would I want to wear your clothes?"

"Hush!" Momma gently pushed Shanell to the floor. "You're too big for this. Get up now. Go do your homework and let me rest for a minute."

I started walking to the kitchen, glancing over my shoulder at her and Momma. She stood behind the chair kneading Momma's shoulders. I shook my head. My sister was a stone manipulator.

3

∾

Tricia

After dinner, Momma hurried out to school. She was in her second term at the University of Phoenix, taking evening classes to earn a degree in accounting. Her dream was to get her C.P.A. and open her own office. At the moment, though, she worked as a bookkeeper in the accounts department for Vincent Aircraft Manufacturers, a large firm that depended on government contracts. Lately, with contracts being awarded to other companies, Vincent started cutting back on their staff. Momma said rumors were flying as to who would be the next to go. This made working there stressful.

Momma talked to me about it because she said since I was the oldest, I should know what was going on and be prepared for whatever happens. So I was aware of the pressure on Momma and tried to do all I could to make home life as pleasant as possible even if it meant hiding my own and Shanell's problems from her.

"I'm going to the studio," I said as I combed my hair back into a French twist and put on some lipstick. "Do you want to come with me?"

Shanell looked up from her books. "Do I look like I want to go?"

"I just thought maybe you'd like to. Anyway, I won't be too long. You know where to reach me if you need to." I headed for the door. "Oh, if Darien calls, tell him to pick me up at the studio."

She didn't answer.

I jogged to the bus stop. It was a warm evening; looking up I could see a few stars in the sky though the streetlights hid most of them. Down the street I saw the bus lumbering in the distance like a tired old man, swaying from one side to the other. If the bus didn't stop at every corner, maybe I'd only be a few minutes late.

The studio was on Hollywood Blvd. in an old building that looked like it was built before the flood. Wide marble stairs led up to a long narrow hallway on the upper floor. Whenever I walked up and down those stairs, I imagined what it would be like to be a movie star with my adoring fans, waiting to greet me and ask for my autograph. The steps had seen better days. They were dirty and in need of a good scrubbing. The studio was on the second floor. Fluorescent bulbs along the high ceiling didn't do much to brighten the cold hallway. Some of the lights flickered off and on as I rushed along. On each side of the hall were wooden doors with numbers stenciled on them; a few had name plates fastened to them. Nobody I recognized. Most of the offices were probably vacant. Harry, our manager, a hustler if there ever was one, rented the studio for us to rehearse.

When I got to the door marked "Markum's Studio," I pushed it open and stepped inside. The studio wasn't very big. A medium size room with a piano in one corner, three mikes set up in the middle, a couple of folding chairs, and a partition separating the control room from the main room. It was kind of drab looking; one spotlight lit up the center area where we rehearsed, leaving the rest of the room in shadows. This wasn't the kind of place you could relax in.

Gracie stood beside the piano following Kanisha as she played the melody of our newest tune. She looked up and waved.

Gracie was twenty-six, plain looking with medium brown complexion and light green eyes that stopped people in their tracks because not many would expect a black person to have green eyes. I liked Gracie. She was a little on the chubby side and all the time in a good mood; she never put people down. She liked to tell jokes she heard from work. Only when she told them, she usually botched them up and that made them funnier. Gracie worked the day shift in a bar on Western. We met when we were members of Bethel Baptist Church choir.

We became good friends even though she was nine years older than me. Don't mean to judge as Momma always said, but Gracie was kinda wishy-washy; I mean we couldn't always count on her. She told me once that she was just as committed to becoming a professional singer as I was. She also said that as soon as she made enough money, she was going see her son who was living with her aunt in South Carolina. She hadn't seen him in five years. We never knew when she was gonna up and leave us high and dry.

Gracie had a great laugh. When she laughed everybody around her would start laughing even though they didn't know the reason. She had a good voice and though not a lead voice, nobody could harmonize like her.

When I came in, Kanisha, the other part of our trio, grunted like she usually did, a permanent scowl on her face. A serious, almost hard looking lady, Kanisha was the type who didn't take no stuff from nobody. She and Gracie were around the same age, maybe a little older. The total opposite of Gracie, she was close to 6 feet, and all skin and bones like somebody from one of those poor third world countries. Practically bald because she had cut almost all of her hair off, she wore long dangling earrings, a nose ring and rings on all her fingers. She dressed in dark tee shirts, black pants and combat boots even when we performed.

The woman had an attitude problem. We didn't get along so well. In fact, if it wasn't for singing, we probably wouldn't ever speak to each other even if we were the last two people on earth. Not that I have anything against her; it was just that she was one of those negative people; always ready to start an argument over the smallest thing. Kanisha smoked weed and did other drugs whenever she could get her hands on them. From time to time, I knew she sold drugs, small time though. But she wasn't hooked or at least I didn't think so and as long as she didn't push anything on me, I didn't care.

Gracie told me once that Kanisha was a whiz on the typewriter. Whenever she felt like it, she worked off and on for a temporary agency. Her main love though was writing songs. She composed and played the piano like she typed. The other good thing I could say about her was that she had a good voice and the three of us together were dynamite.

"bout time you showed up. You know we gotta be outta here by nine," Kanisha said pushing me into a dark mood. If I didn't care about singing, I woulda took off a long time ago. I didn't need nobody jumping on me. But I wasn't in the mood for a fight so I held my peace.

We worked on a new number for about an hour. For some reason, I couldn't get into it and I told Gracie. She helped me through my part and I felt better since we had a gig this weekend. I'd use the money from it to pay for a dress I had my eye on at Marshalls.

Our career was still in its early stages though we'd been singing together for a little over a year. When we started out, we sang at whatever functions popped up, every chance we got—singing contests, and local festivals. Then, some months back through some connection Kanisha had, we started singing backup in recording studios. It was fun, but hard work. Kanisha wrote fantastic songs. Though we hadn't gotten a chance to record anything she wrote for us, we were always hoping. Her reputation as a songwriter was growing, and so was our reputation as a group. She was the one who got us a manager. Harry was an okay manager as far as that goes. I knew he was making money off of us, but we let that slide as long as he got us paying gigs singing backup.

4

&

Tricia

"You want a ride home?" Gracie asked as we ended for the night. We walked downstairs together. The cool air felt good after that stuffy studio. Everybody smoked but me and by the time we finished I felt like I'd smoked a pack of cigarettes.

"No thanks. Darien's supposed to pick me up." I expected him to be at the curb waiting but he wasn't. The boulevard was jammed packed with cars and strange people, a lot of them into heavy metal with powdered white faces, black tee shirts with Iron Maiden or Ozzy Osborn decals on their chests, death head medallions around their necks, and black tights.

"I'd wait with you but I gotta get home by ten. I don't wanna miss seeing this jamming movie coming on. You be careful of these weirdoes. There's a full moon out tonight." Gracie swished down the street. I watched until she disappeared through a long line of people waiting to get into the movie theater.

Where's Darien? I searched the traffic for his blue Datsun 280Z. Usually he'd be at the curb waiting for me when I came out of the studio. Darien's my boyfriend. I called him Mr. Love, not because we did anything stronger than kiss, but because he made me feel loved, like I was special. Though we'd been dating for a few months, I was still a virgin. I knew it was old fashion these days to be a virgin, but I believed in waiting for marriage. Besides, I wanted to make it in the music industry and if I had a kid, I knew I couldn't do both. And I wouldn't give up my dream even for him.

I met him at a party I went to six months ago with Suni, my girlfriend from Compton. She was the type who couldn't walk three feet down the street without getting hit on by some guy. Not that she was pretty or nothing. She just had a look that guys were attracted to. And talk about promiscuous! (I learned that word from one of Oprah's shows), for Suni, hopping into bed with guys she just met was as normal as brushing her teeth. She invited me to a party thrown by some guy she knew. At first I didn't want to go, but she talked me into it. So I put on my dark blue dress and high heel pumps, and made myself look at least twenty. I had to slip out of the apartment before Momma saw me, or she would have grounded me. Anyway, I went and now I'm glad I did because that's where I met Darien.

When this tall, handsome brother walked over to us and sat down, I thought for sure he was interested in Suni. So did she because she started flirting with him right away.   But when he asked me to dance instead of her, I was so shocked I couldn't hardly say anything.

He looked a bit older than most of the guys there. Actually, he was the most finest thing in the room. He had a neatly trimmed mustache and goatee. His wavy hair was cut short.   He looked like a movie star; at least I thought so. Unlike the other guys, he wore a suit jacket, over a gray cashmere sweater, and dark brown slacks. The other guys wore oversize jeans, tee shirts with names of basketball and football teams and name brand sneakers. Most of them sported gold chains around their necks and Kangol caps, which they didn't bother to remove. When he held me close and I smelled his Paco Rabanne aftershave lotion, my head began to swim.

He asked me my name. "Tricia," I said. He said his name was Darien. His voice was sexy and nearly as deep as Barry White's. I figured he must be at least twenty. I hoped I looked older than the other girls there. I know I was dressed differently. Most of them wore short, tight dresses showing too much skin on both ends and cheap looking weaves. My hair was permed. I'd just gotten it done a little over a week ago. Usually I wore my hair in a ponytail, but that night I had it in a French twist.

After that one dance, though, he disappeared - just up and left without saying a word. I guess I couldn't blame him for leaving. Most of the guys at the party were real deadbeats who seemed more interested in drinking and whatever else they were doing in the kitchen, dropping lines on the few girls there - the same line over and over again. "Where have you been all my life? Heaven musta sent an angel like you."

This one guy tried to talk to me. I told him where to go. No sooner did I turn my head did he hand that same line to Suni! Now I was sitting right next to her; can you believe it? She fell for it. Next thing I knew she was on the floor slow dancing with him, letting him feel her up. Then she came up to me and said, "Call you tomorrow," and left with him! Luckily I had my bus pass.

So anyway, I didn't think about Darien until one day Shanell and me went into Music, Music. She had some extra money and wanted me to help her pick out a CD. Who should ring up our sales but Darien! And he remembered me right off.

"You're the one in the dress with all those zippers and the shapely legs," he said smiling at me like we were old friends. I blushed. Shanell was at the other end of the counter looking at some magazines.

"Why'd you leave the party so soon?" I asked, my smile trying to match his. I wished I had worn a dress instead of my old torn jeans and raggedy tee shirt.

"I'm not one for parties. I only told my buddy I'd drop in and when I saw all those guys standing around, I felt even less like staying."

"Excuse me!" the man behind me cleared his throat. "Are you done? I can't stand here all day waiting while you two get acquainted."

"You don't have to be rude," Darien returned. He took the man's purchase and rang it up. I moved over to the magazine rack and waited. A line had formed. He hustled them through, smiling at each one, really being a good salesman. When his line was empty, I went back to his counter. He apologized for the man and asked for my phone number. "Can I call you later when I get off?" And sure enough he did. The rest was history.

"Say Baby, can I talk to you?" This ugly looking guy called me from the other side of the street. I started wishing I had gone along with Gracie. Hollywood Blvd. was not the best place to be by yourself at 9:30 in the evening. Darien, I'm gonna get you for this.

Mr. Ugly came over and I could see he was high. I braced myself for battle but his friends were right behind him. They hauled him off and apologized. Two hard looking sisters strolled by and gave me dirty looks. Long flowing wigs—one blond, the other pitch black—hung almost down to their backsides. Their low cut blouses showed more than half of their bosoms, while short tight skirts hugged their bulky frames like plastic wrap. Their high-heeled boots looked painful, and their faces had so much makeup on, they reminded me of circus clowns. One of them whispered loud enough for me to hear, something about- "working the streets,"

The other one snorted, "Hey, Jailbait, who you think you are working my corner? You betta be gone by the time I get back." They laughed.

What if the police think I'm standing here trying to pick up customers? I started to panic. Maybe I better take the bus, I decide. And just as I was walking toward the bus stop, Darien pulled up in his Mustang.

"Where're you going?" He asked, opening the door.

"Darien, I've been waiting a half hour." I got in and reached over for the seatbelt. I was mad.

"You knew I was coming. I'd never leave my Huggy Bear stranded." He leaned over and kissed me. I started to thaw.

The freeway traffic was heavy. I sat back listening to KJLH, slowly relaxing with my eyes closed. I must have fell asleep because when I woke up the car had stopped, where, but in front of his pad.

"Day, I got a test tomorrow, and I got to get home and study." I protested as he smoothly steered me into his building and up the stairs to his door.

"I promise I'll take you home in a half hour. I just want you to listen to this bad jam I picked up today." I went in reluctantly knowing I'd probably have to fight my way out again.

He lived in one of those secure apartments, the ones surrounded by iron bars. You needed a special card to get into the underground parking lot and building. There was no way to just drop in without the person you were coming to visit knowing about it. No outside bells or intercom systems. I thought it was stupid.

Darien's apartment was so neat. You'd expect a single young man to keep his place like a pigsty. At least that's what I thought. But not Darien. He was a very orderly man. His sister, who practically raised him when their parents died, used to live there, he told me, but moved out when she got married and left the place to him. Luckily the landlord didn't raise the rent. He told Darien he wouldn't if he would do a little maintenance wherever needed for the other tenants. And thanks to his job at Music Music, he was in good shape moneywise and everything else.

There was nothing fancy about the apartment. His sister left him the furniture. A couch, dining room set, a bed, worn but comfortable, sports magazines, and a bookcase filled with books, some paintings Darien did when he was into his "artist period," whatever that is, and an expensive sound system he bought with his first month's salary.

"A half hour," he said. "Just stay a half hour and I'll drive you right to your door, I promise."

"But I was supposed to be home by nine. My mother's gonna kill me."

Darien put on a CD and before long, he had me in his arms dancing to Luther Vandross and moving me toward the couch. The man was all over me, kissing my neck, rubbing his hands all over my body. I knew this was gonna be the night I'd lose my virginity. We were breathing heavy and I felt my insides melting. I wanted him as bad as he wanted me. Then Whitney Houston began to sing "Saving all my love for you," and I knew I couldn't give in. I couldn't let it happen even if I had to lose him. I pushed him away.

"When are you gonna grow up!" he exploded. "We're living in the eighties. What's the big deal?"

"Day, you know how I feel. Why do you make me have to go through this every time we're together? I told you I got a future and I don't want to blow it."

"Blow it! Haven't you heard of the pill, condoms and all the other things they have to keep you from getting pregnant." He shook his head. "I like you a lot but baby, we can't keep going on like this. There are plenty of other girls out there who..."

Now it was my turn to explode.

"Well, you'd better go out there and find them!" I picked up my purse and started for the door. He didn't try to stop me until I got to the street. Then he came running up.

"Hold on. I'm sorry. Wait while I get my car. I'll drive you home."

I was trembling, thinking as he drove that maybe I was wrong. I knew one day he would go out and find somebody else who wasn't such a prude and then where would I be? I really didn't want to lose him.

We didn't say anything when he stopped in front of my house. There was nothing to say.

5

∾

Tricia

"Do you know what time it is?" Momma was sitting on the arm of the sofa by the window, her face lined with worry. "You were supposed to be home by 9:00. What's gotten into you? You know I don't want you out late on a weeknight."

I glanced over at her as I took off my coat. I could tell she wasn't that angry because when she gets mad, her voice gets real low. I told her Darien was late picking me up.

"How did your rehearsals go? When are you all going to start making money from all this?" She got up and began to straighten the covers on the couch. I watched as she dumped out the ashtray and cleared away the dishes—a glass and dish of half eaten strawberry pie.

"I don't know. The manager said some guy wants to hear us sing, so on the weekend, we got to go to a studio over on Venice."

"You just be careful. Those people in the music business can be pretty terrible."

I followed her into the kitchen, opened the refrigerator, took out some bologna and cheese and made myself a sandwich. My mind was on Darien. I wondered how long I'd be able to hold him off. Not that I was a goody two shoes, or anything like that. It was just that I'd seen too many of my friends and girls I used to go to school with get pregnant and have to drop out. Then the guys that they are so in love with dump them and they have to raise their babies by themselves, put the kid up for adoption or have an abortion. I knew a girl that had so many abortions she was sick all the time. And if we started having sex using protection, where would that lead? Would he still respect me or would I become like all the other girls who sleep around? I wasn't even aware that I was alone in the kitchen.

"Did Momma tell you Ma'dear is coming to live with us?" Shanell popped in interrupting my thoughts. She grabbed a pickle from my plate. I slapped her hand away.

"Ma'dear? Why? For how long?"

"That's the same thing I asked," Shanell said. "Momma said she had another stroke and can't stay by herself so she's coming to live with us until she gets better."

In my mind I saw our grandma as she looked when we last visited her in Philadelphia. I always hated going there, but Momma took us every year for two weeks. We never did anything but stay inside because Ma'dear said crime was so bad.

"Your grandmother can stay as long as she likes," Momma said coming into the kitchen.

"But where's she gonna sleep?" Both Shanell and me asked the same question. We waited for Momma to finish her glass of iced tea.

"She'll sleep in Shanell's room." Before Shanell could groan, Momma continued. "You can move your things into Tricia's room."

Now it was my turn. I didn't want to bunk with a silly fourteen year old, going through my things, leaving me no privacy. We'd shared a room since she was born, and up until a few months ago when we moved here from across town.

"I know what this will mean, but you two will just have to do the best you can. Try to get along for me and your grandmother's sake."

Shanell rolled her eyes at me and I did the same to her. I told Momma I'd do my best.

That night, my mind went over what Darien said about finding somebody else. When I finally drifted off to sleep, I dreamed about Ma'dear. Though I loved her, I couldn't help thinking about how our lives would change with her living here. It had always been just the three of us except for about a year when Momma married Donald; and now Grandma....

6

Hazel

Hazel sat at the table for a long while reading and rereading the letter. It was from her brother Melvin. Ma'dear just had another stroke and the doctors said she could no longer live alone.

"Look Sis, I tried to reach you but I couldn't. I'd take her in with Althea and me, but you know we just don't have enough room. Could you take over for a while until things straighten out between us?"

When her mother had her first stroke, Hazel had rushed to her side. But then, she got better and since she lived in a senior citizens complex, Ma'dear assured her that she wanted to stay there rather than move out to California and live with her daughter. The one time she'd been out there had been almost disastrous for Hazel. Ma'dear was always trying to tell her how to raise her children, what to do with her life, showing her disapproval when Hazel met and married Donald. She made Hazel's life miserable. But that was five years ago. They parted on a low note. Though Hazel kept regular contact with her mother, things were never the same. Then when she and Donald divorced, Ma'dear said "I told you so" and things didn't get much better.

Hazel was glad the apartment was quiet when she came in late the next evening. Both Tricia and Shanell were in bed. She kicked off her shoes, set her pocketbook on the counter, and made herself of cup of coffee. When she took out a cigarette and tried to light it, she became aware that her hands were shaking.

"You've got to come get her and let her stay with you awhile." She read the sentence again. When Ma'dear had a second stroke, Hazel hastened to Philadelphia again to get her; however, her mother was adamant. She didn't want to live with her daughter. She preferred to live with Melvin and his wife Althea. Hazel felt hurt but relieved. Since her breakup with Donald, her life was settling down. She had two lovely daughters, a good job, and finally she was able to pursue her dream; everything was falling into place. Now this.

She didn't need the headache of taking care of a person she didn't get along with and who didn't want to live with her. It was almost eleven o'clock. She sighed, there was little else she could do except fly to Philadelphia to get her mother. Since the mornings were hectic, getting the girls off to school and herself off to work, she decided she'd tell them when she came home in the evening.

The next day, Hazel sat at her desk wondering when she should go in to see her boss, Mr. Levine. Things weren't going well. Diana, her co-worker, leaned across her desk and whispered, "Did you hear the latest?" She kept up with everything going on in the building. 5'9, slender, with long red hair, Diana was very friendly with the bosses. Outgoing and flirtatious, she was liked by most of those in the office despite her association with the higher ups.

"Several people in the front office got their pink slips. The big bosses say the company is losing so much money, they have to lay off over a third of the staff. From what I heard, though, we don't have to worry. Our jobs are secure."

"Who're you kidding?" said Monica, her glasses caught the light and threw a glare across the rest of her face. "Just to be on the safe side, I'm looking around for something else. I don't need this aggravation."

Hazel watched as several managers emerged from the conference room, Mr. Levine among them. They had been in a meeting all morning long. The atmosphere around the office was filled with tension though Hazel did her best to avoid thinking about what loomed ahead. Gathering up her courage, she walked haltingly into her supervisor's office.

Looking up from his desk, he smiled his patronizing smile. "Mrs. Porter, What can I do for you?"

After she explained, he said, "We're very busy as you well know. This is a really bad time." Nevertheless, he told her, she could have two days off. Today being Wednesday, she didn't have to report to work until Monday. That would give her enough time, she hoped, to fly back east and return with her mother.

She felt relieved. Tomorrow she would leave for Philadelphia if she could get a flight. Her head filled with plans of things she must do before taking off. Lunchtime she rushed over to her bank to withdraw money for the trip. Her heart sank as she saw the dent this excursion put on her savings. The rest of the day she cleaned up as many papers on her desk that she could knowing the pile would be even higher when she returned. She had a chapter to read for her class if she could get that done. "Hell," she mumbled to herself. She needed a cigarette and maybe even a drink.

That evening she told Shanell. Tricia hadn't yet come in from her rehearsal. Singing was Tricia's passion and Hazel supported her dream. She'd had people all her life telling her how to live, discouraging her from doing the things she wanted to do so she wasn't about to lay that trip on her daughter. And besides, she always knew Tricia had talent. 'Maybe she will be a star one day,' Hazel thought. 'Maybe when she makes a lot of money, she'll buy us a home.' She laughed to herself. 'No, I just want her to be happy, to have a better life than I've had.'

The phone rang. Shanell grabbed it after the first ring.

"Momma, it's for you," she yelled from the kitchen.

Hazel reached for the extension. A deep voice sang over the wire. "Hi baby, you coming over tonight?"

"Hang up the phone, Shanell!" Hazel waited until she heard the line click.

"I can't tonight, Kevin," she whispered. His voice always thrilled her. "I've got to fly to Philadelphia to pick up my mother." She explained her mother's condition.

"What time do you have to be at the airport?" His voice was filled with concern. She told him. He offered to drive her.

Out of all the men that had paraded through her life, Kevin was the one who she could really love. He was the one she should have met in the beginning. Before Martin, before Teddy, before Donald, before all the disappointments, and the bad relationships that hardened her toward most men. At one point, she believed she needed a man to make her feel like a woman. A woman wasn't a woman without a man. That belief had led her to accept any man that walked into her life, and there had been plenty, many more than the three that had passed through and had left an indelible imprint on her. She regretted knowing Martin but not having had Tricia. Teddy was another man she could have lived without. Except for Shanell's resemblance to him, she could barely remember what he looked like.

Don't even mention Donald. That was a mistake from the first. Thank goodness she didn't get pregnant by him. He was the worst. And she'd had the nerve to marry him. It lasted less than six months and almost tore her life apart. Until Kevin came along she was beginning to feel that all men were no good. But by then she had decided that she would never allow a man to come between herself and her daughters again. Never again would she let a man run her life.

Sweet Kevin. He is what a man is supposed to be, she thought as she settled back into her seat on the plane. She cared a great deal for this dark, good-looking man with deep dimples and a crooked smile.

"If only...." She dashed the thought from her mind and looked down at the book she'd brought with her. Accounting Principles, printed in bold letters across the face. Opening it to the chapter she'd marked, she began to read.

7

Shanell

Shanell looked at her profile in the mirror. She pushed out her chest, which was already 34A, a size larger than her sister's. She smiled, pulling down the neck of her tee shirt to reveal the beginnings of cleavage. Already well developed for a young girl of fourteen, she smoothed her hands over her flat stomach and along her waist.

"Stop trying to act older than you are. You're just courting trouble," her mother had warned. She reached for the brush and began brushing her shoulder-length hair. When she piled it on top of her head, she could probably pass for sixteen or older. She brushed it over to one side...or maybe twenty. Despite her efforts, her face still looked like a girl not long into her teens, which she was. She opened

Tricia's makeup case and began to search for color. She applied foundation, lipstick, and rouge. Next she lined her eyelids and put mascara on her lashes. Satisfied, she was beginning to look older. Momma had some earrings that looked great on her. She went into her mother's room, opened her jewelry box and took out a pair of rhinestone earrings. In her mother's closet she found a tight fitting red dress, the one her mother wore when she use to go out a lot. It was too old fashion. Then she remembered the dress Tricia had bought to wear to perform in; a brand new green, sequined tee strap that barely came down to the top of her thighs and fit like a bodysuit.

Yes. She sighed with approval. 'It looks better on me than on her,' she thought. 'And with these high heel pumps—look out En Vogue, here comes Shanell!'

Standing in front of the mirror, she mimicked Gladys Knight. He's leaving, on that midnight train to Georgia, coming from the radio. Her eyes fell on the ashtray on her mother's nightstand. Opening the drawer, she took out her mother's pack of Merit, stuck a cigarette in her mouth, lit it from the lighter laying nearby, and inhaled deeply. She coughed again and again. The lit cigarette dropped from her hand and into her lap. By the time she retrieved it, a small hole was beginning to form on the dress. Shanell panicked. Dashing into the bathroom, she whipped the dress over her head and threw it into the tub, turning on the water.

Her heart beat rapidly. 'Tricia is gonna kill me." She examined the now-soaked dress. A few sequins had dropped off. The hole, though, was barely noticeable. Shanell glanced up at the clock. Tricia would be home any minute. Luckily Momma was out of town and wouldn't be back until tomorrow. She turned on the fan and held the dress up in front of it. 'It'll never be dry by the time Tricia comes home,' she thought. 'What about the dryer?'

Quickly putting back on her clothes and finding a quarter in her mother's drawer, she dashed downstairs to the laundry room. Thank goodness it was empty. She threw the dress into the dryer and inserted the quarter. The drum began to spin tossing the sequined dress from side to side sounding like a jar filled with loose change shattering the silence of the room. Instead of waiting the twenty minutes for the dryer to stop, Shanell rushed back up to the apartment and began straightening up, putting Tricia's makeup case away, hanging her mother's dress in the closet, and opening the window to get rid of the smell of cigarette smoke. Just as she finished, the door opened and Tricia walked in.

"Whatcha doing in Momma's room?" her sister asked going into her room and taking off her clothes.

"Been in Momma's makeup again? And you better take off her earrings. Girl, you can't wait to be grown." Tricia was in a good mood. Shanell glanced at herself in the mirror and saw that the mascara had smeared, as had the lipstick. The rhinestone earrings sparkled in the hall light. She dashed into the bathroom and washed her face. Hurrying back to Tricia's bedroom, she sat down on the bed and watched her sister change into shorts and tee shirt, praying that she wouldn't look into her closet and notice her new dress missing. The dress! She remembered. How to get it back without Tricia finding out?

"I'll be right back," Shanell said.

"Where are you going?" she heard Tricia call as she hastened down to the basement. The dryer had stopped and the dress lay in a heap on the bottom. She picked it up and held it up to the light. It definitely didn't look new anymore. The dress, with the small hole and the missing sequins, was not meant to be washed much less dried in a dryer; it had shrunk. Her heart sank. The dress was ruined. Tricia would never forgive her.

Shanell wrapped it into a ball, put it into a plastic bag she'd found in the trashcan, and carried it upstairs. Tricia was in the bathroom when she entered the apartment. Sneaking to her room, she opened her closet and shoved the dress in as far back as it would go, hidden behind a box of clothes Hazel intended to give to the Salvation Army someday.

"Is something the matter?" Tricia asked as she walked by Shanell's room. "You been real quiet. Are you thinking about Ma'dear coming?" Tricia sat down beside Shanell. "Well, we better start cleaning up your room to get it ready for her."

8

✍

Ma'dear

Everybody treating me like I've lost my mind. As if I can't hear or think. Oh, why did this have to happen? This is the third time. I felt it coming on especially when I had that bad headache that wouldn't go away and when I lost my sight for a little while. I should have gone to Dr. Bryant when it started happening again. But I didn't, and now all I can do is lie here like a vegetable. Can't move my right arm, can't say what I want to say. They're all around me making a fuss and treating me like I'm a child. "Melvin" I say as loud as I can. He doesn't hear me. I'm thirsty. My throat feels like a dusty road. Melvin and Hazel got their heads together, whispering. I can hear! I'm not a child!

"Does she understand what we're saying?" Hazel asks. *She looks good but her suit is too tight and too short.*

"Yeah, she does, I think. She can nod her head. The doctor says she'll get stronger with therapy. Sis. I don't know how to thank you. If you need anything, call. Now I'll just check her out, load her things into the car and drive you and Mama to the airport."

Melvin, I'm thirsty. Can I get a drink of water? Wait, don't go.

"How you feeling, Mama? It's me. Your daughter, Hazel. Don't you know me?"

Course I know you. Somebody get me some water.

"What is it you want? Is there something I can get you?"

Hazel was always so helpless, like I am now.

"I'd better call the nurse." *She pokes around my bed, searching for the call button.*

"How you doing, Mrs. Livingston? What can I do for you? I see you're getting ready to leave us."

"She seems to be saying something but I don't understand.

Of course you don't understand. Why do I have to go with her? Why can't I go back to my apartment or to Melvin and Althea's? Why do I have to be sent halfway across the country to a place of godless people?

"Do you want some water? Here, have a sip. You see. Look at her go. She was just thirsty."

"Nurse, How am I gonna manage when I can't understand what she wants?"

"When you've been around her a while, you'll know. She tells you. Watch her eyes. You'll catch on."

That was good. If I could just go to sleep.

"See, she's tired. She'll be okay. You'll be fine won't you, Mrs. Livingston? Mrs. Livingston? Now you be a good girl. Don't go giving your daughter no trouble."

I wish I could get up and walk right out of here. Melvin comes back. He seems anxious to get rid of me.

"The car's all packed and ready to go. Let's get her into the wheelchair."

I don't remember the trip to the airport. I don't remember even being put on the plane. Hazel stares out the window. I guess she's thinking what to do with me. I hoped they locked my apartment door. I hope Mavis remembers to come in and water my plants. Melvin said he'd take care of everything but he's never been long on memory.

It all happened so fast. I didn't get to say goodbye to Mavis, to any of the ladies in the complex or to Mr. Carter, not to anybody. Did I leave a pot burning? Seems to me I remember I was standing by the stove frying a piece of fish when I felt this sharp pain. When I woke up I was in an ambulance. Was there a fire? I remember hearing loud noises. Must have set off the alarm, like when old man Grover fell and broke his hip; he crawled over to the buzzer and pushed it and everybody came running. They really watch out for you in that building.

Why do I have to go to California? Why couldn't I go home? They could have gotten a nurse to look after me, one of those homecare workers. My children, always doing things half ass. Going to all that expense and for what? I'll be all right in a few weeks. It's a waste of money to take me all the way across country for a few weeks. Why couldn't I have just stayed with Melvin and Althea? I know they fight a lot but at least I'd be closer to home.

"Here's your dinner, ladies. Would you mind lowering your trays?"

"I'm sorry. I'm not very hungry."

What is this mess?

"I'll cut up your meat for you, Mama"

"Would you ladies like tea or coffee?"

I'll have coffee.

"She'll just have water, thank you. I'll have a scotch and soda."

9

Hazel

As the plane descended into LAX, Hazel stretched and glanced over at her sleeping mother. Ma'dear looked so frail, so weak and helpless. Unlike the strong, self-confident poised woman who raised her and her brother alone after their stepfather died. In her attempt to instill independence and discipline in her children, especially her daughter, Sarah Livingston had raised Hazel with a long arm, distant, critical, wanting to prepare her for the world so she would not be defeated. Few affectionate hugs and kisses dwelled in Hazel's memory of her mother, only words of caution, criticism and pride. The one thing Hazel was grateful to her mother for was the fact that she taught her to be proud of her heritage, something she wanted to pass on to her girls. However, somehow, with this business of living, she hadn't had time.

'Now what?' Hazel thought. 'Where do we go from here? How will I be able to manage?' She wasn't sure.

She woke her mother and with the flight attendant's help, they managed to get Ma'dear off the plane, out of the airport, and to a taxi stand.

"Are you comfortable, Ma'dear?" Hazel asked as the taxi driver wheeled into the traffic lanes on the 405 Freeway. It was almost 9 pm, yet traffic was still pretty heavy.

"You'll be surprised when you see Tricia and Shanell. They've grown since you last saw them." Hazel felt she was prattling on about nothing important. And getting no response from her mother made her chatter even more. Ma'dear stared ahead.

"You mind if I smoke? I know you don't approve, but it helps calm me down. And this trip's been so hectic." She rolled down her window as she lit a cigarette, took a deep drag and felt the smoke permeate her lungs. Her mother coughed.

"Sorry," Hazel said as she tossed the cigarette out into the night. "It's such a beautiful night, don't you think? It's been so hot lately..." Stop it! She told herself. Stop talking! She lay her head back against the seat cushion and closed her eyes letting silence fill the empty space between them.

As soon as the driver stopped in front of their apartment building, he jumped out and removed Ma'dear's suitcase from the trunk. Hazel handed him the fare along with a generous tip. Tricia and Shanell came bounding down the steps, rushed over to their grandmother hugged and kissed her cheek.

"Watch out you don't knock her down," Hazel scolded as she helped her mother over to the steps. While Tricia carried her grandmother's large suitcase up the stairs, Shanell reached for her mother's overnight case.

"Run up to Mr. Frazier's apartment and ask if he can help me get Ma'dear upstairs."

"Can she talk?" Shanell whispered to her mother. When her mother didn't answer, she reluctantly turned and went into the building.

A stocky man, Mr. Frazier lived in the downstairs apartment with his wife. Both he and his wife had a down-home friendliness that made Hazel unafraid to call on them when she needed help. In turn, Shanell fed their cat and took care of their plants whenever they went to visit their daughter and grandchildren who lived up north.

After a short while, their neighbor came down immediately and picked Ma'dear up as if she were a 5 pound sack of flour. He carried the old woman up the steps and into their apartment.

"Light as a feather," he said, depositing Ma'dear on Shanell's bed. Hazel thanked him as she walked him to the door. When she returned, Shanell and Tricia had unpacked Ma'dear's clothes, hung them up in the closet, and began helping her into her nightclothes.

"Can we get you anything to eat, Ma'dear?" asked Tricia.

Her grandmother shook her head slightly.

"Ma'dear's tired from the long trip," Hazel whispered. "Now, you all have to be quiet; don't make any unnecessary noises to disturb your grandmother," she cautioned as she shooed the girls from the room.

After turning off the overhead light and switching on the lamp on the nightstand, she moved towards the door.

"If you need anything, just call." 'That was a silly thing to say,' Hazel thought.

Tricia and Shanell were waiting in their mother's bedroom.

"How long is she going to stay with us?" Shanell asked stretching out across Hazel's bed.

"I told you, for as long as she likes." Hazel removed her dress and hung it up in the closet. She pulled on her bathrobe and tied it around her waist. Then she sat down at her dressing table and brushed out her short perm.

"Who's gonna look after her while we're at school?" asked Tricia.

Hazel hadn't thought that far. Could she afford a nurse? Her mother would need a wheelchair, therapy, so much that Hazel suddenly felt overwhelmed. Her two days of leave were up, and she was due to report to work tomorrow. No sense in asking for more days because she knew it wouldn't be granted, not with pay anyway and now with this extra burden, she couldn't afford to take time off without pay.

"Tricia, you or Shanell are going to have to stay home with Ma'dear until the end of the week so I can get things straightened out." Both girls looked at each other.

"But Mom, I'm behind in my assignments. I can't miss any days if I want to graduate."

"I can't either," Shanell jumped in. "They're having tryouts for the new play all this week and I gotta be in it."

Anger flashed in Hazel's voice. "You two had better work it out between you. One or both of you are staying home this week and that's final!"

She stormed to the bathroom and slammed the door. Take deep breaths, calm down. It'll all work out, she told herself as she stared into the mirror. Lines had begun to form around her lips and across her brow, and shadows beneath her eyes were dark from lack of sleep. For two days she'd barely rested. Sleeping on Melvin's lumpy couch had pummeled her body, leaving stiff joints and aches in places she didn't think possible. Added to this, she arose too early, spent every minute at the hospital, and ate whatever she could grab.

Everything fell on her shoulders as soon as her plane landed. Her older brother Melvin and his wife Althea seemed to be in a constant battle, arguing so much it gave Hazel a headache. She was happy to be home, but not happy to have more trouble. She felt ancient instead of thirty-five. After washing her face and brushing her teeth, she slipped into her nightgown. When she came out of the bathroom, her room was empty. Shanell was watching television in the living room; Tricia was talking on the phone, she assumed, to Darien.

"Shanell, don't stay up too late, and make sure Tricia remembers to lock up."

She tiptoed into Shanell's bedroom and peeked in at Ma'dear who was asleep. After kissing her mother's forehead, she adjusted the bedcovers, switched off the hall light, and returned to her bedroom. Diving into her comfortable bed, she gratefully sank into a deep sleep.

10

❧

Ma'dear

Willie Joe, where are you? Why ain't you here with me? Why'd you have to go and leave me? I see you standing over there in the corner. Think you slick. Trying to hide from me. I knew you'd never leave me alone.

You remember the time we danced all night at Rockland Palace, and my feet swolled up? We could really go. Hottest couple on the dance floor. That was when we first met. I remember when I first laid eyes on you. You were standing with your buddies over in the corner and I was with my girlfriend Sadie holding up the wall, waiting for somebody to ask us to dance. You came over and real gentlemanlike asked me. A Billy Eckstine song. The singer sounded so much like Billy, I swear he even looked a little like him. Oh, but dancing with you made my heart almost stop. You took us home in a cab afterwards. You were so handsome in your army uniform.

   Wait, where you going? You can't leave me now. You gotta wait 'till I'm ready. Willie Joe...wait for me....

11

❦

Tricia

"Wake up, Ma'dear. I brought you some breakfast.   I'll move these things off this table." Ma'dear looked at me as if she didn't know me.

"I'm Tricia, your granddaughter." I managed to get her to eat some of the oatmeal I made. It was like feeding a baby. I tested it first; then I pushed it into her mouth and wiped off what didn't stay in. I'd rather feed a baby; I could feel my stomach turning over. It must be hard growing old and being helpless like you're a baby only you're not. You lived your life, been married, raised children, had a home of your own, then, all of a sudden, you're like a child again.

"There. All gone. You want something else?" Ma'dear just stared. I wished I knew what she was thinking. "I'll be right back, soon as I wash these dishes."

Shanell made me so mad this morning. I was supposed to go to school and get my assignments for the rest of the week. But no, she pitched a fit. To keep the peace I said I'd stay home. I hoped when I got to school the next day, once I explained the situation, my teachers would let me make everything up, especially Mrs. Stern, my English teacher. Tonight, though, with this gig on Sat., I had to be at the studio. I didn't mind missing school, but I wasn't going to miss our rehearsal.

Darien called me last night. He asked me if I'd come over after rehearsal. I told him I couldn't. I didn't want to go through a wrestling match with him again.

I went back into Ma'dear's room; straightened up a bit. "Ma'dear, You want to watch television? I can bring my little TV in here so you can watch. Shanell and I need to be studying anyway." I brought the TV into the room and placed it on the dresser. I turned on "All My Children" and watched it a while with her. From time to time I glanced over to see if she was paying attention and she seemed to be.

"Want me to comb your hair?" Ma'dear's got fine hair, a beautiful pearl gray. When I took down the bun, her hair fell to her shoulders. "I wish I had hair like yours," I said. "My hair is coarse, and if I didn't have a perm, I'd have to keep a hot comb in it. Mama said the reason my hair doesn't grow is because I keep doing things to it. When I can afford to go to the beautician I have it permed. I like to dye it different colors. If it was like yours, I'd let it hang over my shoulders." I brushed out her hair and spread it out over her shoulders. It was soft and full. "I never seen you with your hair out. Why don't you ever wear it down?" She must have been beautiful when she was a girl. "You must've been a knockout when you were young. Huh?" She didn't say anything. I wondered if she understood me.

I spent the entire morning and afternoon trying to entertain Ma'dear. I sang one of the songs we were working on, read to her from an old Bible Momma kept in her drawer, and we watched all the soaps. I couldn't believe it. I even emptied her bedpan.

Caring for her wasn't so bad. She was nice, much nicer than she was on our last visit to her home. Then, I had made up my mind that that was the last time I'd go there. I told Momma and she said she understood. It was terrible.

At four thirty Shanell came home.

"It's about time!" I lit into her before she closed the door. "Where've you been? You were suppose to come home right after school."

"I went to drama auditions. Momma said I could." She threw her backpack on the floor and plopped down in front of the TV.

"That was before Ma'dear came. You were supposed to go to school and come right back home." Shanell didn't answer. Just went into the kitchen, pulled out the bread and the leftover roast beef.

"That's for dinner."

"So what am I suppose to eat?" She went into my room carrying her sandwich and milk.

"Oh no you don't!" I followed behind her. "Yl9ou can't eat in my room."

She threw down her plate and glass, ran into the bathroom, and slammed the door behind her.

I don't have time for this! Let her act like a spoiled child if she wanted to. I had to get ready for tonight. Gracie called and said there would be a big shot in the recording industry at the studio to listen to us. If he liked us...I didn't want to think about what that would mean.

I went into my room and started to look for something to wear. I pulled out my purple tee shirt and matching pants. The ones I bought last year when I worked part time at Kate's Boutique. They had the best clothes and didn't charge an arm and a leg for them. The owner let me put things on layaway. I bought my whole wardrobe from Kate's. I had the reputation of being the most stylish person at school.

All the girls were jealous because I never wore the same thing twice in three weeks. I wish I hadn't quit, but I needed time to rehearse.

Right now I needed to get into the bathroom and Shanell still had her little butt in there. I banged on the door. "Shanell, I need to get in there. You gonna be much longer?" She didn't answer. I banged again. I heard the toilet flush; then the water running in the sink. Finally, the door opened and Shanell came out as cool as can be. She walked past me without a word.

"You should go in and see how Ma'dear is doing. At least let her know you're home from school," I said.

"What for?" But she did. When I came out of the bathroom, Shanell was sitting by Ma'dear's bed. She'd made her a sandwich and they were both watching TV together. I shook my head wishing I could understand my sister. Sometimes she could be so frustrating, and then at other times she could be really sweet. Those times were few and far between.

I left the apartment before Momma got home. It was Shanell's turn to make dinner. All she had to do was warm up the pot roast from last night, make some mash potatoes, and heat up the spinach. I'd grab a burger from McDonald's when I got downtown.

I heard Kanisha and Gracie singing in two-part harmony as soon as I walked in. I threw my jacket on the chair and rushed across to where they were at the piano and I jumped in and we did our thing. I felt good whenever we sang, like I was floating on a cloud or riding on a wave. Singing helped me forget my problems, school, Darien, Shanell, Ma'dear. I was high on harmony. Then we got to a part calling for a solo and Kanisha tried it but it was too high for her. She handed the words to Gracie. Gracie passed it over to me. I tried it and it was just in my range.

"Girl, you sound too good," Gracie said.

"You were off key. Do it again, and this time pay attention to the piano," Kanisha said.

We went through it again. I thought it sounded even better. Not Kanisha, though. She made me do it again until I'd just about had it with her.

The door opened and in walked Harry with this middle-aged white man dressed in a three-piece gray suit, with thick gray hair slicked back looking like a used car salesman.

"Girls, I want you to meet Mr. Donovan. He's from Capital Records and he's here to listen to you sing."

"Yes, Harry has told me about you," His voice was raspy like he'd been eating sandpaper. He pulled a handkerchief out of his back pocket, blew his nose, and mopped his forehead "Now don't let me disturb you. Go right ahead with what you were doing."

Harry took him over to the side and after he sat down, Harry brought over a bottle he always kept in his briefcase and poured the man a drink in a paper cup. I felt a little nervous. Capital Records, I thought. We were on our way.

Gracie was just as excited as me. Kanisha didn't give him a second look. She lit a cigarette and began playing chords on the piano.

"This may be our chance for a recording contract," I whispered to Gracie.

"Yeah child. I can see us now. Our names in lights traveling all over the country, doing concerts, making money, that's all I want-the long green.

"You don't believe this man is really from Capital, do you? He's just another one of Harry's schemes. Else he wouldn't be drinking that cheap booze Harry keeps in his briefcase. Probably one of his bookies," Kanisha said throwing cold water on our enthusiasm. I glanced over at Harry and Mr. Donovan. They were drinking and having a good time, not paying attention to us.

"You may be wrong, Kanisha. What if he is from Capital?"

"You're too naive for words. You'd believe anything anybody tells you. Anyway. We're here to rehearse, so let's go."

"That's okay honey," Gracie patted my hand. "We'll make believe he's from the record company and sing our hearts out."

And we did. When we'd run through three or four numbers, I watched the man get up; Harry followed him to the door.

"I'll be right back, girls," Harry hollered at us and went out.

"Well, what do you think? Do you think he likes us?" Gracie was enthusiastic. "Yeah, we're in!" She reached over and we high fived.

My fingers crossed behind my back, I was all smiles and wishing. Kanisha just kept playing chords. Then she broke out into a blues tune she'd been fiddling around with lately.

"What do you think?" Gracie asked Kanisha who ignored her. "Oh, you're always so damn moody." She waved her off and ran to the door. "I'm gonna see where they went."

"What's that you're playing," I asked Kanisha. The tune was beautiful. I tried to hum the melody, but she stopped playing and glared at me. Then I wandered over to the window and looked out at the boulevard. Harry and the man were still talking on the sidewalk. A taxi pulled up and Mr. Donovan got in. After the cab disappeared down the street, Gracie rushed over to Harry. She saw me at the window and waved. Whatever he told her, I could see her shoulders slump and the light go out of her face.

They came back upstairs.

"He says he'll let us know," Harry said. He scratched his ear and reaching into his jacket pocket, he pulled out a cigarette and lit it, exhaling a cloud of smoke. "Tricia, can I see you in the hall for a moment." Surprised, I glanced over at Gracie and Kanisha. Both stared back at me. Then Kanisha began playing again. After Gracie gave me a nod, I followed Harry into the half-lit hall.

Harry was a small man. I guessed he must have been around forty-five. From what I learned from Gracie, he had always been in the business having started out singing big time with a famous group I never heard of. She said, he made a lot of money and even got a chance to sing on TV. Then Harry almost got killed in a car accident. Some of the other members of the group died. He didn't know much of anything else except the music business, so he decided to manage. From what Gracie said, he managed some other singers though I never met any.

From time to time I heard other people say he was a small time hustler. One time, we were singing at this place and he got into a big argument over what, I never found out. The guy called him something that made Harry real mad. I'd never seen him mad before but when I looked around, the man was on the floor. And the man was a lot bigger than Harry. Gracie said we needed him. Harry protected us. A lot of people in the music business would take advantage of us, beat us out of money and steal our material. He got us some jobs and collected ten percent of what little we made. On the side, I suspected he had some shady dealings, else how could he manage to live on the little he got from us.

Harry turned to face me when we were in the hall.

"Look Tricia. Donovan is only interested in you. He says you got real talent and he wants you to call him."

I was shocked. "But what about Gracie and Kanisha? We're a group. I can't go off without them." I shook my head. I could just see them, especially Gracie who brought me into the group. No. If there was anything I valued, it was loyalty.

"Do you think they wouldn't go off without you? Are you interested or not? Just give him a call," he said, holding out a business card. "He owes me a favor."

I took Donovan's card and promised Harry I'd call. We went back in. I didn't say anything to the girls. Neither did he. When Gracie asked me what he wanted, I told her he wanted to borrow five dollars from me. Harry was always borrowing money from us so it wasn't unusual. I could tell that she didn't believe me. I felt like a traitor, but at the same time, as I walked to the bus stop, my heart was beating fast.

Imagine, a big time person in the industry was interested in me. My head would be in the clouds for days.

12

۶۵

Ma'dear

Precious Lord, Take my hand. Lead me on, Let me stand. I'm tired...

I'm tired. Why do I just want to sleep all the time? I don't feel no pain, just a numbness in my legs and my right arm. I wish I was home. Why can't I go home? I don't want to be here in this godforsaken place. Never did like California.

I remember when I got a letter from my brother Bud, well, not really a letter, a picture postcard from when he and his wife came out for vacation. It was a picture of Grauman's Chinese theatre in Hollywood, that place where famous actors put their hands and feet in cement. Didn't mean anything to me. People in California act like fools. Why Hazel would want to live here is beyond me. But she was always wild, had a mind of her own, couldn't tell her nothing.

If I was to die tomorrow, I wouldn't have no regrets. I did the best I could and I believe I led a good life. I don't have nothing to be ashamed of. I could stand before my maker with my head held high. Who you think you're fooling? You suddenly got an attack of forgetfulness? You forgot already about all the things you done, all the men you been with?

But that was long ago. I paid for that. I paid in full.

Oh yeah! What about Fred and Willy Joe? What about Sadie Washington, your best friend? What about her? You're responsible for her death...

Stop! I don't remember no Sadie Washington, Willie Joe, or Fred. Besides, that was a long time ago. Stop now! Let me rest. I want to rest.

13

❧

Hazel

Hazel glanced at her watch. It was a little after 5 P.M. She covered her typewriter, slowly cleared her desk, pulled her purse out of the bottom drawer and opened it. Taking out her compact and lipstick, she touched a few strands of hair into place, powered her face and applied a fresh layer of lipstick.

"Got a hot date?" Monica asked as she prepared to leave.

"No. I'm just not in a hurry to get home." Hazel lit a cigarette after looking around to make sure the supervisors had left. "No smoking" signs dotted the room. She blew the smoke away from Monica, keeping the cigarette out of sight.

"You must really be in a bad way, smoking on the floor like that. If I wasn't in a hurry, I'd join you." She laughed. Coming closer, her expression grew serious.

"Having a hard time huh? Look, if there's anything I can do to help, just let me know. You know we sisters got to stick together."

"Nothing I can't handle." Hazel gathered up her things and together they walked to the elevator. When they reached the ground floor, Monica rushed off. "Call me, any time," she flung over her shoulder as she disappeared around the corner.

Hazel stood for a moment before heading towards the parking lot. She got into her car and started for the freeway home. Just before she got to the Slauson Street exit, she turned off and headed back to Crenshaw, then over to Adams where she stopped in front of a small one-story house located back from the street. Dwarfed by huge five bedroom houses in a neighborhood once known as Sugar Hill, which sported the likes of Ethel Waters, Sammy Davis Jr. and others, the tiny structure looked like an interloper.

Hazel turned off the engine and waited. At 5:45, a green Mustang drove up, the garage door opened, the driver smoothly cruised in. The man got out walking towards her with a dimpled smile on his face. He was tall, around 6 ft., handsome, muscular in his beige cotton polo, brown slacks and slender waist, with skin the color of dark chocolate; his curly hair glistened in the waning sunlight.

"Hazel, what a welcomed surprise. Why didn't you tell me you were coming?"

"I just decided as I drove home from work." He held open her car door for her to step out. His arm encircling her waist, he steered her up the steps and into his house.

"I'd better call home," she said as she reached for his wall phone and dialed her number. He disappeared into his bedroom.

"Shanell, how's everything going? Tricia went to rehearsals? Did you give Ma'dear something to eat? I'll be a little late. See you around seven. " She hung up and poured herself a glass of water. She could hear the shower running and heard Kevin humming. She sat down on the couch and waited for him.

His house was neat and orderly, though you could tell a bachelor lived there because while on the surface everything had its place, a thin layer of dust lay over everything as if it hadn't been dusted in a while. The curtains must not have been cleaned in a long while because they looked worn and dingy. Once she had offered to take his curtains home and wash them but the thought annoyed him so she never mentioned it again.

Kevin was 38 years old, had been married once but divorced after two years. He worked as an insurance investigator and spent a lot of time out of town, chasing down those suspected of committing fraud. He and Hazel met three years ago when she got into a minor car accident and he was sent to investigate her claim. He asked her out for a drink and their relationship developed quickly after that.

He came out of the bathroom with a towel wrapped around his waist. Taking her in is arms, he kissed her neck and began to steer her towards the bedroom.

"Wait, Kevin, I'm not in the mood." She pulled away. "I just needed somebody to talk to.... Maybe later," she added noticing a frown cross his face.

"Would you like something to eat?" he asked pulling on his robe. He opened the refrigerator and began pulling out remnants of food. He was a good cook. He loved to try new recipes especially Thai recipes that called for special ingredients like lemongrass, ginger, and vanilla bean. She sat on a stool and watched him put together their meal.

"It's Ma'dear, my job, school, everything. I'm not sure how I'll manage having Ma'dear with me."

"But she's your mother. What's there to handle?"

"I left home when I was seventeen. She drove me away actually. Said I was wild. Didn't like much about me, she told me one day. Especially when I was pregnant with Tricia. She sent me to live with my aunt, and after all these years, we haven't gotten along for more than five minutes. And now I may have to take care of her for the rest of her life. It scares me."

She talked for over an hour and when she finished, she felt relieved. This time when he invited her to his bed she consented. It was 8 P.M. when she turned the lock in the door to her apartment.

As usual Shanell was on the phone, Ma'dear was asleep, and Tricia was at rehearsal. She took a bath, read a magazine, and as soon as her head hit the pillow, she fell fast asleep.

14

☙

Shanell

"Course I know you. I seen you around school plenty of times. How many boyfriends do I have? Now why should I tell you that? How many girlfriends do you have?"

Shanell giggled into the telephone. Just hearing his smooth voice sent chills up her spine. Shay called me! Wait until I tell Babe. She's not gonna believe this.

Shay was the most handsomest boy in school, one of the star players on the basketball team. She hadn't ever seen him without a girl on his arm.

"What about Cheryl? I thought you and her was tight." He told her they'd broken up. He said his friend had told him about her and had given him her number.

"What's your friend's name?" she tried to make her voice sound sophisticated, rich like she'd heard Tricia whenever she talked on the phone to Darien. "No, I just wanted to know who it was. Am I a virgin?" She blushed. "You're not supposed to ask a girl that?" Her stomach did a flip-flop. "I can't go out during the week. To the movies on Saturday? I'll have to ask my mother if I can." If she says no, I'll go anyway, she told herself. He said something she couldn't quite catch; then he said he had to go. "See you in school tomorrow." She hung up.

I gotta call Babe. She's gonna die when she hears this. She dialed her friend's number but got a busy signal. Hanging up, she glanced up at the clock. 7:15 pm. Momma and Tricia were still out.

Not wanting to disturb her, yet needing to talk to somebody, she peeked into Ma'dear's room. A wave of disappointment washed over her when she saw that her grandmother was asleep. She tiptoed in and began to gather the soiled dishes. A glass dropped from the tray and rolled beneath the bed.

"Shit!" Shanell whispered before she could stop herself. Glancing quickly at Ma'dear, she saw that her eyes were open.

"I'm sorry. I didn't mean to disturb you," she said quickly hoping her grandmother hadn't heard curse. She only did it at school or when she was with her friends. Sometimes though, it slipped out at home and when it did, her mother and Tricia usually took her to task about it.

"How you feeling? Can I get you anything?" She just lays there and stares at you. I wonder can she hear me? I wonder how it would feel to be paralyzed?

"You thirsty? You want some water?" Suddenly she realized she was yelling. A smile began to form on Ma'dear's face. Shanell laughed. Sitting down beside her grandmother, she stroked her hand.

"You know what happened in school today? My drama teacher, Mrs. Clark, said I've got a good feel for acting. I auditioned for the part of Peter Pan in the school play and it got down to me and this girl named Loretta. She's got blond hair and blue eyes and everybody just knew she was gonna get the part because she plays the lead in just about all the school plays. Well, Mrs. Clark said I did such a good job that even though Loretta got the part, I'm gonna be her understudy. You should've seen me, Ma'dear. I had memorized my lines down to a tee. You wanna hear me recite them? I'll be right back."

She dashed out of the room and retrieved the script from her backpack. "I gotta set up the scene first." As she began describing the scene, her glance fell on her grandmother. Her eyes closed, her breathing rhythmic, she was asleep. Shanell's shoulders   slumped.   "Maybe   tomorrow,"   she whispered.

Gathering up the tray with the soiled dishes, she carried them into the kitchen. After putting them into the sink, she decided to call Babe again. This time when she dialed her number, Babe answered immediately.

"It's about time, girl. Who was you talking to? You'll never guess who called me...." Deep in conversation, she didn't hear the door open and her mother come in.

"Have you done your homework?" Hazel hollered as she passed the kitchen. "Make sure you clean up the kitchen before you go to bed tonight. And don't stay on that phone too long. Other people would like to use it sometime." Shanell heard the door close to her mother's room.

"Can you believe? He asked if I was a virgin?" She giggled. "I didn't say I was or that I wasn't."

15

❧

Ma'dear

I remember when I was a little girl. Every Sunday Mama would dress me and my baby sister Johnnie up in real nice clothes and the whole family would all go to church together. I loved to go to church. Sunday was my favorite day. Afterwards, we'd come home and Mama would cook a big dinner. While Papa read his paper on the porch, Sammy, Bud, Johnnie and me would play out in the yard until she called us to come in for dinner. Johnnie was the youngest, and though my brothers teased us a lot, they protected us, made sure we were safe.

At fourteen, Sammy was the oldest, full of energy, always in trouble for doing something dangerous like climbing trees and diving from rocks into the small stream not far from our house or walking along the railroad track and jumping off just before the train came.

One Sunday, Sammy was swinging on that old tire Papa hung up in the yard. He accidentally fell off the swing and nearly cut his ear clean off. Papa grabbed him up, jumped in our old rickety car, and sped off to town. We sat around for hours waiting. Finally, when it was real dark, Papa came back with Sammy. He had a sad look on his face like he had been beat. Sammy's face was wrapped in bandages. Mama put him to bed and told us all to go to bed. But I snuck downstairs and heard Papa tell Mama what happened in town.

Seems that when Papa took Sammy into the hospital, they asked him what he wanted; then they said they didn't treat no nigger child; that he'd have to carry him to the Negro hospital in the next town. Papa raised such a fuss, they threatened to call the sheriff. They threw him and Sammy out. By the time he got him to the other hospital, his ear was infected.

Mama tried to calm Papa down. He said he was sick and tired living in the South where "they always trying to steal you manhood." I didn't understand what he meant by that. That was the first I remember when Papa started moving away from us. He came home from working at the sawmill every day, but he started drinking more and more.

From that day on Sammy had problems with his hearing. His condition got worse until he lost his hearing in both ears. The infection spread and Sammy died. A little while after that Papa left. Went to work one day and didn't come back.

Mama got a set look on her face until I can't hardly remember if I ever heard her laugh again. And she used to laugh all the time. She had one of the happiest laughs I'd ever heard. But when Papa left, she didn't hardly ever crack a smile anymore. She started cleaning up white folks home and we children had to practically raise ourselves we were alone so much. Children should never be left alone to raise themselves. Look what happened to me.

Shanell comes in. She's got a pretty face but I don't know why young girls got to wear pants all the time and that skimpy top. Why do Hazel let her dress like that? I bet she's fast like her mother. What's she doing? Look out, she dropped a glass. Reminds me of myself. Wish I could let her know I hear her. She's yelling at me like everybody else. I wonder why people think I can't hear. It's just my voice. That's all. There's pressure on my vocal chords. That's what the doctor back in Philadelphia said.

So my granddaughter wants to be an actress. I hope not. Reminds me of myself when I was her age....

Sadie, why don't you leave me alone! I never done nothing to hurt you.

16

ॐ

Tricia

I called Mr. Donovan and he told me to come to his office tonight. I knew Momma would be mad especially since I'd been out almost every night this week. I hadn't been able to make up all my assignments. Mrs. Stern threatened to call Momma if I fell asleep in her class again. I tried to keep awake, but whenever I did, I'd get so annoyed at the way the other students kept up so much noise in class. They acted like kids and it made me so mad. The other day we had a substitute teacher and Larry and Tiny started bagging on him real loud. It was so funny I had to laugh. When I saw he couldn't handle it, I shouted at those fools. That quieted them down, but they gave me dirty looks. Really, sometimes I wondered why they even came to school. I could hardly wait to graduate. Sometimes when I looked at the students in my class, I felt so old. Like I didn't really belong there. Just a few more months I told myself.

My history teacher was lecturing as usual and writing notes all over the blackboard, which I could barely read. Tearing a sheet of paper from my notebook, I wrote,

"Dear Mr. Love, It seems like years since I last saw you. Why haven't you called? I called you the other day but all I got was your answer machine and you haven't called me back. I'm sorry about the other day. Call me, please. " I signed it "Your Huggy Bear."

I folded it up and tucked it into my purse. I looked up just in time to see Mr. Jordon coming down the aisle, handing out papers.

"As soon as you finish this test, you may start on your homework." Oh shit! I forgot to study.

Lately, it seemed like everybody was mad at me. Shanell was always mad so she didn't count. Gracie and Kanisha found out that Mr. Donovan was interested in me and not them. Take last night. They gave me funny looks. Even Gracie would stare at me whenever she thought I wasn't looking. Kanisha was harder on me than usual and usually Gracie was on my side. This time, though, she agreed with Kanisha. If Donovan offered to help me, maybe I'd be better off going it alone.

I rushed home after school, and dashed into the bathroom to shower and change clothes. I knew I had hours to wait but I was anxious to see what this was all about. Momma hired a nurse to look after Ma'dear while we were in school and give her some physical therapy. When I came out of the bathroom, she was finishing up and about to leave. She was a short, thick woman with dark brown skin, a short Afro, and a wide grin. She was always grinning, which made me suspicious. But what I mostly didn't like about her was that she treated Ma'dear like she was a child.

"We had a good day today, didn't we? We ate all our food and now we're taking a little nap."

The first time I heard her all I could do was shake my head. She sure was strange. I asked Momma where she got her, but all she said was to just be grateful we don't have to miss any more school. Anyway, Miss Strange waved at me as she closed the door. "See you tomorrow," she yelled.

I wanted to take off early for Mr. Donovan's office in midtown, so I was ready as soon as Shanell got home. Before we could get into an argument, I left. I took two busses before I reached his office near Alvarado. I was kind of nervous, partly because I'd never been to this part of town. The only time I'd been through this area was on the bus on my way downtown. It looked ugly and crowded with so many people it almost made my head spin. Storefronts sold cheap goods, house wares, and electronic equipment. There were plenty of fast food places, Taco Bell, Jack in the Box, and Tommy's Hamburgers.

I walked as fast as I could to the address on the card. Mr. Donovan's office was in an old building that must have been something in its day. The entrance looked all carved with sculptured statues, like something I'd seen in my history textbook book on ancient ruins in Rome and when I looked up I saw gargoyles glaring down at me. The building looked dingy and in serious need of a bath. Why do people in the music business have their offices in ancient buildings in the seedy part of town? I wondered.

A security guard asked me who I was going up to see, and made me sign in as he gave me a close inspection as if I was from outer space. Then he pointed me to a broken down elevator a few feet from the entrance and went back to reading his magazine. I spotted a naked woman with big boobs on one page. I wished I had asked Darien or somebody to come with me.

The elevator creaked slowly up to the third floor as if it was on its last legs. Not seeing anybody else in the building except the security guard and me made me even more nervous. Maybe I shouldn't have come, I thought. But I hummed a Whitney Houston song to help steady my nerves as I hurried down the dark corridor.

"How do I know if he really loves me..."

I pictured myself onstage surrounded by lights and applause.

At a door marked D and D Promotions, Inc. I stopped. Reaching into my purse, I took out my compact, checked my hair and makeup, and popped an Altoids in my mouth. Then I turned the knob and went in. The lights were on and I heard the sound of jazz music coming from a radio, but nobody was behind the reception desk. I sat down and waited. Photographs of recording artists lined the walls. I picked up a copy of billboard magazine from the table and flipped through the pages. The clock on the wall said six thirty. My appointment was for seven.

I hoped he'd see me early. I wanted to get out of here before dark. No such luck. The clock ticked away but nobody came. Finally it was seven and still nobody came. The phone rang several times. I was tempted to pick it up but I didn't. After a while, I got up enough nerve to go to the door leading to the other room that I guess must be Mr. Donovan's office. Putting my ear against the frame, I listened. Then I knocked, no answer. I tried to turn the doorknob. It was locked. I sat down and waited some more. I started to feel jumpy and annoyed at the same time.

The clock moved to seven thirty; then to seven forty-five.

Disappointed, my heart sank. He wasn't coming. I was mad now. Finding a scrap of paper in my purse, I wrote him a note telling him I came. I took some scotch tape from the desk and taped my note to the door. Then I left.

The hallway was dark and filled with shadows. I pushed the elevator button listening to the elevator squeak as it headed for the fifth floor above me. I heard the gate open and close. But the elevator didn't start back down. I looked around for the stairs. It was only three flights down to the street. I was beginning to get really scared. My body shook. I felt sweat break out under my arms. The longer I waited, the more nervous I got.

Finally, the elevator came; pushing back the gate, I stepped in. My heart raced as I imagined the security guard gone home leaving me stuck in this building for the night. As the elevator creaked to a stop on the first floor, I slid back the gate and practically ran to the door almost falling down with relief when I spotted the security guard sitting on a stool smoking near the door.

He unlocked the door and as I rushed through, he tipped his hat and said, "Have a nice night." I heard the bolt being thrown behind me. As I hurried to the bus stop, I thought, 'I should've stayed home. '

When I stepped into the apartment, Momma was waiting by the door, a frown on her face.

"Where've you been? Shanell said you went to rehearsal but you didn't tell me anything about that this morning. You've been going out every night this week and it's got to stop. You may think you're grown, but you're not! You're seventeen. I've got enough to worry about without you adding to my worries!"

I told her about my appointment with Mr. Donovan.

"You know better than to go into that area alone and at night. You want to be a singer so bad that you'll put your life in jeopardy, and for what? You need to be more careful."

I apologized, went to my room and took off my clothes. Momma followed, sitting down on Shanell's bed, she watched me undress. I saw some of the anger and tension seep out of her face.

"By the way, Shanell said Darien and a Mr. Donovan called...." She went on, but I was too worn out to listen. I got into bed and pulled the covers up around my shoulders. She turned the light out and closed the door as she left.

17

❧

Hazel

Hazel woke up feeling tired as she had been feeling of late. Reluctantly she rolled out of bed. 5:30 a.m. A half hour before she had to start waking Shanell and Tricia. Stumbling into the bathroom, she washed her face, brushed her teeth, turned on the shower and waited for the water to warm. The spray felt good, waking her up at least, but not quite ridding her of the tired feeling. She knew she was stressed out, badly in need of a vacation. Maybe she should take a few days off and take the girls and her mother to the beach or someplace together. They hadn't spent any time together in a while and it was telling. They lived like strangers in the same household. What with her going to work and school; Tricia always out at rehearsals, Shanell always on the telephone, her mother...Hazel thought about Ma'dear and how few times she'd spent more than a minute with her. She felt ashamed. But I don't have time, she thought. I've hired a nurse that I can hardly afford. Shanell and Tricia keep her company. It's all I can do to make ends meet. I don't have time; she rationalized again. She felt at war with herself. As she reached for her morning cigarette, she heard Tricia's voice in her mind telling her that she smoked too much.

Yeah, I could rent a cabin in Crestline and maybe get away. We need to become a family again. Her spirits lifted as she prepared herself for work. Stopping at Ma'dear's room, she peeked her head in and was surprised to see her mother awake. Their eyes met.

"Good Morning, Mama," she said from the doorway. "Did you sleep all right?" There was something in her mother's eyes, an accusing look that made her duck her head.

"I've got to get the girls up. It's late. I'll talk to you later."

Closing the door hastily, she leaned against it as she tried to stop her body from trembling.

Pulling herself together, Hazel entered the girls' room. Tricia woke immediately, tumbled out of bed.

"Mornin'," she mumbled as she staggered into the bathroom, eyes still closed. Shanell, lying on the cot, turned over and pulled the covers over her head.

"Com'on now. It's time for school."

"Aw, Momma. I'll get up when Tricia's out the bathroom."

"Alright then. But don't let me have to come in here again to wake you," Hazel said. Before she closed the door, she noted how messy one side of the room was - clothes thrown on the floor amid sneakers, papers, books and even a glass from the kitchen. On the other side, Tricia's side, everything was neat and in its place. With two growing girls sharing the same room, it was cramped. Well, I don't have time to deal with that.

"How would you like to go on a vacation?" she asked the girls when they came into the kitchen. Tricia looked well groomed as she always did in her short skirt with a matching knitted vest, dark stockings and suede boots. Her face carefully made up, her hair stylishly combed in a flip. She's a young lady all ready, Hazel thought. I'll be losing my little girl soon. Shanell wore the dress of the day - denim jeans with holes in the knees, black tee shirt with Bob Marley's face stenciled across her chest, and dirty sneakers. Hazel watched as Tricia poured herself a glass of orange juice and buttered one slice of toast.

"We're almost out of cereal and milk," Shanell said shaking the last of the Cornflakes into her bowl.

"I'll have to go grocery shopping tonight. So what about it? Easter's coming and I'll have a few days off. How would you like it if we all went away for a little vacation?"

"Can't," Tricia said. "Too busy. We're hoping to cut a demo soon. And Harry's got a lot of things lined up for us."

"Me, too, I don't want to leave my friends. Besides, I got plans. Sorry," Shanell said.

Hazel felt her shoulders slump. "Maybe I'll go by myself, then."

"You taking Ma'dear with you?" Shanell asked.

"Since you're both staying home, I'll leave her with you." Hazel knew her voice sounded harsh. When she rose from the table, her chair almost toppled over. Both Tricia and Shanell looked up from their food. They exchanged glances.

Hazel rinsed out her coffee cup, picked up her purse, and started for the door.

Shanell followed her. "Momma, you forgot to give me lunch money." As Hazel counted out $2.00, Shanell went on. "Next week their taking class pictures and I'll need..."

"You should have told me about it yesterday. I don't have time now," she snapped.

"But I got to turn it in today or I won't get my picture in the yearbook," Shanell whined.

"Can't you see Momma's late," Tricia said. "You pick the worst times."

As Hazel ran down the step, she barely missed bumping into the nurse who was climbing up.

"Good morning Mrs. Porter. Looks like it's gonna be a lovely day."

"Good morning," she responded. "The girls are still upstairs. I'm late. Excuse me." She dashed to her car.

I've got to get away, she thought. Everything seems to be closing in on me.

She'd missed so many evening classes; she hoped she wouldn't have to drop out of school. Every day at work no one knew whether it might be their last. The tension was heavy. As she drove through the early morning traffic, she became aware of tears slipping down her face. She wiped them away with the back of her hand. Suddenly she spotted a phone booth. Without thinking, she pulled over, got out and called her office.

"I can't come in today," she said to her supervisor. "It's my mother, she's taken a turn for the worse," she lied, hoping she wasn't courting bad luck.

The supervisor was sympathetic, told her to take as much time as she needed. After she hung up, the thought of how long it would be before she would be let go, fluttered past like a persistent bee along with the thought of searching for another job, and not being able to pay the bills. She tossed the thoughts aside as she turned the car around and drove back home.

By the time she reached her apartment, the girls had gone. Except for her mother and the nurse who were in the bedroom, no one was around. She undressed quickly, slipped under the covers and quickly fell into a troubled sleep.

18

ঔ

Ma'dear

Sadie was my best friend. When Mama said I was too wild and threatened to send me to live with my aunt in North Carolina, it was Sadie who came up with the plan to run away to New York. She was having a hard time with her folks, too. Her stepdad used to beat her and her mother. She told me once he tried to rape her. So she planned to leave home as soon as she could. When she told me what she was planning to do, I decided to go with her. Though I knew it would hurt my folks, I just couldn't go to North Carolina. That's even further down South than Virginia and Lord knows I couldn't stand them folks in Virginia. I guess I was pretty wild.

We left one afternoon when everybody was at work. Papa Jones, Mama's second husband, worked at the sawmill, Mama at the canning factory. My brother

Bud had joined the army as soon as he came of age, my baby sister Johnnie was staying with Mama's sister in Delaware for the summer. Nobody was home but me. I told Mama I wasn't feeling well so she didn't press me about going to work in the field that morning. As soon as they left, I put my few belongings into the one old cardboard suitcase we had and headed down the road to Sadie's. Didn't even think about leaving a note. I was a fool, didn't think about nobody's feelings but my own. I was ready for a new life and nothing and nobody was going to stop me.

It was a warm spring day and as I walked down the road carrying my old piece of suitcase, I didn't even hear the birds singing or see the butterflies or the bees, or smell the blooming flowers. The road was empty. On each side were cornfields and I suppose if I looked hard enough I'd see people working in the fields planting crops, tomatoes, beans, and grapevines. I was trying to kick up as little dust as possible to keep from getting my legs dirty. I carried my shoes. Figured I'd put them on as soon as we got to somewhere with sidewalks. Then I'd throw these old sneakers away and start acting and looking like somebody who didn't grow up in the sticks.

Sadie was waiting for me down by the big oak tree. She had her belongings in a pillowcase slung over her back.

"Girl, we can't start no new life like that," I said when I saw how countrified she looked. I wore a brown skirt and white blouse that looked pretty decent. I had packed my Sunday best, the only nice dress I owned. I'd saved up for it and ordered it from the Sears and Roebuck catalogue. Sadie wore overalls and sneakers with holes in the toe. "I got plenty of room in my suitcase. Put your things in here and we'll take turns carrying it."

Getting a hitch to town wasn't too hard. Most of the colored men who stopped didn't mind giving two young girls a ride in their truck or wagon. They'd ask us questions about where we was going and why. We usually made up a lie that we were sisters and going to see a sick relative in the next town. They'd tell us to be careful.

Never thought we'd reach the next city alive, though. We had to fight our way out of automobiles, trucks, and wagons, men ready to offer us a ride and as soon as we hopped in within a few miles, they wanted us to pay for the ride in you can guess how. Lord have mercy, if it wasn't for us being together, I don't know what woulda happened. But we made it.

We was lucky to find jobs in the city working for white folks, cooking and cleaning. Sadie cooked and I would clean, babysit, and do laundry. Determined to *get out of the South, we'd stay just long enough to save up bus fare to the next town.*

We worked our way through Virginia, Maryland., Delaware, D.C, New Jersey, until finally we reached New York City. Stepping off the bus at the Port Authority downtown, we had to ask passersby how to get to Harlem. After telling us where to find the subway, a man told us to take the A train up to 135th Street. Talk about a scary ride, we were petrified. It took us several months from the day we left Virginia, but we finally reached Harlem, the colored capital of the world. Wall to wall folks going bout their business. Nobody paying us no nevermind. All around us was sounds, people laughing, talking, music coming out of saloons, that early in the morning; we were shocked.

We stood on the corner of 135th Street and Lenox Avenue, staring up at the tall buildings, blocking out the sun. But that didn't matter, us carrying all we owned in my cardboard suitcase, trying not to look like two scared girls straight up from the sticks. We was so excited just to be there. I think between us we had about enough money to rent a room. It was nearly noon when we found one.

The landlady rambled through the rules, no men up in your room, no smoking or cooking in your room, doors are locked at 10 p.m., no this, no that; neither of us would remember half what she said as soon as she said it. *We settled in right away, went out to see the city.*

Harlem at night was a wild woman's dream. The city was alive with those same sounds we'd heard when we first set foot on the street early that morning, only more so at night. It didn't take Sadie and me long to make ourselves at home. The landlady told us about her cousin who worked in Bronxville cleaning rich folk houses.

A few days later, he took us to the people he knew who were looking for help. Since we had a lot of experience in that department we got hired in no time. Sadie worked for a family about a mile away from where I worked. Every morning we caught the bus out to Bronxville along with all the other maids, butlers, and chauffeurs who lived in Harlem.

Thursdays, our day off, we'd go dancing. In no time Sadie and me had men running after us, taking us places, showering us with presents like nylons and candy, and promising us the world just for a kiss. Child, we was something else.

Then one night up at Rockland Palace, Willie Joe walked into my life and drove a wedge between Sadie and me big enough to run a train through. Things went downhill fast after that.

"Why'd you let it happen? You coulda done something."

"What could I do? Sadie, It wasn't my fault. Why you blamin me?"

"You coulda done somethin."

"Stop trying to make me feel guilty. It was just as much your fault as mine. Now you just stop saying that!"

"Mrs. Washington. Mrs. Washington. What's the matter? Why are you crying? Something hurting you?"

"Ma'dear. Wake up, Ma'dear. You're having a nightmare. I'll take over, nurse. You can go," said Hazel.

As she put on her coat and gathered her things, the nurse explained. "I was just sitting here, watching TV. Must've dozed off. She was fine. Then all of a sudden she starts making this noise and acting like she's having a fit, shaking her head and all. That's why I started to call you. I didn't know you were at home."

"I came back early, a bad headache. I'll take care of her. I'm sure she'll be alright." Hazel walked the nurse to the *door and held it open for her.*

"I'll be back tomorrow bright and early."

"Yes, tomorrow." Hazel closed the door and went back to Ma'dear's room. She seemed to have calmed down. Hazel stroked her mother's hair and rested her hand on her forehead for a moment. Then she sat down and watched her mother's even breathing.

"What could have upset her?" Hazel wondered. "I wish she could talk, tell me what's happening."

19-

❧

Hazel

The phone rang startling her. She rushed into the kitchen.

"Hey baby. I called your office and they told me you were out sick. What's wrong? Anything I can do?"

Of all the people in the world she didn't want to hear from it was her ex husband. She felt her voice drop. "No, Donald. There's nothing you can do. My mother's here with me now. I stayed home to look after her." What have you ever done for us, she thought sarcastically. "So, is there a reason for this call?" She asked, her voice formal, distant.

"No, baby. Just wanted to hear your voice. See how you're doing." His was like drowning in 50 year-old cognac. She hated his smooth, syrupy sweet tone.

"We're fine. You never worried about how we were doing before. Now what's the real reason for the call?"

"Why does there have to be a reason? You know how much I care about you."

"Listen, Donald. If you've called about money, I don't have any."

"Why does it have to be about money? See, that's what's wrong with you. You were always jumping to conclusions. Always ready to think the worst of me."

She listened to him go on and wondered what she ever saw in him in the first place. How could she have ever married him?

"I've got to go. My mother's waiting for me."

"Before you hang up, there's a favor you could do for me.

"I told you I don't have any money."

"It's not gonna cost you anything."

She sighed, "Well, what is it?"

"I was wondering if you'd let me use your address."

"My address. What for? Don't you have your own place?"

He explained that he was starting a business and needed a place separate from his own where he could receive mail orders. "I mean, if you'll just put my mail in a box and I could come over and collect it once a week, no strings, promise."

It didn't seem like much but still...

"I won't be in your way. I'll call you and if you want, you could just set the box outside your door and I'll pick it up. Don't even have to bother you."

Reluctantly, she gave in. Donald was always a smooth talker. A salesman, he could convince you to sell the clothes off your back. Always involved in some type of scheme, on the edge of being legal, though some she wasn't sure of. But she wasn't one to stand in the way of a brother making a living, she told herself; as long as she didn't have to be involved. Returning to her mother's room, just as she settled in the chair, the door opened and Shanell peered in.

"What're you doing home so early?"

"I didn't go to work today," Hazel said, getting up. She looked down at her sleeping mother. "You stay with her while I go fix dinner."

"But Momma, I brought my friend home to do homework with," Shanell stammered. "I can't leave him out there alone."

"Well, tell him you've got to help your mother. Or do you want me to do it."

"No. That's okay. I'll do it."

As soon as Shanell returned, Hazel went into the kitchen, her mind, a bundle of emotions. The rest did some good, but now, she thought, I don't know what's worse, having Mama stare at me with that accusatory look or having her asleep all the time. Whatever it is, I've got to deal with it. She pulled out a package of chicken from the freezer and slammed it down on the counter.

20

❧

Tricia

Have a date with Darien tonight. He's taking me to the movies. When I told Momma, she got mad, telling me that I'd better not be falling behind in my school work or I could kiss my singing career goodbye. But I promised her I'd keep up. I could see she was just talking to be talking. She looked so tired lately. Shanell said Momma didn't go to work today. I was surprised because she almost never calls in sick

I wished Ma'dear would get better and go home. Not that I didn't love her; it was just that life changed since she came to live with us. It seemed like something was always going on. I never had a moment to myself. And having to share a room with Shanell was really getting on my nerves.

The doorbell rang and I heard Darien's voice talking to Momma. She liked him, thank goodness. I heard them laughing at something. I made a last minute check in the mirror.

He stood when I came into the room, looking gorgeous in his leather jacket, green pullover and slacks. The man could dress. I smiled at him as I walked to the closet to get my jacket.

"You look pretty," Momma said touching my hair. "Don't you think that blouse is a little low cut?" She whispered in my ear. "No, Momma." I frowned. As Darien helped me put on my jacket, I caught a whiff of his cologne. I was swooning. I put a scarf around my neck to hide the low cleavage and to please Momma. We headed for the door.

"Don't keep her out too late," Momma said.

"I won't. Night." Darien smiled and closed the door behind us.

The night was mild; the sky filled with stars and the moon was so bright it was like a spotlight lighting up the street. With his arm around my waist, Darien helped me into his Mustang. We didn't say much as he whizzed down LaBrea to the Baldwin Hills complex, his tape player jamming with the Four Sounds. I rested my head back and listened, my eyes closed. The night felt very special.

I don't remember the movie. As usual we sat in the back row where all the lovers sat and kissed. I slapped his hands from my breast. He slid them down between my legs.

"Stop," I said as I pushed his hands away.

After the movie, Darien took me back to his apartment. We still hadn't said more than a few words to each other all night. It felt good just being with him though something in the back of my mind said I should stop before it was too late.   He turned off the lights, put on R. Kelly, and we danced.

Seems like you're ready...Girl are you ready...to go all the way...

We were doing some heavy petting when he propelled me towards his bedroom and before I knew it, he had my blouse unbuttoned. I felt all gooey inside not able to stop him or myself. He pulled my clothes off and then his. I tried to stop him but at the same time, I didn't want to. He pushed me down on his bed and started pulling at my panties.

"Wait," I protested, trying to hold him off.   "I can't"

"Com'on now. I won't hurt you." His breath came rapidly. I struggled beneath him suddenly realizing what was about to happen.

"Darien, please. I can't. I'm not ready."

"Yes you are. You're just scared. Ain't nothing to be scared of."

In a panic, I managed to push him off me, catching him off balance. He slid to the floor. Grabbing my clothes and holding them in front of me, I walked back toward the door.

He got up and sat on the bed. Through the darkness, I could feel his anger. I started to put on my clothes. "I'm sorry," I apologized. His breathing slowed. He got up and put on his shorts.

"I'm sorry, too," he said, his voice sending cold waves over me. "I'll take you home. Give me a minute." He went into the bathroom. I finished dressing in the living room and sat down on a chair to wait for him. I felt ashamed. I shouldn't have come up to his place if I wasn't going to do it with him. I should have stopped it before we got to this point. I could understand him being mad at me. I was a tease, I could hear him thinking.

I didn't look at him when he came out. We didn't say a word as he drove me home making me feel even worse. I wanted to explain but what could I say? He dropped me off in front of my building, mumbled, "goodnight," and drove off before I could get my key out of my purse to open the outside door. I couldn't go inside like that. Removing the key out of the lock, I sat down on the stoop and cried. I was glad the street was empty, even though it was just 11 pm on a Saturday evening.

A virgin at seventeen, I laughed bitterly. Who did I think I was, some kind of saint? Was I so different from other girls my age? I wanted to tonight. I wanted to go all the way with him, but I couldn't and I didn't know why. Scared, I guess. All the things Momma drilled into my head as I was growing up, about being a good girl, about men not respecting a girl who sleeps around, about getting an education and on and on came back and sat on me hard. I wanted to spit them out, vomit them out onto the street right then and there. Her words were like a chastity belt holding me down, weighing heavy on me, keeping me from truly being with the one I loved. And, I hated to admit that I might lose him, or maybe I'd already lost him.

Suddenly I wished there was somebody I could talk to; somebody who wouldn't judge me or put me down. Momma would have a fit if I even brought up the subject. Shanell would laugh. Gracie would say go ahead. It's about time. She thought I was weird. As it was, she got pregnant before she was sixteen.

My head was spinning. I got up from the cold steps and let myself into the apartment. I felt drained. I stole past Momma and Shanell who were watching

TV, and into my bedroom. I quickly undressed, and slipped into bed.

I dreamed I was on stage singing solo and all of a sudden my voice cracked right in the middle of the song. I couldn't remember the words either. The audience started to laugh. I opened my mouth and nothing came out. The people began to throw rotten tomatoes, and they booed me. I broke down and started to cry.

They shouted, "Get off the stage. She can't sing. She's a phony.

The more I cried, the louder they got. My tears fell until they flooded the floor. I couldn't stop crying. The spotlight stayed on me. I saw Darien jump up from the front row, turn his back on me and shout, "She's a fake!" Then he laughed louder than the rest. The tears fell even harder, and it seemed like they turned to rain; my clothes were drenched. I tried to run but the spotlight kept following me, the voices kept laughing and shouting for me to get off the stage.

Suddenly I was awake. The room was dark. Shanell was asleep on her cot, her breathing steady. My pajamas were soaked with sweat. I stumbled out of bed and into the bathroom, took off my pajamas, and stood before the mirror, looking at my naked body.

"If he ever calls me again, I'm not gonna be scared," I vowed.

21

❧

Shanell

Though she sat beside her mother watching the TV screen, Shanell's thoughts were far away. Her mind was on Shay, the boy she met a few weeks ago. Even though they went to the same school, she'd seen him in the hallway and at his locker, but he never gave her a second glance. Captain of the basketball team, he had girls fluttering all over him like bees searching for honey. Then one day, out of the blue, he called her and she agreed to meet up with him.

Her stomach fluttered as she remembered the first time they spent the day together. She'd told her mother she was going to the movies with her girlfriend Babe, but instead she met him at the McDonald's on the corner. He bought her a Big Mac and fries, and then they went over to the arcade where he treated her to Donkey Kong. Naturally he beat her score several times over. She wasn't good at video games.

She enjoyed just being with him. Next they took the bus over to World on Wheels and skated for a while. It was so much fun. But the best part was when they ran into his ex girlfriend and he put his arms around Shanell's waist and kissed her right in front of the girl. Everything happened so fast. She smiled at the memory.

"What are you smiling about? Did you hear the door?" Hazel's voice broke into her thoughts. When Shanell didn't answer, Hazel went on.

"Must be Tricia. Anyway, I feel like having some popcorn. Go make us some."

She hopped off the sofa and started for the kitchen.

"And while you're at it, look in and see if your grandmother wants anything."

Shanell couldn't believe it. She didn't feel any different. She checked herself in the mirror and she didn't look any different from how she always looked. You really can't tell whether a girl's a virgin or not, at least not by looking at her, she thought. Well, one thing I know. Tricia still is, she laughed smugly.

At first it had hurt like hell and it was over so quick. 'I don't see what the big deal is anyway.' One thing she did know was that she was in love, really in love. Not like those schoolgirl crushes she'd had many times before. No, this was different. She was Shay's girl now. The finest boy in school. All the girls were after him.

"Shanell, how's that popcorn doing?" Hazel yelled. Burnt. Shanell peered down at the burnt kernels sticking to the insides of the bag and dumped everything into the trash. Luckily there was one last bag.

She called Shay the day after but his mother said he wasn't at home, and she hadn't been able to catch up with him at school. She glanced over at the telephone wondering if it was too late to call. It was 11:30 pm. Should she take a chance? If somebody else answers, I'll just hang up.

She dialed his number and listened to it ring. On the fourth ring, a man's voice answered. "Hello," it was fuzzy with sleep. "Hello." Shanell held the receiver trying to get up enough nerve to ask for Shay.

"Who the hell is this calling this time of night?" Bam! The line went dead. Smelling the burning popcorn, she hung up the phone and rushed over to the microwave. "Damn," she swore. "Momma, I burned the popcorn," she yelled.

"I can smell it all the way in here," Hazel responded. "Well, get another bag and hurry up."

"I burned the last bag, too."

"Can't you do anything right?" her mother said. "Forget it, the movie's back on."

22

❧

Ma'dear

"*Y*ou *sure one fine looking thing," Willie Joe held me close as we danced across the floor. My eyes was filled with stars. Then the music changed and suddenly he swung me loose and I almost fell. He caught me and we jitterbugged to Louis Jordan's orchestra.*

"*He was rocking, he was rolling. Never seen such jumping to the break of dawn....*"

When I got off that floor, sweat was pouring down my face. My clothes was wringing wet and I could hardly catch my breath. Sadie gave me a dirty look when Willie Joe brought me back to the table. She jumped up and threw her arms around his neck, pressing her body into his.

"*Willie Joe,*" *she purred in that voice she uses when she's trying to get a man.* "*Dance this one with me,* honey." *Willie Joe smiled down on her, pulled out a big handkerchief, and wiped the sweat from his face.*

"Y'all women trying to wear me out." He winked at me and escorted Sadie to the floor. She would have to pick a slow song so she could get close to him. I sat there sipping my drink trying not to notice them. Then Willie Joe's buddy Mack, asked me to dance. A short man with a big stomach, his breath smelled like fried pork chops and beer. When he smiled at me, I noticed he had several gold teeth. His arms held me tight as he leaned his sweaty face against mine. I stiffened as I pulled away trying not to offend him or make him mad. He seemed to get the message because he loosened his grip. Then he started asking me questions about Sadie. Where she from? How old is she? Does she have a boyfriend? Stuff like that. I gave him all the particulars including some I made up. By the time the song ended, he got the impression that Sadie was after him. He spent the rest of the night trying to get her to dance with him. 'Course, both our eyes was on Willie Joe.

Sadie and me spent most Thursdays together on our days off. We rode the train from Bronxville back into the city to the room we kept for use on our day off. On Thursdays we'd party at Rockland Palace with all the people who worked in service, and got that day off.

Willie Joe didn't work in service. I'm not sure what he did for a living. Whatever it was he was always there and he always had plenty of money. Sadie and me would vie for his attention though he told me he favored me. Probably told her the same thing. I didn't know it at the time that he was playing us. Whenever we'd see him at the Palace, he'd ask both of us to dance, both of us fools thinking we was the light in his eyes.

After meeting up with him and his buddies at the Palace a few times, Willie Joe called me up and asked me to go to the ball game with him on my day off. We went up to Yankee Stadium to see the Monarchs play and after that, we took the train to Coney Island and spent the rest of the evening going on one ride after another. We rode on the Ferris wheel, the bumper cars, and even the roller coaster that scared me out of my wits. Just before it was time to go home, he took me on a ride through the Tunnel of Love. He held me in his arms and kissed me. It was the nicest evening.

Like I said, I didn't know much about him. What I did know was that he was a gentleman; at least he was with me. Tall, handsome, well built, he had a dark complexion, the color of dark chocolate with a head full of tight curly hair and a sweet smile. He made me laugh and he flattered me, telling me I was the prettiest thing he'd ever seen. He was so easy to talk to. I told him about my life, how me and Sadie had come up from Virginia and worked our way to New York working in service. He said when he got out of the army, after

WWII, he didn't know what to do with himself. A friend told him about getting a job as a sleeping car porter. He worked the rails for a while and got to see the country from one end to the other. What he hoped to do one day was move to California, get married, and have a house full of children.   He set me to dreaming, too.

I didn't tell Sadie about Willie Joe and me seeing as how every time I mentioned his name, she'd talk about him like he was a dog.

"Why you want that no account man. He ain't interested in nothing 'cept what he can get from you," she'd say. "I don't trust him. What he want with you anyway?"

She'd run him into the ground so much that I wouldn't tell her nothing about him and me.

Sadie and me worked for a while for the same rich family in Bronxville. I was hired to be the live-in upstairs maid. Sadie was their cook. When I first saw how these people lived, I wasn't that impressed. I'd worked in white folks' homes before in the South with their huge mansions, swimming pools and all.

The Bloomsteins lived in a large house with a grand piano in the downstairs living room, a tennis court in their backyard and a swimming pool. But they were the messiest people I ever saw. They'd just drop their clothes wherever they fell. I guess I would too if I knew there'd be somebody to pick up after me. Mrs. Bloomstein had a closet full of clothes and more shoes than she'd ever wear even if she wore one pair a day for a year. I tried to get my feet in a few, but gave up when I almost busted a nice pretty green pair of suede pumps trying to get my size eight foot into a size six shoe.

I didn't get to see much of Sadie, she being downstairs and all. I'd sneak downstairs from time to time whenever the head butler wasn't around. He was in charge and you'd think he was the master of the house the way he kept an eye on us with his uppity ways. You know how black folk can be when you give them a little authority. He even talked like the Bloomsteins.

I didn't realize how much Sadie was stuck on Willie Joe until six months later when we was having a conversation on the train riding back to Bronxville. I happened to mention that Willie Joe asked me to marry him. I didn't know that much about him, but it didn't matter. I was nineteen and to me he was the world. Whenever we was together, nothing else existed. He could make me laugh, cry, rage and sing. The man made me want to sing all the time. He was all I wanted or thought I ever wanted. So I was bubbling all over with the news and though I knew Willie Joe and Sadie went out together a few times, it didn't matter to me. Willie Joe wasn't no saint. He told me he liked women,

*but he said I was special and he wanted me to be his
wife.*

*"You a damn fool," Sadie said in a harsh whisper.
"The man's no good.   How could you ever think of
marrying him?"*

23

❧

Hazel

Letters and packages began to arrive shortly after Hazel told Donald he could use her address. All were addressed to E&M Inc. Hazel glanced at them and dropped them in a shoebox and set it by the door. At first she was curious; they all were, but as she valued her privacy, she respected others. She stopped Shanell and Tricia from steaming one envelope open when they first began to arrive.

Donald called about a week later and asked if he could pick them up. And today, as she came in from work, she saw his car, a brand new shiny BMW with a personalized license plate, parked in front of her apartment. Her arms loaded with groceries, she struggled to insert the key into the outside lock. The door swung open and Mrs. Frazier stepped out. She was a woman in her early fifties, a bit on the heavy side, bosomy, with broad hips that made her waist look small. Her salt and pepper hair was short and neatly pressed. Always a pleasant smile on her face, she was shorter than Hazel by about 3 inches. Her legs reminded Hazel of tree stumps.

"Evening, Mrs. Porter. Just getting in from work?"

Hazel smiled as best she could, hoping to slip upstairs before becoming engaged in a long conversation.

"Need any help with your groceries? I can call Mr. Frazier."

"No thanks, I'm fine." She started up the steps.

"That's a handsome looking car out front. Mr. Norris got him a new car?" Mrs. Frazier said. She was well meaning and a great help to Hazel at times, but she was also quite nosy. There was nothing she liked better than to question Hazel about her personal life and gossip about everybody else in the building.

"No, I don't know who it belongs to," she said. Who else would have "HYROLA" for a license plate but Donald! That was one of their biggest problems - his gambling as well as his scheming, always trying to get something for nothing. But she wasn't about to tell Mrs. Frazier her business.

"I saw a well-dressed, handsome young man go upstairs about a half hour ago. I wonder who he came to visit?"

Hazel shrugged. Her arms felt like they were about to fall off. "If you'll excuse me, I've got to put these frozen vegetables in the freezer before they thaw."

"Don't they spoil quick. Well, don't let me keep you. I was on my way to the store. Do you need anything? I don't expect you do. I'll let you go. Tricia and Shanell sure are growing. You got your hands full." She laughed. As she stepped cautiously down the outside steps, holding tightly to the banister, she muttered, "My arthritis is acting up again."

Hazel pressed her head to the door of the apartment, listening. Donald's booming voice drifted out to her. She hesitated before putting her key in the lock. When she opened it, everybody's eyes turned to look at her. Tricia and Shanell sat on the couch, Donald in the recliner. He jumped up and tried to take her packages.

Waving him off, Hazel said, "That's all right. The girls can manage." She handed the groceries to them. They carried them into the kitchen glad to be relieved of the burden of holding an conversation with a person they didn't think much of.

"Woman, you still looking good enough to eat. Lemme take a look at you. Hmm, hmm, hmm." He shook his head, a broad smile on his lips.

Donald was barely five feet nine with a shoulder length Jheri curl. Neatly dressed in an expensive looking suit that didn't hide his muscular build and slender waist. He was thirty-two, three years younger than Hazel. Women found him attractive. He had a devastating smile, and a sparkle in his eyes, one that made a woman think that he belonged to her solely— that is, before you got to know him. Hazel fell for his smile and his smooth talk, and against her better judgment and her mother's advice, married him thinking he'd be a good father to the two girls. Too late, she realized that she was actually driven by loneliness, the same thing that propelled her into all her relationships.

"Donald," Hazel said, sitting down on the sofa and kicking off her shoes. "Have you been here long? Did the girls offer you anything to drink, ice tea or juice?" She tried to maintain a level of disinterest in her voice. "Shanell," she called, not waiting for his response. "Bring Donald a glass of ice tea."

Shanell brought the glass and set it on the table beside him. He smiled up at her and took a sip. After she had gone he said, "They sure have grown. How long has it been, a little over year?"

He sat opposite her, seeming to undress her with his eyes. He knew too much about her, she thought., nervously uncrossing her legs and pulling her skirt over her knees.

"I've got your mail. It's in this box by the door. The girls should have given it to you so you didn't have to wait." She jumped up and strode over to the door, picking up the box.

"I wanted to see you, that's why I waited." As he took the box, barely glancing down at its contents, his hand brushed against hers. He covered her hand with his and held it. She pulled away and sat back down on the sofa.

"Yes, long time, no see. Anyway, Donald, what have you been up to? And you never explained just why you needed to use this address."

"I told you. I'm starting a business and until I get a post office box, I needed some other address other than my own. I sure like that outfit you're wearing. You always knew how to wear clothes." He sat down beside her. "I really miss you." He ran his fingers along her neck and reached over to kiss her hand. She jumped up.

"You got your mail. Now, if that's all. I've got to see about Ma'dear."

"That's right. Tricia said something about your mother staying with you. How's she doing? Not that I care. She never liked me and the feeling was mutual."

"She's fine.   From now on, I'll leave the box outside the door.   That way you won't have to come in." She opened the door indicating for him to leave.

He transferred the envelopes to his briefcase and stood up. "I appreciate your doing this for me. I promise you, as soon as I get a P.O box, I won't bother you anymore." He brushed close to her and reached out for her hand again. She didn't resist. Bringing it up to his lips, he kissed it. Staring into her eyes, he whispered in his most seductive voice,

"Maybe we can have dinner sometime. We were magic together, remember?"

She remembered, blood flooding into her face. That was the only good thing about him, the way he made love, a man who had had a lot of practice. He knew how to make a woman feel good. She shut her mind at the thought. Before she could reply coldly, he was gone.

Just as Hazel closed the door, Tricia and Shanell scurried back into the room.

"Were you girls listening again?"   Hazel said. "What did I tell you about eavesdropping?"

"We weren't listening. We were just ready if you needed us. For defense," Tricia said sliding easily down on the sofa, a magazine in her hands.

"What did he want?" Shanell asked, following her mother into the kitchen. "We wasn't gonna let him in at first. Then Tricia remembered you had said something about him coming by to pick up some letters. Momma, I don't see what you ever saw in that man."

"Peel these potatoes while I get dinner started." After washing her hands in the sink, she opened the refrigerator and took out a package of chicken breast.

Taking the peeler from the drawer, Shanell picked up a potato and began to peel it. "Ugh! I can't stand his cologne. It smells stronger than Tricia's cheap perfume. And did you see all that jewelry? I hate men who wear flashy jewelry, gold necklaces and diamond rings. He must got a lot of money from somewhere."

"It's not any of our business where he gets his money from," said Hazel, tying an apron around her waist. She glanced up at the clock. It had struck her that Donald seemed to be on the good side of his luck. One of the last times she'd seen him was when she walked out on him almost a year and a half ago. He hadn't had a job in months and didn't seem interested in getting one. He'd lie around the house and sleep all day until evening when he'd go out and stay half the night. Or when she'd come home from work and he'd have some of his hoodlum friends in, playing cards, smoking, drinking, and with music blaring. It seemed like all they did was argue until one day, she had had enough. It wasn't a healthy atmosphere for Tricia and Shanell.

For weeks she searched and found an apartment for her and her daughters. And when he went out for the evening, they quickly packed their things, taking whatever could fit into her car and left, leaving no forwarding address.

He called her at work until her supervisor told him "Mrs. Porter is no longer allowed to receive outside calls except in an emergency." Then he'd be waiting for her when she came out of the building pleading for her to come home. Finally she threatened to get a restraining order against him. She filed for divorce. The last time she saw him was in court when the divorce was granted. He still asked her to forgive him but for her, it was over. After seeing him today, she began to have regrets about allowing him back in her life. Oh well, it was too late now. She just hoped he'd get a P.O. box soon and that would be the end of it.

24

ॐ

Tricia

Not a word from Darien since that night. I went by Music Music where he worked but all I did was look through the window at him. He didn't see me and I didn't have the nerve to go in. I tried to call him a few times. As soon as I heard his voice, I'd hang up without saying anything. I missed him.

The other night I went to the studio to rehearse. I told Gracie about my problem and she said, "Forget him. There're enough men out there to ring your chimes a thousand times over."

"How can you just forget somebody you love?" I asked. She didn't have an answer to that. She just laughed. Kanisha came in and we started to rehearse.

Since that incident with Mr. Donohue, it was tense for a while but it was back to normal again. The girls knew I wouldn't just walk out on them. We worked out some great arrangements and we practiced new routines so that we'd be ready for our next gig. Harry had us booked at a local club down on Florence for Friday night. We would be singing backup for this old singer Harry said use to be popular back in the 1960s. He needed backup singers for this one night engagement. The pay wouldn't be much, but I could sure use it. With Momma not sure about whether she'd be laid off, it was just a matter of time.

Momma called Shanell and me in for a family discussion. We didn't have family discussions often; only when something serious was about to happen like when Ma'dear was coming, or when she decided to leave Donald.

"You all know there's been cutbacks at my job. I may be the next to go," she said. I looked at Shanell who was about to say something but Momma stopped her.

"I know what you're going to say. How are we going to survive? Well, I don't know myself," she said. Her voice was shaky. Shanell reached out and grabbed her hand.

"Momma, don't worry about a thing. I can quit school, get a job and help out," I said.

"I hope it won't come to that. I just wanted you to be aware of what might happen. That's why I've been kind of hard on you two lately. I've got so much on my mind."

She wiped a tear from her cheek. At this moment I wished I was out of school and had a good job so that I could take care of all of us. I hated to see Momma going through so much by herself. I put my arm around her shoulder.

"Everything'll work out. You'll see," I told her. But I wasn't so sure.

After school the next day, I had to meet Gracie and Kanisha at Club Zanzibar at 4:30 PM. to rehearse with Big Jim Thornton. I was nervous because I heard some pretty bad things about Big Jim. I heard he was hard on backup singers. Kanisha said he was a perfectionist, that if you sang one wrong note, he'd stop everything and embarrass you in front of everyone. He might even ask you to leave right then and there.

Club Zanzibar was one of those clubs that had been around for ages. I heard some big names use to play there, people like Billy Holiday and Dinah Washington, old singers I read about in some old Jet magazine I borrowed from the lady next door. Mrs. Rose saved everything. She had a garage that was too full to hold her car. It was stuffed with old magazines and newspapers that probably went back to the Civil War.

The Club use to be one of the top clubs in its day. I walked in and right away my eyes were drawn to the walls. They were covered with black and white autographed photos of Nat King Cole, Ella Fitzgerald, Charlie Parker, Fats Waller and others. I stared up at them.

"Can I help you, little lady? You looking for your daddy? You ain't the police are you? Trying to take away my license," he laughed. I jumped as I turned around. The man looked like a scarecrow, all skin and bones, with a bald head and a nice crooked smile. He wore a rumpled suit jacket and navy blue pants that looked a size too big.

"I'm looking for my friends, Kanisha and Gracie. We're supposed to sing backup for Big Jim Thornton tonight. We're going to rehearse," I said, my voice shook.

"Ain't seen nobody. At least not yet. Say, how old are you?" He raised his eyebrows, inspecting me like I was a juicy piece of steak. "You old enough to be in here?" Taking off his jacket, he went behind the bar, hung it up, and rolled up his sleeves. In spite of his skinny frame, his arms looked strong like iron pipes. He switched on the TV mounted above the bar.

I glanced down at my hands. "Do you mind if I wait over by the jukebox?" I asked, knowing I sounded like a little child and wishing I could disappear into the shadows. My stomach fluttered as I moved quickly across the floor to the jukebox.

"Say Hey man. What's happening? Gimme a double bourbon on the rocks and make it quick. Working for the man gives me the shakes. Gotta have something to calm me down." I watched a tall heavy-set man who looked like a bear in a pin stripped suit stroll up to the bar. On his face was a wide grin that grew wider when he looked over at me. On his head he wore a leather cap that he tipped at me.

"Give the little lady whatever she wants, too."

"Down, Jackson. She's a minor. Your eyes must be getting bad. Don't give me that jive about working for the man. You ain't done a day's work in your life. Least wise nothing that would even break a sweat across your brow."

The bartender gave him a drink and he strolled over to where I was standing. "My name's Jackson. What's yours?" I told him. He held out his hand and took mine gently stroking it. "You sure got pretty hands, soft delicate." He stared at me. "What are you doing in a place like this?" He gestured towards the room.

"We're singing backup tonight for Big Jim Thornton."

"How old are you? You not twenty-one are you? If you're not, you better not let anybody catch you. Don't want my man Sam to lose his license." He put his hand in his pants pocket and pulled out four quarters. "Play anything you like."

While I was looking over the songs, a woman walked through the door.

"Hey Jackson," she called over to him as she slid onto the barstool. "Come over here. I got a bone to pick with you."

She lit a cigarette and crossed her legs. She wore a dress that looked just a little too tight and emphasized the bulges around her middle. Though she glanced over at me, she didn't say anything. Jackson waved at her as he walked towards the bar.

"I'll send you over something, non alcoholic," he said over his shoulder.

A few minutes later, the bartender brought over a glass of coke filled with ice. I thanked him.

"Say, little miss. When you finish, I'd feel much better if you would leave. You're not allowed in here unless you're twenty-one," Mr. Sam said.

"But I'm waiting for some people. We're supposed to sing here tonight," I protested. Damn, I wish I hadn't been so anxious to see this place. If I had waited and come with Gracie and Kanisha, then maybe nobody would have noticed me. I really wanted to do this gig. Just as I was about to leave, Gracie and Kanisha walked in. I rushed over to meet them.

"The bartender said I have to leave because I'm underage."

"You didn't tell him how old you are, did you?" Kanisha asked. "She's gonna screw up this gig for us," she said to Gracie. I felt myself getting annoyed.

"You can always get somebody else." I started to walk out.

"Not at this late date. You should have waited for us before you went in."

"Don't worry," Gracie said. "The bartender leaves at five. And he won't be here tonight. We'll have Tricia fixed up and looking like she's thirty when we come back. I'll go over and talk to him. Maybe he'll let us rehearse for a while. Get used to the place. I'll make up something. Y'all wait here."

I stood by the door. Kanisha went with Gracie and I saw them talking to the bartender. After a short while, they came back. Gracie was smiling.

"He says it's okay. As long as you stay in the background."

We went over to the piano and Kanisha began to run through some of our songs. A half hour later, Big

Jim Thornton walked in. He was a huge man who looked just like his picture. He was over six feet and looked like he weighed at least 300 lbs. He sweated a lot and kept a towel hanging out his waistband. He greeted us with a wave of his hand and started ordering his musicians around, three guys—a saxophone player, a bassist, and a drummer. They set up quickly and Big Jim sat down at the piano and warmed up.

"Let's see what you girls can do," he said after he'd played through one of his numbers. "You've heard my recording of "Swamp City Blues," haven't you? All you got to do is do what you heard on my record."

He jumped off into the song; his band leaped in after the first four bars. Gracie, Kanisha and I found our note and ran after him. At first it was going great, then suddenly he stopped and banged down on the piano.

"What the fuck's going on? Somebody's off key. I thought you girls knew what you were doing?"

I was confused. Nobody was off key as far as I could tell. Gracie, Kanisha and I looked at each other. Kanisha started to say something but Big Jim cut her off.

"I don't want to hear no goddamn excuses. You either get it right or get the hell out." Then he demonstrated what he wanted us to do. I was shaking in my boots through the rest of the rehearsal. He didn't stop anymore. I guess we did all right because he said he'd see us back at the club tonight at 8:30 pm. He mopped his forehead, grabbed his jacket and hat and headed towards the bar. Mr. Sam handed him a shot glass of something. He drank it in one gulp, set the glass on the counter and walked out.

I hadn't paid any attention to the musicians until now. The saxophone player came over and apologized. "Sorry. Big Jim's like that. Don't let him scare you. Just do what you did today and everything'll be all right. By the way, my name's Hi C." He put out his hand for each of us to shake. "Hi C," Gracie asked. "What kind of name is that?" She laughed.

"Named after my father. His name was E flat." We all laughed, Gracie and me, that is. Kanisha was in the telephone booth. Gracie whispered she had to use the little girls' room. As he was putting his sax in a case, he asked me, "Your first time singing backup?" I told him this was the first time we would be singing in a nightclub. "But not the first time we've sang back up. Mostly in the studio. And we've never backed up anybody as famous as Big Jim."

He looked like he was in his late twenties, younger than the other guys. He was short, a little taller than me and stocky, not fat, just solid. On his head was one of those African hats made of Kente cloth. He had on a Dashiki to match and dark pants. I liked his smile. He smelled like cigarettes and aftershave lotion. He said he'd been playing with Big Jim for about a year. "Big Jim's on his way out. This'll probably be my last gig with him. I'm thinking about starting my own jazz combo. You like jazz?"

"I don't get a chance to listen to it much. But I do like Phyllis Hyman and Al Jarreau." We went on like that until Gracie came back and said they were leaving.

"See you tonight," Hi C said and left along with the other musicians.

"He's cute," I said to Gracie.

"Forgot Darien already? You go girl. Anyway, we gotta be coordinated. What color should we wear? I got this cute pink number."

"Pink!" I said. "I don't have anything pink. Besides, we gonna be in the background. We can't be standing out."

"You're right. How about dark green? I think I can find something green in my closet. See if you can find a green blouse, or skirt; something sexy and that makes you look older. Drop by my pad and we'll come down here together." Kanisha joined us as we walked toward Gracie's car. Gracie told her what color we had decided on. "Hop in. I'll take you home."

Kanisha jumped in the back seat. I sat in the front beside Gracie.

"The man's a trip," Kanisha said settling in the back. She pulled out a joint and started to light it.

"Girl, don't be starting that shit in my car. You want to get us busted?" Gracie yelled. I rolled down my window.

"Don't be so scared. Nobody gives a shit about what I'm doing. Besides, I need to come down."

Gracie pulled over to the curb. "You put that mess out right now or you can get out and walk. There's a time and place for everything."

Kanisha took one last draw and gently rubbed it out in the ashtray. She wrapped the butt in a tissue and put it in her purse. We drove on for a while not saying anything. I hoped Kanisha wouldn't get stoned by evening though I knew she'd be high. She usually was. At least when she was wasted she was not so much of a bitch as she was when she was sober. Gracie dropped her off first.

"I hope she's not too high tonight," Gracie said like she was reading my thoughts. "I think I'd better pick her up early just to make sure."

When she dropped me off, I barely waved goodbye. I thought about what I was going to wear tonight for my first important signing engagement. Even though we were just singing backup, you never know who might be in the audience. Suddenly it came to me. I knew what I'd wear. My new sequined green dress, the one I bought a while ago and had been saving for just this occasion.

25

 ✑

Shanell

Shanell put her head down on the desk at school. She heard her teacher call her, but she didn't feel like answering. All she could think of was the way Shay passed by her in the hall and didn't even look her way. He had his arm around Paulette's shoulder. Paulette with her long blond hair and creamy white skin was a cheerleader and very popular. They were laughing at something he had whispered in her ear. Shanell was tempted to say something to him. Instead she shrank back into the corner of the hall and prayed Shay wouldn't notice her. He didn't. Now in class, all she felt was a sinking feeling in her stomach. She wished she could leave the planet, disappear, go to another school, get away, anything but be here at this time.

"Shanell, the teacher's talking to you." She heard her friend Babe's voice. Babe pushed her arm. Shanell raised her head. Mr. Kravitz was looking at her as was everyone else in the class.

"What year was the Suez Canal built, Miss Porter? You should know this." His voice stern, he turned to address the entire class. "Pay attention to this review. It's going to be on the test tomorrow." Again, he focused his attention on Shanell. "Well, we're waiting."

Her head ached and she felt like she was going to throw up. She had to get out of there. Slowly, she got out of her seat and made her way to his desk. "Mr. Kravitz," she leaned towards him and whispered. "I don't feel well. Can I go to the nurse's office?"

"Are you trying to get out of class again?" The look on her face made him hastily write her a pass. He didn't want her vomiting all over his desk.

The nurse took her temperature and told her she could lie down on the small cot in her office until the end of the period.

"Can't I just go home?"

"Is there someone there who can pick you up? I could call your mother. What's her work number?" The nurse flipped through her files. Shanell thought of her mother rushing to the school to get her and decided.

"I think I can make it through the day," she said.

"Are you sure? You have a slight temperature and you may be coming down with something," Nurse Finch said.

"No, I guess I just needed some air. I'm feeling better already," Shanell said. She smiled weakly.

"Well, here's a pass to get back into class." The nurse scribbled a note and handed it to Shanell. She took it and started down the hall towards her classroom. When she came to the door to exit the building, she slipped through it, ran down the steps and into the bright sunlight.

She ran along the street until she came to a park. Sitting down on one of the benches, she watched a group of toddlers playing in the sandbox and mothers pushing their babies in strollers.

"Come here, Tommy. Don't put that in your mouth!" A young girl got up from a nearby bench. Carrying her infant in one arm, the girl who didn't look much older than Tricia, yelled at the toddler who was putting a shiny object into his mouth.

"Dammit, Tommy, spit it out!" She snatched at the child's arm. Tommy screamed and tried to pull away. The girl raised her hand and smacked the child hard on his bottom. She grabbed his arm and pulled him toward the bench next to where Shanell was sitting.

"These kids 'bout to drive me wild. I shoulda had my head examined...."

Shanell watched as she placed the infant in her carriage, reached into her bag, and took out a banana. She peeled it, and gave it to Tommy.

She glanced over at Shanell. "You got any kids?" she asked. She was dressed in jeans, a tight tee shirt and sneakers; her dark hair, elaborately braided, hung down almost to her waist. In one nostril was a small diamond jewel. All along the outside of her earlobes were gold hoops that ranged from tiny to large. Her fingernails were long and painted a bright green. Shanell wondered how she found time to care for herself and her kids.

Shanell shook her head. "I'm only fourteen."

"Shit. I was fifteen when I had Tommy. He's three and a half. Say, shouldn't you be in school? Whatchu doing here in the park? They let you out early?"

"No, I wasn't feeling well so I left."

"Ditched, huh? I know. I use to do that all the time. Now I wish I'da stayed in school and not had these kids. Tommy, come over here! Don't throw no rocks at them birds. Had to drop out of school to take care of my kids. Hold her for me, will you?"

Before Shanell had a chance to say anything, the girl handed her the baby and took off after the child who had disappeared behind a distant shrub. The baby suddenly began to cry. Shanell held her and rocked her gently, putting the pacifier in the baby's mouth. The cries grew louder as the baby pushed the pacifier away.

"Don't cry. Your mommy will be right back." But the baby continued to cry and squirm in Shanell's arms. Feeling helpless, she looked around for the mother and saw her some distance away with Tommy. Just then two elderly women strolled by and glancing at Shanell and the crying baby, shook their heads in disapproval. Shanell could read the look on their faces. She wanted to say, "This ain't my baby."

"Thanks, I'll take her." The baby's mother took the child and shoved a bottle into her mouth. The baby ate greedily. Tommy, thumb stuck in his mouth, climbed up on the bench beside his mother and lay his head in her lap.

"By the way, my name's Gloria. What's yours?" Shanell told her. "That's a pretty name. I was gonna name my baby Chanel like the perfume or LaToya. But then I decided on Chemise. If I have another girl, I'll name her Lanika. Not that I plan on having another baby soon. My mama almost killed me when I had Tommy. Then I got pregnant with Chemise."

"Does their father help you take care of them?" Shanell asked.

"Are you kidding? Tommy's father is in jail. Don't know where Chemise's daddy is. Probably out getting some other girl pregnant. If I had it to do over, I'da stayed in school and left the men alone, least until I got my education. You can't do nothing without an education. What time is it?" She looked down at her watch.

"Almost noon. You hungry? I don't live far from here. Why don't you come home with me and I'll fix us something to eat."

Shanell thought about going home but knew that she couldn't until 3 P.M. The nurse was there with her grandmother and she was sure to question her about why she wasn't at school. Besides, there was nothing to do at home.

"Okay, if you don't mind. Here, I'll help with Tommy." She took the little boy by the hand and walked beside Gloria as she pushed the baby carriage out of the park and down a few blocks until she came to a large house.

"I live in the back," she explained. "Got me a little place after my mother kicked me out. It ain't much but it's home." They walked around the side of the two-story old Victorian house down the driveway, passed the garbage cans and a huge bougainvillea that almost obscured the structure in back. The tiny house looked as if it had once been used as a storage shed but had been converted into living quarters. It was badly in need of paint. Other than that, to Shanell, it looked great.

"I tried to fix it up a bit. When Mama was speaking to me, she brought over things, helped me put up some curtains," Gloria said as she unlocked the door.

They entered a large rectangular room that served as living room, bedroom, and kitchen, and a small room off to the side that Shanell assumed was the bathroom.

"Just put Tommy down on the couch. I'll let him sleep awhile." Tommy had insisted Shanell carry him and he had fallen asleep in her arms. Grateful to be relieved from her heavy load, she lay him gently down on the couch and pulled a knitted colorful afghan over him. Then she sat down on an overturned box near the table and watched as Gloria undressed the sleeping baby, put a clean diaper on her, and place her in her crib.

After the baby was settled, Gloria lit a cigarette and walked over to the refrigerator, peered inside, and withdrew a package of lunchmeat, a loaf of white bread, and a jar of mayonnaise.

"You want a beer?" She held a Budweiser up to Shanell. "Course you don't." Popping the tab, she tilted her head back, took a long swallow, and burped.

"Only thing else I got is water and the baby's milk. I could send you to the store for a soda."

"No, that's alright. Water's fine," Shanell said. She picked up a magazine, Sepia Romance, and flipped through the pages. "My boyfriend is in love with his best friend" was the title of one article.

"Sorry I don't have a TV. My boyfriend said he was gonna get me one but he hasn't yet." Gloria handed Shanell a bologna sandwich and a jelly jar filled with tap water.

They talked a while about everything from boys to babies and before Shanell realized, it was 1:30. Both Tommy and Chemise had awakened and been fed. Gloria smoked several cigarettes and drank another can of beer. Shanell drank more water.

At one point she asked to use the bathroom. She had trouble closing the door. Closing the bathroom door was a problem as it also served as a closet, she observed. Some clothes hung on the back of the door, some were piled on the overflowing hamper, and some littered the floor.

It was fun talking to Gloria especially about boys. Gloria had a great sense of humor and loved to talk. She laughed a lot except when one of the children upset her. Then she'd reach out and smack them. Actually she smacked Tommy hard on the bottom several times and shook the baby when she cried too much. Suddenly, it was 2 P.M.

"Would you mind looking after the kids while I run to the store for a minute? It's easier to shop alone than to drag them along," Gloria said as she stepped out of her jeans and took off her sneakers. When she went into the bathroom, Shanell heard the water running. When Gloria came out, she was wearing a short dress and after putting on makeup, she slid her feet into a pair of high-heeled wedgies. She looked a lot older than eighteen; especially when she tied her braids back with a black ribbon.

"I won't be long," she said as she closed the door behind her.

It didn't dawn on Shanell until an hour later that Gloria wasn't dressed for grocery shopping. She played with Tommy, read him a story, changed Chemise's diaper and gave her another bottle. After picking up the clothes Gloria had thrown all over the place, she folded them and placed them on the end of the table. Then she washed the pile of dishes stacked in the sink. It looked as if they'd been sitting there a long time. Finally she swept the floor.

When the clock struck 4 P.M. she began to worry. She looked out the window; however, all she could see was the bougainvillea and the lengthening shadows.

Where is she? I gotta get home. What if she don't come back? What am I gonna tell Momma when she finds out I ditched school? Her mind chattered as she tried to read another article in Sepia Romance Magazine, but she couldn't concentrate on "Pregnant by my stepfather."

Tommy began to get cranky. "I want my mommy!" His cries grew louder. Shanell made him the last of the bologna sandwiches that calmed him while he ate. Chemise began to cry. She could find no more bottles of milk for the baby. The diaper bag held one more diaper. After changing her, she picked up the baby and walked around the room, hoping the child would fall asleep.

Again she thought, 'what if she don't come back? What do I do with the children? I can't go off and leave them alone.'

Suddenly there was a loud knock on the door. "Gloria, open up. I know you in there!" A man's deep voice demanded. "If you don't open up this damn door, I'm gonna kick it in."

Trembling, Shanell opened it a crack and said, "Gloria ain't here." A dark-skinned rough looking man in his late twenties stood just outside. He had a scar that ran along his nose and under his eye. He wore a heavy sweater and black jeans. On his head he wore a skullcap and dark sunglasses.

"Where she be?" he asked. Shanell heard a trace of a West Indian accent.

"I don't know," Shanell said. She heard something fall behind her. She glanced over her shoulder and saw Tommy had knocked over a lamp. Chemise began to howl again.

"When she get back, tell her Raymond stopped by. Tell her I want my fucking money!"

"I'll tell her," said Shanell her heart racing as she closed the door. The clock struck 6 o'clock.

26

✍

Ma'dear

*W*illie *Joe and me got married early one Thursday morning at the Justice of the Peace. Then we went out to Coney Island and spent the rest of the day riding the Ferris Wheel and going through the Tunnel of Love. When it got dark, he took me to his room on 128th Street off 5th Ave.   He lived on the first floor of a rooming house.   I'd been there just once before for a quick minute but now this was to be my home.   He had a big bed right in the middle of the room, a dresser on one side near the window, a closet stuffed with his clothes, and one chair that stood beside a small table. It had a communal bathroom and kitchen. Willie Joe kept a hotplate in his room.   The landlord wasn't too crazy about him bringing me there, but when Willie Joe told him we was married, he said it was okay.*

He carried me across the threshold and carefully set me down. I looked around. "Honey, where am I gonna put all my stuff?" I laughed. "This is gonna be mighty small for the two of us."

"Don't you worry," he said. "Before long we gonna find us a larger place. I got my eye on one." He sat down on the bed, pulled me down beside him and kissed me.

We stayed in bed the whole weekend. Only time we got up was to get something to eat from the Chinese restaurant down the street. I called Mrs. Bloomstein Saturday morning and told her I was in bed with the flu.

She said, "Take your time getting over it. Don't want you spreading it around."

I thought about taking a week but then I figured we needed the money especially now that we was married.

It was a year before we moved. I got so use to living in that box that when we moved to a one bedroom flat, I almost didn't know what to do with myself.

But about Sadie. She didn't take it none too lightly. That Monday after we was married, Sadie approached me when I got to work. She came upstairs and sat on the chair, watching me picking up Mr. and Madam's *clothes and straightening up the room. I could feel her eyes following my every move. I hadn't told her.*

"You didn't come home the entire weekend. Had to go to Rockland Palace by myself. Didn't see Willie Joe neither. Was he with you?"

I hadn't planned on telling her just yet but what else could I do?

"Willie Joe and me got married Friday," I said, not looking at her.

I caught a glimpse of her face in the mirror. The look she gave me made me shiver. I tell you, it scared me. She didn't say a word at first. Then she smiled a funny kinda smile. And just as sweet as can be, she reached out and hugged me.

"Congratulations, I hope you two will be very happy together."

I felt relieved when she said that though I still had a strange feeling inside.

"Guess I'll have to get me a new roommate," she said as she went back down to the kitchen.

She asked me and Willie Joe over to dinner a week later. She fixed up a real feast: pork chops, mashed potatoes, and collard greens, cake and ice cream for dessert, and coffee. We had a good time that night. We all was in a good mood. Willie Joe bought a bottle of scotch and after dinner, we drank our fill. He told us some jokes and had us laughing. I was grateful because

I wasn't sure about how Sadie was taking our marriage. When I talked to him about how I felt, he said I was letting my imagination run away with me.

"Sadie don't mean you no harm."

I quit working for the Bloomsteins shortly after we married and went to work as a cleaning woman at Macy's Department Store. Since I worked in town I got to go home regularly. I worked nights. Willie Joe had settled down just after we got together. He was a gambler, he told me, but being a married man, he felt he needed a steady job. You can't count on gambling. He found a job as a doorman at a big hotel downtown.

It was about a few months later when I started feeling like something was wrong. Willie Joe started turning away from me. When I asked him what was wrong, he said it wasn't nothing. But I noticed every time I'd reach out to hold him at night, he'd move away. At first I thought it had to do with something at work. We was doing right fine, that is until he started turning away.

When I'd come home from work early in the morning, we usually had a few hours together before he had to get up and go to work. They were precious hours. One day, I came home and fell in bed beside him. When I reached for him, he got up.

"What's the matter, honey?" I asked watching him light up a cigarette and sit in the chair. It was still dark outside with just a trace of gray.

"Nothing," he said, putting his head in his hands. He wouldn't look at me.

I got up and tried to sit on his lap. I wanted him to hold me. When I reached out for him, he pushed me away.

"Don't," he said. He started putting on his clothes. "I'm going for a walk." It was almost 6 AM. He didn't have to be to work until 8. He was gone before I could open my mouth. I fell asleep and when I woke up, I saw that he'd come back, ate and gone off to work. Just before I had to leave, he came in. It was like nothing had happened. He was his old self again. We made love just before I had to run out the door. I had worried about him all day as I cleaned up the room and made dinner. When I left for work that evening, I felt everything was all right. It must have been something on his job that he didn't want to talk about.

When I came home the next morning, though, he turned away from me like he did the previous morning. This went on for weeks and it seemed to be getting worse. Before long, I was on pins and needles wondering what was going on. Whenever I asked him, he'd say, nothing was wrong. The weeks went by and he wouldn't touch me. I guess we started getting on each other's nerves. Then I discovered I was pregnant. When I told him, he almost cried. We went out and searched for an apartment and found a nice kitchenette on 143rd Street. Didn't take us long to move in as we didn't have much to pack. This would be a new beginning, I thought. But it wasn't.

Willie Joe stopped eating the food I cooked for him. I'd find the plate of cold food still sitting where I left it. This made me so mad we started arguing. We argued day and night. One day I looked at him and saw how thin he was getting and how the circles under his eyes was getting darker. I told him he should go see a doctor. He said he couldn't afford one and besides, I was making a big thing about nothing. Those was the worst months in my life.

I had to talk to somebody about it so one day I called Sadie. I went over to our old room and it was the first time I'd laughed in months. We talked about the good old days and when I told her about what was happening between me and Willie Joe, she said, "Didn't I tell you you couldn't trust him. Probably got some hoe on the side."

It almost cut my heart in two to think about that. I went home feeling worse than before I came. Only this time Sadie had planted a seed that Willie Joe's actions fertilized. There's nothing worse than a suspicious wife. Every time I looked at my husband, all I could see was him taking another woman to bed and me carrying his child. I didn't like myself then because I lived and breathed just to find out who he was cheating with. I searched his clothes for telltale signs. One day I called in sick from work and followed him. When I discovered he was going to Sadie's place, I nearly died. I told him what I'd learned when he came in that evening. He was shocked to find me home. We had a big fight. I told him to get out and I never wanted to see him again. He got down on his knees and begged me to forgive him.

"I don't know what's happening to me. I don't want to cheat on you. I love you," he pleaded. "I just can't help myself. Please. Give me another chance. I promise it'll get better."

I thought about our baby. What chance would I have trying to raise a child alone? And besides, I still loved him. I told him he could stay.

27

✑

Hazel

The doorbell rang and Hazel, thinking it was the girls, opened it without asking the usual, "Who is it?" or looking through the peephole. There stood two men, one short and the other tall, both overweight, ugly and wearing rumbled suits that looked as if they'd slept in them. The short one flashed a badge.

"I'm Detective Garvey and this is my partner, Detective Bowler. We'd like to ask you a few questions. May we come in?"

Hazel's heart jumped. She clutched the collar of her robe. "Has something happened to one of my girls?" she asked in a trembling voice.

"No Ma'am. May we come in? It won't take long. We'd just like to ask you a few questions?"

Hazel stood aside and allowed the two men to enter. Detective Garvey sat down on the couch. From his breast pocket, he withdrew a small notepad and pen. Detective Bowler, the taller of the two, walked over to the window and glanced down at the street. He took out his handkerchief, blew into it, stuffed it into his back pocket and leaned against the wall. Hazel noticed he was carefully surveying the room.

She sat on the arm of the chair, wondering if they could hear her heart thump.

"Do you know a Donald Porter?" Garvey asked.

A wave of relief flooded her. *It's about Donald, not my girls.*

"Yes, he's my ex-husband," she responded.

"Have you seen him lately?" Garvey did the talking while Bowler moved from the window to peer at the photographs hanging on the wall.

Hazel's mind raced. "Is he in some kind of trouble?"

"Let's just say we want to ask him some questions. It's nothing that concerns you, Ma'am."

"When was the last time you saw him?" Bowler asked, standing near the kitchen door and peering in.

Hazel, recovering her composure, straightened her shoulders. "It's been a while," she said vaguely. *What was Donald into now? Whatever it was she needed to find out.*

"If you see him or hear from him, give us a call," Garvey said as he struggled to get off the couch.

"Can you tell me what this is about?"

"Sorry to disturb you, Ma'am," Garvey said ignoring her. He strode to the door. Bowler followed. Garvey reached into his breast pocket and handed her his card. They left.

After closing the door, Hazel went to the closet and picked up the box with Donald's mail. The box was almost full. She had expected him a few days ago as he came every two weeks; however, it had been weeks since she'd last seen him. Having no way to get in touch with her ex husband, she was torn whether to open the envelopes or throw them away. Oh well, she thought, replacing the box. It's his problem. But this is the last time he's going to use my address.

The ringing phone startled her

"Hey Baby." It was Donald.

"Two detectives were here looking for you."

"What did you tell them?"

"I didn't tell them anything. I don't know anything. Donald, what have you been up to?"

"I told you I'm in business. It's legit. I swear."

"Well, you'd better take your legit business somewhere else because I'm not going to have my home used as your mailbox anymore."

"Yeah, I know. I was calling to tell you I got my post office box."

"That's good. So when are you coming to pick up your mail?"

"There's a slight problem. I can't get over there. You gotta do me a favor. Could you bring it to me?"

"Why can't you come and get it?"

"I don't have transportation at the moment."

"What happened to the BMW? Donald, what are you really up to?"

"I'll explain it to you when you come. Can you meet me at ten o'clock tonight at the pier in Santa Monica?"

"Are you kidding? You're asking me to drive all the way to Santa Monica at ten tonight? You must be crazy."

"Hey, you want to get rid of me, right? This is the last time, I swear, Baby. I won't bother you no more."

If this is what it takes to get rid of him, I'll do it, she reasoned. She thought about asking Kevin if he'd go with her. After calling him and getting no answer, she left a message for him to call her. The door opened and Shanell walked in.

"Young lady. Where have you been? It's 6:30."

"Over at my friend's house," Shanell answered, throwing down her backpack and heading for the kitchen. Hazel knew she should get on Shanell about coming in so late, but her mind was still racing about the police's visit and Donald's call.

She prepared a tray for her mother, and then went into the kitchen to continue cooking dinner. As she entered the kitchen, she heard Tricia singing.

"Got a gig tonight, Mom. This may be my lucky break."

Tricia peered under the lid of the pot and stuck a fork in to taste the stew Hazel had simmering. Shanell was cutting up salad greens. Tricia grabbed a slice of tomato. Her sister didn't protest.

"Tricia, stop that!" Hazel said. "Dinner's almost ready. Set the table and tonight is your turn to wash dishes."

"I'll wash them when I get back from the gig." Tricia continued to sing as she set the table. "Can we make this quick. I've gotta get dressed."

Dinner was a quiet affair. Hazel couldn't concentrate; her mind on Donald and the police. Shanell's was on her day at Gloria's. Tricia's was on tonight's engagement. When they finished their meal, Shanell helped Hazel clear the table while Tricia went to her room to get dressed.

At 9:30 Hazel started out for Santa Monica. It was a mild evening; stars filled the sky; a bright moon bathed the street in shadows. There was little traffic as she drove along Venice Blvd. to Lincoln. She turned off on Ocean Avenue and down a side street where she searched for a place to park. She was still a ways from the pier, which was lit up with the newly restored merry-go-round, eateries and wall-to-wall people. A gentle breeze blew against her skin.

Though it was late April, Hazel shivered as she strode quickly towards the pier. How was she going to find Donald in this crowd? She'd put his mail in a shopping bag. Carrying it to the end of the pier, she stopped near the railing and waited not daring to sit down on the benches stained with the remains of the day's fishing, and the droppings from the gulls. Few people ventured to the end of the pier at this time of night.

The food kiosk was closed and stood like an abandoned hovel. A few lovers, their arms tightly around each other's waist, kissed, stood for a while, and then walked back to the lights and the crowd.

She noticed a man coming towards her. At first she thought it was Donald but as he passed under a lamppost, she saw he was thin, medium height, and sported a beard. He wore a dark blue hoodie, and of all things, dark glasses. She wondered how he could see. Stopping a few yards from her, he lit a cigarette. She began to feel uneasy as she turned away. If Donald isn't here in five minutes, I'm leaving, she thought. Glancing down at her watch she saw that it was 10:15. When she turned around, she had the strangest feeling that the man had moved closer. Maybe it was her imagination.

She thought about the girls at home and the argument that had broken out over Tricia's dress. She couldn't find her new dress or something like that. She had accused Shanell of taking it. Tricia had turned the place upside down looking for it. To quiet the storm, Hazel loaned her a dress she could no longer wear. It had gotten too snug. Reluctantly, Tricia put it on. She looked pretty good in it, and with her face made up, she looked older than her seventeen years. Hazel cautioned her to be careful and as usual, she waved her mother off. "Oh Momma, You worry too much. I can take care of myself."

The man had moved closer, Hazel wasn't mistaken. Now he was barely an arm's length away. Suddenly he reached out for the shopping bag.

"Gimme that," he said, as he tried to grab her arm. His breath smelled of liquor. Jerking her arm away, she swung at the man with her purse hitting him in the head. He stumbled. Just then a couple appeared from the other side of the darkened kiosk seemingly unaware of what was happening. Hazel didn't wait. She began to run back towards the lights and the people, and didn't stop until she reached her car.

Once inside, she locked the doors and drove, her body trembling, not sure where she was going. When she stopped her car in front of Kevin's apartment, she was still shaking. Once inside, he held her in his arms until her heart stopped racing and her breathing slowed.

"Drink this," he said, handing her a shot glass of Southern Comfort. The mellow liquor coursed through her body warming her insides and relieving the tension. She relaxed in Kevin's arms with her head on his shoulder, not speaking for almost ten minutes.

"Now, tell me what happened," he asked gently. She told him about her appointment to meet Donald that evening at the pier, about the police earlier that day, and about the man who grabbed her arm.

"I don't see the connection. Some drunk tried to steal your bag. That happens all the time especially that time of night. You know you shouldn't have been out there alone in the first place."

"What was I gonna do, Kevin? I just want to get rid of Donald once and for all."

"You don't owe him anything. You shouldn't have agreed to accept his mail. You told me he was a hustler. Why would you let yourself become involved with him again?"

Hazel listened patiently while he scolded her. Then she said, "You're right. I overreacted." She got up to leave. "I must be watching too much television."

She turned down his suggestion that she stay the night. "You've got to be up early in the morning to catch a flight. Besides, Shanell's home with Ma'dear and I need to get back."

"What are you going to do about his mail? If I were you, I'd toss it. Like I said, you don't owe him a thing." He walked her to her car and kissed her deeply. "I'll call you when I get back." He had to fly to San Francisco in the morning on an assignment.

It was midnight by the time Hazel reached her door. Tricia hadn't gotten in yet, she noted with annoyance. Shanell and her mother were asleep. She undressed for bed, but before settling down she went into the kitchen and dumped the contents of the shopping bag onto the table. Then she began to open the envelopes.

28

Tricia

What a night! When I found my brand new, never-worn dress balled up in the back of the closet, I was ready to kill Shanell. She pretended that she didn't know anything about it but who else woulda done that? So finally, she admitted that she did it and even apologized. Momma put her on punishment, but that didn't help me. I needed something to wear that would make me look older and sexy. Momma dug into her closet and pulled out one of her classy dresses that she wore when she and Kevin went out nightclubbing. She said it had gotten too tight. It was a sleeveless, lime green velvet shift with a scoop neck and fringes along the hemline. Since I was a little bit smaller than she was, she pinned it up and when she was through, it didn't look half bad though my own dress would have been just right. She loaned me a pair of her earrings and single strand pearl necklace and helped me do up my hair. I slid my feel into a pair of wedgies that made me look taller and accented my legs.

"Now, don't go thinking you're grown because you're still underage," she said.

"But Momma, I'm almost eighteen."

"Not for another month. You be back at a decent hour." She made me turn me around and nodded her approval.

I called Gracie and told her I was on my way to her house. I didn't have to wait long for a bus, and thank goodness, it wasn't crowded. When I got to her apartment, Gracie was putting the finishing touches on her makeup. She wore a low cut green sweater that showed plenty of cleavage, and a long black skirt that had a split that went up to her thigh.

"Girl, where'd you get that dress? It's jamming," she said as she walked around me. I told her it was my mother's. "My mom never had clothes that look like that.

"When we get to making some real money, we can start buying outfits that match. For now, we do the best we can." She stepped into some high heel black shoes. "These are gonna kill my feet, but what the hell. It's only for tonight." She grabbed a pair of sandals, "just in case. On second thought...." She changed from the high heels to the sandals. "Until we get there."

I redid my makeup, adding more mascara and rouge. Gracie combed my hair into a different style and I had to admit I looked good. We got into her car and she drove over to Kanisha's.

"Wait here while I run up and get her," Gracie said as she parked in front of Kanisha's building. It was almost 7:45 and already my stomach was bubbling over with that nervousness I always got when I had to perform. Somebody said that was good because when you're on edge, you do better than when you're all relaxed. I certainly wasn't relaxed. When I spotted a group of guys hanging out near the end of the block, I checked to make sure all the doors were locked and prayed they didn't notice me. I slid down low in the seat. The last thing I needed was to be hassled.

Suddenly I heard Gracie calling me. I rolled down the window and looked up. She yelled for me to come up. She needed my help. After locking the car, I walked up to Kanisha's apartment on the third floor. Gracie opened the door quickly and I followed her to the bedroom. Sure enough, Kanisha was stretched out on the bed sound asleep.

"Damn door was wide open and she's half dressed and dead to the world. Can you believe it?" Gracie shook her and yelled at her while I went into the kitchen and made some instant coffee.

We managed to get her dressed and poured the coffee down her throat. Though she was still high, at least she was awake enough to help a little. Between Gracie and me, we got her into the car. By the time we reached the club, she seemed to have gotten herself together. Both Gracie and me decided that this was the last gig we'd do with Kanisha. Talk about being pissed off!

The nightclub was crowded; the air thick with cigarette smoke and a mixture of smells, alcohol, perfume, cologne and who knows what else. A man reached out for my hand as I tried to keep up with Gracie and Kanisha on our way to the stage. We passed a table full of women who looked us up and down. One of them whispered to the other and they burst out laughing. "Don't pay them no mind. They just jealous," Gracie said.

Just then I heard the announcer introducing Big Jim. The big man, dressed in a white suit, mopped his brow as he walked out on the small stage. We put our things down behind a curtain and rushed after him. Three stools were set up along the side, near the back of the stage. That's where we sat- out of the spotlight with three mikes in front of us.

We were seated by the time people stopped clapping. Big Jim started off with his hit, "You got me blowing my mind over you." The crowd loved it. I looked over at Gracie. We were thinking the same thing. Once on stage, even though we were in the shadows, it was like magic. Suddenly Kanisha was wide-awake and on fire. That's the way she was. We didn't have any trouble following Big Jim. Everything went great. The feeling in the air was electric.

Between sets, I saw Hi C at the bar talking to a lady. They were holding hands and he was whispering in her ear. I didn't hang around. I followed Gracie, Kanisha and the bass player to the alley behind the club where they lit up. The bass player passed around a pint of whiskey and a joint. Gracie and Kanisha took a swallow. They didn't offer me any.

When the gig was over, Kanisha told us about a party going on across town. Gracie was ready. She was always ready to party. I remembered my promise to be home at a decent hour so I said, "I think I'd better go home."

"Take the little kid home before her mommy comes looking for her," Kanisha said.

Gracie turned to me. "I'm not gonna stay long, but if you're sure you want to go home, I'll drop you off." I felt bad about spoiling their fun so I gave in.

We all piled into the drummer's car. Everybody was in a good mood, even Kanisha. The party was at somebody's apartment in Compton and it was in full swing by the time we got there. The place was wall-to-wall people, loud and stuffy. Some people sat on a gray couch that looked like it had seen better days, some leaned up against the wall, a few even sat on the floor. About three couples in the center of the room tried to dance. The music was so loud you had to yell to be heard. I stuck close to Gracie. Kanisha disappeared somewhere. Somebody passed around a bottle. "Try it, just a sip," Gracie said. I frowned. "Come on, Tricia, loosen up."

I took a sip. It tasted terrible; I almost gagged. Then Gracie handed me a glass of soda.

"Dump the liquor in. It'll taste better."

I felt myself relaxing and before long I was laughing like a fool. I was surprised when Hi C came up and asked me to dance. I hadn't even noticed him there. It was a slow song playing on the stereo and he held me so tight I felt like I was gonna pass out. I thought about Darien and wished he was here. I rested my head on Hi C's shoulder and felt him nuzzling my neck. I didn't stop his hands sliding over my butt.

"So, Jailbait. What's your next move?" he whispered. His breath smelled like cigarettes and spearmint gum.

"What do you mean?"

"I mean, have you graduated from high school yet? Are you planning to stay with your two friends or are you going to strike out on your own? You got talent, you know."

"How do you know? You never heard me sing alone," I asked, feeling bold and relaxed.

"I can tell. I'm a musician, remember? I heard your voice. If you decide to go it alone, give me a ring. Maybe we can work something out."

Just then the song ended and just like that, Hi C. was gone.

Suddenly I heard shouting and a loud crash. Everybody rushed toward the kitchen.

"You betta get your friend out of here before I kick her head in. Don't nobody be messing with my woman."

I pushed through this circle of people and saw Gracie pulling Kanisha by the arm. Her hair was all messed up and her dress was torn. Blood seeped from the corner of her mouth.

Gracie saw me. "Come on, Tricia. Help me get Kanisha out of here." Kanisha didn't protest. She didn't say anything while Gracie went back in to find the drummer and get him to take us back to the parking lot where Gracie left her car. He was mad, but he drove us back to the club, running a couple of red lights and a few stop signs. I was grateful to get back in one piece.

We got Kanisha to her apartment. As Gracie drove me home, I asked her what happened.

"Kanisha was in the kitchen talking to some chick. Next thing I know, the chick's boyfriend comes in and socks Kanisha."

"Just for talking to her?" I asked. It didn't make sense to me.

"Well, maybe they were doing more than talking," Gracie said. "You know how Kanisha is."

I knew Kanisha preferred women to men. It was no big deal to me as long as she didn't try to hit on me. When we stopped in front of my apartment building, Gracie reached into her purse and handed me $20.00. "That's for tonight's gig. That SOB made twenty times that but that's all I could get out of him. At least we don't have to split it with Harry."

I put the bill away. "Every little bit helps," I said as I shut her car door.

"See you tomorrow. Rehearsal's at seven."   She waved as she pulled away from the curb. I felt tired but the excitement of singing in a nightclub was still with me.

I stopped humming one of Big Jim's songs as I opened the apartment door. It was 1 AM and I was surprised to see the kitchen light on. I tiptoed to the kitchen and stepped back in shock. Momma was sitting at the table, a stack of bills beside her, and she was thumbing through a small book.

29

℘

Ma'dear

Willie Joe was dead. It was the darkest day of my life. How could a man die before he reached thirty years old? One day he seemed to be the healthiest man alive and the next day, he was lying in a hospital bed taking his last breath. The doctors couldn't find nothing wrong with him, nothing that was causing him to lose so much weight. Food wouldn't stay on his stomach. He just wasted away.

I didn't have long to grieve, though, because a few days after I buried him, Melvin was born. He was the spitting image of his father. I stayed off from work for as long as I could, but I had bills to pay. I asked a neighbor lady to look after baby Melvin while I went to work. For months all I did was go to work, come home, and just sit by the window and stare down at the street, thinking about Willie Joe.

Then I got a letter from my mama. She wrote me and told me to come home. I didn't realize how pitiful I looked or how I'd let everything go until I took the Greyhound back home to Farmville.

"You better get yourself together. You got a child to raise," Mama said to me one day. "First thing you should do is get out of that place where you and Willie Joe lived. Too many memories. Then you should fix yourself up and start living again."

"I just need a little more time," I told her.

"Child, sitting around here ain't getting you nowhere. Go on back to New York and start living again."

After a few weeks in the South, I felt strong enough to leave. I left my baby with Mama and took the bus back to New York. I'd been gone so long I lost my job. Didn't matter 'cause cleaning jobs weren't that hard to find. After a week of looking, I found another job cleaning up buildings at night. During the day, I worked as a nurses' aid in St. Vincent's Hospital downtown. I don't know how I did it, but I managed to save enough money to look for another place. I found a small kitchenette over on 143rd St. and 8th Avenue in Harlem. It was little more than a room with a Murphy bed, a half kitchen, and bathroom. The rent was something I could afford. It would suit me until I had enough money to go back down south and get my baby.

I went back to our old place to clear out Willie Joe's and my belongings. In the year we'd been there we'd accumulated a few things. The apartment was furnished, so mostly I just had to get rid of his clothes and pack mine up. My friend, Esther came over to help me. Willie Joe and I used to play cards with her and her husband and every now and then, we would go to the picture show. She was real helpful to me when Willie Joe got sick.

One thing about Esther, though, was that she was very superstitious. She believed in spirits and ghosts and was always talking about stuff like that. Herman, her husband, would always tell her she was a fool. Willie Joe would just laugh. I tried to laugh at it but it scared me half to death.

When Willie Joe started losing weight and acting funny, Esther said somebody had put a spell on him. I didn't believe her. One day she made me so mad I told her not to come round no more. And she didn't. We'd pass each other on the stairs and hardly speak. She and Herman moved away about a month before Willie Joe passed. She showed up at his funeral. I don't know how she knew he had died, but I was grateful.

On the day I went to clean out the old apartment, I ran into her on the street. I told her I was getting ready to move and she asked if she could help. Sure, I said. I needed the company. We packed up my things in boxes.

She said she knew some people she could give Willie Joe's clothes to. Then we started to clean up. She swept the floor, while I wiped down the woodwork and washed the windows. Just when I thought we was through, I remembered I hadn't emptied the water from under the icebox. I got down on my knees and grabbed hold of the tray and pulled. It was filled with water so I was careful as I pulled it out.

Something else was in that tray besides water. It was a dirty brown sack no bigger than a small egg tied up with a string. I dumped out the water in the sink and took the bag over to Esther.

"Now what could this be?" I held the sack up to her. Water dripped from it. Esther stopped sweeping and leaned over to get a closer look.

"Child, where'd you find that?" she shouted, jumping back and wiping her hands on her apron. "Get some newspaper and wrap that thing up. Don't throw it away. Looks like the work of the devil."

Suddenly I felt a chill run down my spine. "Esther, you scaring me." I did what she said.

"I know a lady over on 8th Ave. Let's take that thing over to her."

We left everything in the middle of the floor. I wrapped the sack in newspaper, put it inside a shopping bag and followed Esther to a building on 8th

Ave. We walked up the steps and into the dark hallway. On the second floor she stopped and looked around.

"Just wait a minute until my eyes adjust to this darkness. I can't see the numbers on the doors." She peered at each number and then she knocked on the next to the last door. I heard a woman's voice yell, "Who is it?"

"Esther Garvey," Esther answered.

"Just a minute, Esther. I'll be right with you."

The door opened and there stood a skinny woman who didn't look much older than me. She had a scarf tied around her head and an apron covering a yellow cotton dress. Her complexion was the color of sage honey. Freckles sprinkled across her nose.

"Come on in," she smiled. "I was just cooking me up some dinner. Would you like something to eat?"

She must have been from the West Indies. Her accent was thick and welcoming. Esther introduced us. "We can't stay long, Madame LaFontaine. We want you to take a look at this."

Esther handed Madame LaFontaine the shopping bag. After peering into it, Madame reached into the bag, carefully took out the newspaper holding it between her thumb and fore-finger, and placed it on a nearby table. It seemed like she took forever to unwrap it. She examined the muslin bag without touching it; bending over the sack, she sniffed at it. Then she looked up at me, wiping her hands on her apron. The smile she had when she first greeted us was gone. She told us to have a seat on her sofa. "Tell me what's been happening?" She asked as she sat down opposite us.

I told her about Willie Joe. When I finished, she said, "Somebody's been working roots on you and your husband."

"Didn't I tell you that when Willie Joe was alive," Esther said. "But you didn't believe me."

I felt like somebody had taken my breath away. I gasped for air. Madame put her hand on my shoulder.

"You want a glass of water, honey?"

I couldn't think of who or why anyone would want to do anything to me and Willie Joe. I told her this.

"Is it over?" I asked, hoping she would tell me that it was.

"Not as long as you got this thing her." She pointed to the muslin bag. "Bad luck," she murmured rubbing some kind of oil on her hands and opening the bag carefully. Inside was a chicken bone, a piece of hair, Willie Joe's or mine, I couldn't tell, and a dirty napkin rolled up in a ball.

"Can you take the spell off?" Esther asked Madame.

"I can't take it off, but I can turn it around to the person who put the spell on you. Who was it? Think hard."

"No. I don't know of anybody who would do this." I couldn't think. I just wanted to get out of there.

"Well, when you know who it was, you come see me again. I can turn the spell around, but it's gonna cost you."

I nodded. This wasn't real. I was having a nightmare. Nothing made sense.

"Have Esther bring you back when you got the money."

Esther helped me up. I must have been in a trance because I don't remember going back to the apartment. She talked the whole time, but I don't remember what she said. We finished cleaning up the place and after she helped me load my boxes into Willie Joe's old car, she gave me her number. I drove over to my new place, unpacked, and tried to sleep.

30

❧

Hazel

"$10,000. Momma, we're rich!" Shanell shouted.

"Be quiet, girl, before you wake your grandmother."

"Where'd you get all that money?" Tricia wanted to know.

"It's not my money." Hazel pointed to the stack of envelopes beside her. "It's Donald's. I opened his mail."

"Why would people be sending him money like that?" Shanell asked. "And to think it's been sitting around here all this time."

"What are you going to do with it?" Tricia stifled a yawn. "You can't keep it."

"I don't plan to keep it. I can't get a hold of Donald. I'm just not sure what to do with it."

"What's this?" Shanell picked up the little black book that was almost hidden beneath the envelopes. She flipped through the pages. "It's full of numbers."

Tricia looked over her shoulder.

Looks like Donald's little black book, thought Hazel. She'd heard of men keeping little black books with all the numbers of women they slept with.

Tricia grabbed it. "Let me see if our number is in it." After leafing through the pages, she handed it to her mother.

"It's way passed bed time," said Hazel, glancing up at the clock. "You all go to bed. I'm gonna put this money away. Tomorrow I'll try to get hold of Donald and find out what's going on."

In the excitement of discovering the money, they'd forgotten to ask her about her meeting with him at the pier several hours earlier. She was glad, because she didn't want to worry them. Shanell stretched and yawned as she followed Tricia to their bedroom. "See you in the morning, Mom," they whispered as they left.

Hazel looked around the kitchen for a place in which to hide the money. Her eyes landed on a small door above the cabinets. Unless you knew it was there, you'd never notice it. She'd discovered it one day when she was cleaning and wondered why anyone would build a door so high up and as far as she could tell at the time, completely useless.

She picked up the black book and flipped through the pages. They didn't look like telephone numbers, just page after page of letters and numbers that made no sense to her. Taking a manila envelope from the drawer, she stuffed the book and money in it. Climbing up on the kitchen stool, she opened the door and tossed the envelope inside. She looked around the kitchen one last time; satisfied, she turned off the lights and went to bed.

The next morning the sun streaming though the curtains woke her. It was Saturday. For a moment she had forgotten all that had taken place the night before. She got up reluctantly, peeked in on her mother and the girls. All were sleeping soundly. She headed for the kitchen and put on a pot of coffee. Then she went into the bathroom and ran her bath water. It wasn't until she was soaking in the tub that she remembered the money, the book, and Donald.

A shiver ran down her spine when she relived that moment at the pier when a man reached for her bag. Earlier that same day, the police had come looking for Donald. They wouldn't say why. Donald had called her and told her to bring his mail to him at the pier, yet he hadn't shown up. What was going on? Whatever it was, she didn't want herself or her family involved. Kevin had tried to reassure her, but it hadn't worked. She was more concerned now than ever before.

"Momma, you gonna be in there long?" Shanell's voice broke into her thoughts. "I gotta go."

"I'll be right out." She finished her bath and putting yesterday behind her, she focused on her present chores. Today was the nurse's day off, so she would have to look after her mother. Maybe she'd dress her and take her to the park while the weather was still mild.

It was difficult getting her mother bathed and dressed, but with both Tricia and Shanell's help, she managed. And thanks to Mr. Frazier, the neighbor who practically carried her mother downstairs, they were on their way.

"I'm taking you to the park, Ma'dear? It's about time you got out and got some fresh air." Hazel pushed the wheelchair along, nodding to everyone who looked her way as she passed. Some ignored her, but a few smiled or nodded back. Like many on the city street, she, too, was always busy, either coming or going, always moving. Having a leisurely stroll on a warm spring day was something she seldom had a chance to do. "I need to do this more often," she noted.

Another thing she realized was that she wasn't really connected to the community in ways that mattered. She seldom went to any of the surrounding churches unless someone invited her. Nor did she belong to any of the civic organizations like the NAACP. As far as attending PTA meetings or even back to school nights, those were not on her list of priorities. She made a note to take some time away from her busy schedule to become involved. It would help the girls, she thought. However, she knew she was only fooling herself. The likelihood of this happening was probably less than none, yet it was a nice thought.

Hazel felt good as she wheeled her mother down the block and across the street to the park, chatting about nothing in particular, a one-way conversation since her mother showed little reaction and no verbal response. She stopped near a park bench and watched the children play on the teeter-totter and climb the monkey bars. Hazel wanted to light up a cigarette, but she knew her mother would disapprove. Instead she pulled out a stick of gum.

Ma'dear's health had improved a bit since she came to live with them more than a month ago. Hazel remembered how she'd suddenly awakened. A few days earlier she had been on the phone to Kevin when she heard her mother's voice calling her as soon as she hung up. Running to the room, she pushed open the door. Ma'dear's eyes were wide open and though it was barely above a whisper, Hazel heard her call her name.

"Yes, Mama. What's wrong?"

"Water, I want water. So thirsty."

Tears flowed from Hazel's eyes as she rushed to the sink to fill a glass with water and bring it back to Ma'dear.

"Mama, you're awake. You've come back to us."

Since then, her mother seemed to stay awake longer and seemed to be aware of her surroundings. Still, she had a long way to go before she would completely recover. Nonetheless, Ma'dear was making steady progress.

Hazel took a sidelong glance at her mother. "Well, where do we go from here?" she said aloud. "I wish you could understand me, Mama. I wish I knew what you were thinking. There's so much I want. I want my girls to grow up to become nice young ladies, to go to college, to find good husbands and get married. I'm taking an accounting course and when I'm through, I'm going to try to start my own business. I bet you never thought I'd get serious and settle down?" She laughed nervously. "You always thought of me as a flake, right? That I'd never amount to much? Melvin was the light in your eyes." Stop it!

Just shut up! She thought, feeling a knot form in her stomach. "What is it you use to tell me? That I would always be looking for somebody to take care of me." She looked down at her mother who showed no response. "I wish I did have somebody to take care of me and my girls now."

To hell with it, she thought. She reached into her pocket and pulled out a pack of cigarettes. Lighting one up, she inhaled deeply, exhaling a long trail of smoke. Her mother coughed. Hazel took another long drag and dashed the cigarette out. They sat for a while saying nothing. Suddenly she jumped up.

"I guess we'd better be heading home," she laughed nervously. "We need to do this more often."

As she approached her block, she saw a police car parked in front of her apartment building. A small crowd had gathered. Her steps quickened as she saw Mr. Frazier talking to one of the policemen.

"What's going on here?" she asked as she pushed the wheelchair through the crowd. Her heart beat rapidly. "Has anything happened to my girls?"

"Tricia and Shanell are all right," Mr. Frazier assured her.

"A break-in," the young officer said. "Are you Mrs. Porter? You live in Apartment 3?"

"Yes," Hazel responded her voice rising. "Where are my girls?"

"In my apartment. My wife is looking after them. They're alright." Mr. Frazier helped Hazel take her mother to his apartment to wait.

Tricia and Shanell jumped up from the sofa and rushed to Hazel's side. They hugged. "Momma..." Shanell started.

Hazel stopped her. "You both stay here with Ma'dear. I'll be right back," she said, and followed the officer upstairs.

The lock on the door had been completely shattered as if it had been kicked it. Hazel entered cautiously behind the policeman and Mr. Frazier. The furniture was not disturbed but every drawer had been pulled out and its contents dumped on the floor. It was a hurried job, as if the thief were looking for something in particular. "Probably money to buy drugs," the policeman said. "Can you tell if anything is missing?"

"I don't know," said Hazel as she surveyed the apartment. "What do I do now? Does somebody come and take fingerprints or what?"

"I can take a report and send you a copy to give to your insurance company. I'd like to talk to your daughters about what happened," he said.

"They weren't here at the time," Mr. Frazier responded. Hazel felt a sense of relief.

After the officer had gone, Tricia and Shanell helped put things back in order before bringing Ma'dear upstairs. After several phone calls to the manager, he came and fixed the lock. While both Tricia and Shanell stayed with their grandmother in her room, Hazel went into the kitchen, climbed up on the stool and checked the shelf above the cabinet. The money and the book were still there. Once everything had quieted down, Hazel called the girls in and asked them what had happened.

"We went to the market like you told us to," Tricia said, "When we came back, we noticed that the door was open."

"We went downstairs and told Mr. Frazier who called the police," Shanell said. "Then you came back."

"Do you think it has anything to do with Donald's money?" asked Tricia.

"I don't know," Hazel said with a sigh. "I hope not."

31

❧

Ma'dear

I dreamed of Willie Joe that night. In my dreams I saw him standing in front of me wearing the same suit I buried him in. He was holding out his arms and saying something to me, gesturing like he wanted me to come to him. Then just as suddenly I was in a empty room all by myself. The walls were blue and there weren't any windows. In a corner I saw something that looked like mist. I couldn't see clearly. I heard voices but I didn't see nobody. I spied a door and I ran to it and tried to open it, but I couldn't. It was locked. When I turned around it seemed like the mist had gotten thicker and was rolling towards me like it wanted to cover me. I started running, trying to get away. It kept getting closer and closer. Then I screamed so loud, I woke myself up. My nightgown was soaked and I was trembling.

I got out of bed, walked over to the kitchen sink, and drew a glass of water. I stood by the window looking down at the empty street. Sleep had gone. I knew I'd be awake the rest of the night. My thoughts was on Sadie and Willie Joe and what Madame LaFontaine had said about the spell. "I can't take the spell off but I can turn it around to the person who put it on you." Sadie. I was sure it was her that took away my husband and deprived my son of a father. If it was the last thing I did, I vowed I'd get back at her.

It took me a few months to get up enough money to go back to Madame. I sold Willie Joe's Buick and some other things, saved every penny I earned until I had enough. Then I went back to her apartment.

"Course I remember you, Honey. You Esther's friend the one whose husband had that spell put on him. I was wondering if you'd come back."

I handed her the money and waited while she counted it. She stuffed it in her bosom and told me to sit down. "Would you like some tea?" she asked. "I'll be right back." She disappeared into another room.

When Esther first took me to Madame's, I hadn't paid any attention to her apartment. But now as I sat there alone, I looked around. An old upright piano sat against the wall. On it was a lot of pictures, of her family, I supposed. Some dressed modern; others looked like they had been taken long ago because the people in them had on clothes like they wore in the last century. There was a big picture of Marcus Garvey hung on one wall and on another wall, a picture of Christ on the cross. The room was crowded with furniture, too much for the size of the apartment. Most of the furniture was covered with brightly colored throws. Next to the sofa was two overstuffed chairs, a coffee table with a strange looking lamp on it.

On the windowsill were about fifteen colorful bottles. A breeze blew through the curtain

It was a cheerful room though I didn't feel in no way cheerful wondering if I was doing the right thing. My stomach was bubbling over. I heard a man's voice and some children laughing, reminding me of little Melvin. I wanted to see him so bad. It had been a while. When I get this mess cleared up, I promised myself I'd go down south, get him and bring him home.

"Here we are." Madame LaFontaine set down a tray with two cups, a teapot and a plate. "And here's some cookies I thought you might like."

Next she handed me a small box. "Don't open it now! When you get home, take out the powder, and sprinkle it on some dollar bills. Then give the bills to the person you want to put the spell on."

"That's all I have to do is give her some money?"

"That's all. Watch you don't touch the powder!" She cautioned. Then she smiled. "Now let's have some tea and cookies," she said pouring the hot brewed tea into my cup. I hesitated. She laughed. "Don't be afraid. I ain't trying to poison you."

When I got home, I set the box on the table. I hadn't talked to Sadie in over a year. In fact, I wasn't even sure where she lived or if she was still in the city. What am I gonna tell her I'm giving her money for? So many thoughts went through my mind. I started to open the box. It was so small, like a box a ring would come in. How could something so small contain something that could turn a person's life around? I wasn't superstitious, at least not like Esther. No, I decided. I'll leave revenge up to God. Didn't it say in the Bible.

"'Vengeance is Mine', saith the Lord." I put the box up on the shelf in the back of my closet, went into the bathroom and took a bath.

A few months later as I was coming up out of the subway, who should I run into but Sadie. She was strolling along Lenox Ave. with her arm linked through the arm of a man I vaguely remembered. When she saw me, her face lit up.

"Sarah, Lord have mercy. I ain't seen you in ages. Heard you had gone back down South." She hugged me and gave me a peck on the cheek. "I'm so sorry. When I *heard about Willie Joe, I was shocked. Forgive me for not calling you."*

My heart was beating fast. The thought about what she may have done to Willie Joe flashed through my mind. I couldn't think of a thing to say. On the outside, I smiled but on the inside, I trembled.

She was dressed in a tight flowered dress and high-heeled pumps. On her head was a blue pillbox hat that matched her purse. I glanced down at my drab gray dress and low-heeled work shoes. My hair, pulled back into a bun, made me look twice as old as she. The run in my stockings seemed to be creeping up my leg as we talked.

"You remember Harry from way back when." The man beside her looked familiar to me but I couldn't place him. He squinted his eyes at me. Then a big smile spread across his face.

"Sarah? Yeah, I remember now. Didn't you use to go with Willie Joe?"

"We was married," I said, a thick lump gathering in my throat.

Sadie held out her hand to show me a small diamond ring.

"Harry and me's married." Her arm linked through his, she batted her eyes at him. "You should come over and visit with us sometime. We can catch up on old times."

"I just remembered. Willie Joe left some money for me to give to you," I said. I don't know where that came from. It just popped into my head.

"Money?" Sadie frowned. "Willie Joe didn't owe me no money. But I can always use some. Not that my baby don't keep me well supplied." She pulled him closer and gave him a peck on the cheek. He squeezed her shoulders. "Here, let me give you my address." She opened her purse, pulled out a scrap of paper, wrote her number on it and handed it to me. "We gotta go. It sure is good seeing you."

We made a date for me to visit her on Sunday. I watched them walk away. Then I rushed home.

Reaching into the closet, I felt for the small box I'd put there. I carried it over to the table. Taking five one-dollar bills, almost a week's wages, from my purse, I spread them out on newspaper. For the first time, I lifted the lid from the box. In it was a tiny amount of white powder, about a tablespoon full. After putting on the rubber gloves I use when I'm working, I sprinkled the powder over the bills, shook off the extra onto the newspaper. Then I placed the bills into an envelope, sealed it shut and placed it on the mantle until Sunday. Next I tossed the gloves into the trashcan, took the newspaper over to the stove and burned it along with the small box. Sunday was three days away.

32-

๛

Tricia

Momma got ready for school. As she ran out the door, she cautioned us, as usual, about not opening the door to strangers and making sure we looked after Ma'dear. It had been a while since she went to her classes at the University and since she had only a few more weeks before school was over, she hoped to finish up and not have to drop out. It had also been several weeks since that trouble with Donald and whatever he was involved in. Things seemed to have calmed down.

Graduation was only a month away. If I wanted to graduate, I knew I needed to buckle down, so I put my singing engagements on hold; not that there were many. Actually I hadn't heard from anybody since that gig with Big Jim. I talked to Gracie a couple of times but then she went South to see about her little boy. Kanisha had dropped out of sight. So everything was cool.

Ma'dear was making steady progress. She was able to sit up and watch TV. Still she couldn't talk without a lot of effort. I was beginning to like having her live here with us even if I did have to babysit her when I came in from school. Is that the right word, babysit? Do you babysit a grown up? Shanell liked to go in and watch TV with her. The other day, I heard her talking to Ma'dear. I couldn't tell if she was listening. She seemed to be asleep, but Shanell was babbling on and on about boyfriends. I admitted I felt jealous that she could talk to Ma'dear and not to me and I was her big sister. Then I shrugged it off. At least with Shanell talking to Ma'dear, she spent less time arguing with me.

One time I was standing outside the room. I heard Shanell asking Ma'dear about having babies. I mean, she came right out and asked Ma'dear how do you know if you're going to have a baby? I don't think Ma'dear was even awake. When I walked in, she changed the subject.

But I was curious. My sister had been acting funny lately. Sometimes I'd hear her in the bathroom throwing up and when I asked her about it, she'd say it was something she ate. So when I heard her talking to Ma'dear about babies, it suddenly hit me; Shanell must be pregnant!

As soon as we were alone, I asked her. She glanced at me with her mouth open, looking like I hit her. Tears spilled down her cheeks.

"Why you ask me that?" All of a sudden she was busy picking up her clothes and things in the room and putting them away. I waited until she stopped. Finally she lay down on the bed, her face hidden in the pillow. "I don't know," she muttered. "I think so."

"Who's the father? Was it that boy I caught you with a few months ago?"

She didn't answer. I sat down beside her on her bed and stroked her back. As if we didn't have enough trouble, I thought, now this. Suddenly she looked like a little girl. I wanted to hug her like I use to do when she was younger and got hurt.

"Are you sure? When was the last time you had your period?"

"I can't remember. Maybe over a month ago. What am I gonna do?" she asked.

Every month Momma questioned us about our period. We had to tell her when it started, because she was afraid we'd get pregnant. She cautioned us over and over again. I remembered Shanell told her just last week that she was menstruating.

"Tricia, you gotta help me!"

I wanted to say, 'serves you right' but I didn't. This was news Momma didn't need to hear. Since this is the first time Shanell had asked me for help since she became a teenager, I couldn't let her down. My mind raced. Shanell was only fourteen, too young to care for a child. She could hardly take care of herself. Her future would be messed up. Putting a child up for adoption would be hard. Then I thought of Gracie. If anybody would know what to do in a situation like this, she would. I looked up her aunt's number in South Carolina and called her. Luckily I reached her.

After she filled me in on how things were going with her and her family, she said, "Child, this place is so boring. I can't wait to get back to civilization. Sometimes I wonder if these white people know slavery ended long ago." When she finished complaining, I told her why I called.

"Gracie, do you know any place where they give abortions without a parent's consent?"

"Girl, don't tell me you and Darien finally did it?"

"No, it's not for me. It's for my sister Shanell."

"You're kiddin." she said, "Isn't she only fourteen? Girls these days are too fast, though I had my son when I was fifteen." I heard a crash in the distance. "Hold on a minute," Gracie said. She dropped the phone. "I told you not to climb on that chair! And stop pulling on that cord or I'm gonna smack your behind." She came back on. "Sorry about that. Off hand I can't think of the name of the place I went to once. Maybe it'll come to me. How far along is she?"

"I don't know. She's not showing or anything."

"That don't mean much."

I'll probably catch hell from Momma about the phone bill, but once Gracie got talking, it was hard to get her to stop. Right in the middle of telling me about a man she met, she remembered the name of the clinic. I grabbed a pencil and wrote down the name. After I hung up, I looked up the name in the yellow pages. It was way across town, in the neighborhood where we use to live.

"I'll meet you right after school and we'll go over there together," I told Shanell.

"But what about Ma'dear? The nurse leaves at 3:30 and we can't leave her alone."

"I'll have to think of something," I said.

The look Shanell gave me made tears come to my eyes. She didn't say anything as she hugged me.

After school the next day, I hurried over to Shanell's school which wasn't far from mine. She was waiting for me by the front gate.

"The clinic closes at 5:00. We won't have time to go home to see about Ma'dear and make it there before it closes."

This morning I told nurse we'd be a little late getting home. I asked her if she'd stay and she said we'd better be home by 4:00 because she had other things to do.

We caught the bus to south Central. It let us off in front of a raggedy looking building. I could tell Shanell was scared. I was, too. The clinic was on the first floor; the room was crowded mostly with women who stared at us. The receptionist behind a glass panel asked us what we wanted. She didn't look very friendly. Handing me a form to fill out, she asked what medical insurance we had.

"We don't have medical insurance. How much does it cost for an exam?"

When she told me, I knew we couldn't afford it. I felt like I had let Shanell down.

"Maybe if find a gig that'll pay enough money..." I said.

"That's alright, Tricia. I appreciate your help. I guess I'll have to tell Momma."

It was 4:45 when we got home. The nurse was fit to be tied. She said she was gonna tell Momma and she was charging us overtime. "You young people have no sense of responsibility! Don't think about nobody but yourselves." She slammed the door behind her. I looked in on Ma'dear and saw she was sound asleep.

I couldn't understand why the nurse was so upset. Ma'dear doesn't cause any trouble. And we weren't all that late.

Shanell was sitting at the kitchen table with her head in her hands. She wiped tears from her eyes and looked up at me when I came in.

"I'm gonna tell Momma tonight, Tricia."

"Wait, give me a few days and I'll come up with something. Momma's got enough to worry about without adding this to it." What about the money Donald left? I could take what we needed and get it back when I could. It was a thought.

Shanell agreed to wait until Thursday.

That evening when everyone was asleep, I sneaked into the kitchen, pulled the stool over to the cabinet and climbed up on it. I reached into the envelope where Momma had put the money and drew out $300.00. That should be enough.

The next day, instead of going to school, I took Shanell back over to the clinic. This time she got to see the doctor. He examined her, gave her a test, and said he'd call us in a few days. I told him I'd call him.

As we rode home, a thought suddenly struck me. Shanell was only fourteen and no longer a virgin. She was still a kid. I was almost eighteen. What was I saving myself for?

33

✍

Hazel

The phone rang waking her from a sound sleep. Without thought, Hazel reached for the lamp and switched it on. Glancing groggily at the clock she saw that it was 3 AM.

"Baby, you got to help me. That black book... I need it." It was Donald. Anger surged through Hazel. She sat up.

"You got some kind of nerve. First of all, I drive all the way out to Santa Monica and you don't show. Then you wake me up at this ungodly hour!"

He feebly apologized. "Something came up. I really need that book, it's insurance."

"Insurance, insurance for what?"

"I don't want you involved in this. I just need that book."

"What about the money, Donald. $10,000. Where did you get it?"

"Fuck the money. The book is worth ten times that," he said.

Hazel told him all that had happened. "You can have the money and the book. I'll never forgive you for involving us in your mess."

"Yeah, Baby. I'm real sorry. I'll take everything off your hands. But the cops aren't the only ones watching your apartment. Can you meet me..."

Before he could finish his sentence, Hazel shouted, "I'm not going to meet you anywhere. You're putting our lives in danger!"

"Right, I said I was sorry. Okay. Take down this number." She reached for a pad and pencil and wrote down the address he gave her. "Tomorrow, around lunchtime, go to that address. Ask for a man named Foster. Tell him I sent you and hand him the book. I swear I won't ask you for nothing else. You can keep the money."

After he had hung up, Hazel couldn't get back to sleep. What kind of game was Donald playing? She got up, went into the kitchen, and made a cup of hot chocolate. Retrieving the black book from its hiding place in the cabinet, she opened it and began trying to decipher the entries. Beside each number were two or three letters. The numbers were random. She couldn't figure out the pattern. It must be some sort of code. Shaking her head, she concluded this was some scheme Donald was mixed up in.

Tomorrow she would follow his instructions and turn everything over to some man named Foster. At least it wasn't too far from where she worked and it was during the day, unlike that late night excursion. She'd be happy to put it all behind her. Tomorrow. What could happen during the day?

Hazel glanced up at the clock. Almost noon. She reached into her desk drawer and checked her purse. Inside was an envelope containing the black book.

"Where are you going for lunch?" Monica asked. "I know this neat little Indian restaurant over on 12th. The food is delicious and the service is quick."

Hazel apologized. "I got some errands to do, but I'll catch you tomorrow."

"There's an important meeting after lunch so don't be late," Monica said as she dashed off to the ladies room.

"What are you doing for lunch?" Diane sat down on the edge of Hazel's desk. Hazel told her the same thing she told Monica. Diane's strong perfume quickly engulfed Hazel's space. Swinging her legs back and forth, she leaned over and whispered; "I heard the boss is going to be handing out more pink slips this afternoon."

"Do you know who's going to be cut?" Hazel asked, her stomach muscles tightened.

"I know who it's not going to be." Diane tossed her long red hair and hopped to the floor. "Don't worry, darling. It probably won't be anybody in this department."

Hips swinging from side to side, she strode off down the aisle. "Have a nice lunch."

Hazel hastily gathered the papers she was working on and stacked them neatly in a pile on the side of her desk. Then she took a quick glance in her compact mirror, she applied a thin layer of makeup and rouge, reapplied her lipstick, and grabbing her purse, she headed for the elevator.

It was a warm day; spring was everywhere. Trees and shrubs were in bloom, people were seated in various spots outside the buildings, on low retaining walls, on concrete steps, and on the few benches scattered around the complex. A few people even sat on the neatly mowed grass.

Hazel walked quickly to her car, jumped in and drove over to Olympic and Broadway. She had an hour for lunch and she figured all she had to do was to find the place, give the black book to a man named Foster. At least that part would be over. Donald hadn't said what to do with the money. One thing at a time, she thought.

It was 12:15 by the time she found the building, parked and went inside. An old structure, it inhabited the lower floors next to garment factories and discount dress shops. There were probably sweat shops in the rear, she thought as she maneuvered passed the workers taking their break outside, some lined up in front of the street vendors selling hot dogs, chips, and sandwiches.

The elevator looked decrepit and dangerous with its sliding gate and slow, squeaky movements. Hazel hesitated, thought about taking the stairs but decided time was of the essence. Foster's office was on the top floor.

It wasn't difficult to find his office as there was only one other door and it was a fire exit. Turning the knob, she walked in. The receptionist, an elderly lady with a gray, unkempt look, dressed in a brown cotton dress peered at her over her bifocals. Her thick fingers were poised above the computer keyboard. Noticing the food stains on the bodice of the woman's dress, Hazel's eyes shifted to the wall behind the woman. A poster of a racehorse hung in the center of the wooden panel.

"I'm here to see Mr. Foster."

"Do you have an appointment?"

"Well, no. I was told to deliver something to him."

"I'm afraid Mr. Foster is out at the moment," she said in a slight southern drawl. "I should hear from him soon. Take a seat if you wanna wait."

She gestured to the chair behind Hazel; dark brown like the woman's dress, stained, worn and uncomfortable looking. Hazel sat gingerly on the edge of the cushion and watched the woman type. From time to time, the receptionist peered over her glasses at Hazel. After a few minutes of silence she offered Hazel a cup of coffee.

"I just made a fresh pot," she said.

"Thanks, I've already had my quota for today," Hazel responded. What kind of place is this, she wondered looking around the tiny space. Nothing indicated what type of business Mr. Foster was in. The clock was approaching 12:45.

"Will Mr. Foster be much longer?" Hazel asked with growing anxiety.

"Oh, he should have called by now."

"Called. Isn't he coming in?" Hazel asked.

The woman laughed. "Here? Mr. Foster coming here?" She looked curiously at Hazel. "Mr. Foster never comes here. This is an answering service. We just take messages. Didn't you see the sign on the door?"

Hazel didn't remember seeing any sign on the door.

"Probably not," the woman laughed again. "Probably couldn't read it anyway. I've been here so long, I never noticed whether it's legible or not." She wrote something on a pad. "Next time I see Max, I better remember to tell him to redo the sign."

Exasperated, Hazel almost exploded. "I thought you said he'd be here soon."

"No, I said I'd probably hear from him momentarily."

"Well, where can I reach Mr. Foster? I have a package for him."

"I can send it to him. We're not allowed to give out his address, sorry." She turned back to her typing. The phone rang. She answered it.

Hazel waited until she hung up. "Can you tell me Mr. Foster's first name?"

The woman looked thoughtfully, "Don't you know it?"

"My boss gave me this address and told me to deliver a package to Mr. Foster and only to Mr. Foster. He didn't tell me anything else." She glanced down at her watch. She had to be back at her desk in five minutes. She knew she'd never make it.

"His name's Leonard," the woman said peering more intently at Hazel.

"One more question. What kind of business is Mr. Foster in?"

"How should I know? Maybe you should ask your boss. Now, if Mr. Foster calls, who should I say was asking about him?"

Sensing the woman becoming more hostile by the minute, Hazel let out a long sigh and turned towards the door. "Tell him Donald Porter sent me and he can reach me at this number." She wrote her work number down on the back of a receipt she found in her purse. Then she added her home number should he call after five.

As she rode the rickety elevator to the first floor, she resolved to find Foster and give him this book. "Better yet, I'm gonna find Donald and wring his neck!"

Hunger pangs reminded Hazel she hadn't eaten since breakfast. The line in front of the vendor's stand was almost empty, but she had no time. She hopped into her car, lit a cigarette, inhaled deeply, and stepped on the gas. It was 1:15 by the time she pulled into the parking lot of her office building.

34

◈

Ma'dear

Sunday morning. I woke up before dawn. It was hard to sleep knowing what I had to do. Suddenly I felt so old, much older than my twenty-three years. I got up, took a quick bath, made some coffee and a piece of toast and waited. I wasn't expected at Sadie's until 3 PM. I thought about going to that little church up the street. I hadn't set foot in a church since before I left Virginia. If there was anything I wasn't, it was a hypocrite. I couldn't go to church and turn around and hurt somebody.

All night long I tossed and turned, my mind chattering about Willie Joe, Sadie, and whether I was doing the right thing. "'Vengeance is mine,' saith the Lord." That kept going round in my head. Then I remembered what Madame LaFontaine said. The spell couldn't be taken off even though Willie Joe was dead. I didn't care about me, but what if the spell hurt my little son Melvin? What if it was passed on down through the generations to all the males in the family? No. I had to put an end to it. It would serve Sadie right. Nobody should mess with roots. You never know what it'll do.

Time passed slow that morning. Finally it was nearing time to go to Sadie's. I put on my best outfit-the dress I wore to my wedding to Willie Joe. I smiled at his picture on my dresser.

"This is for you, honey."

Even though Sadie lived about ten blocks from me, I could've took the bus. Instead, I decided to walk. By the time I got there I was so nervous, I didn't feel tired after the long walk. I climbed the stairs to their fourth floor apartment and knocked on the door. Sadie opened it right away.

"Girl, you right on time as usual. You ain't changed a bit." She hugged me and took my coat. I followed her into the living room. "Now, you just make yourself at home."

I sat down on the couch. It was a small room, with beige colored walls; two comfortable looking chairs with crocheted doilies each on the arm, and one larger doily in the center of their coffee table. A couple of wedding photographs of the happy couple hung on one wall, a poster of President Harry Truman on another wall and over the mantle, a picture of Jesus Christ on the cross. Sitting in one of the chairs was her husband Harry. He was listening to the radio, a drink in one hand, a cigarette in the other. He looked at me with a grin on his face. He must've had quite a few, I thought. I started to feel uncomfortable, him looking at me in a unhealthy way.

"So, how's Willie Joe?   Ain't seen him in a long time," he said, after Sadie had gone to the kitchen.

"Willie Joe's been dead over two years now."

"No," he said leaning forward in his chair, almost tipping over the glass he was holding. A few drops of liquor dripped onto his pants. "What'd he die from?"

"The doctor's said something about heart failure?" I looked toward the kitchen hoping Sadie would come back.

"Sorry to hear. You sure are looking good." He puffed on his cigarette and blew a cloud of smoke my way. "Would you like a drink?"   He yelled to Sadie to bring in another glass.

She came hurrying in with a tray and a glass filled with ice. Harry poured almost a full glass of scotch whiskey and handed it to me though I'd already told him I didn't want nothing. Something about the way his hand touched mine made me shiver. I didn't like it one bit.

"I gotta run to the store for a minute," Sadie said, pulling on her coat and grabbing her purse. "See if I can scare up a loaf of bread. Thought I had everything, but I forgot the bread. It won't take me long. You make yourself comfortable. Harry, be a good host and entertain Sarah." I offered to come along with her but she waved me off.

She stood in front of Harry, her hand out. Without saying a word, he reached into his pocket and drew out a hand full of bills. That reminded me. I opened my purse and carefully pulled out the envelope with the tainted money. "Here's the money Willie Joe left for you." I tried to hand it to her. She pushed my hand away.

"There's plenty of time for that. Now, I'll be right back. You make yourself at home."

No sooner did the door close when Harry came over and sat down next to me.

"You look good enough to eat," he said, his hand reaching for mine. I got up and moved to the chair. He followed. Sitting down on the arm once again, he tried to put his arms around my shoulders.

"Look here, Harry. If you don't stop, I'm gonna have to leave." I pushed him away.

"I'm just trying to be friendly." He reached for me again.

"It ain't right for you to be chasing me around like this. Sadie wouldn't like it."

I moved back to the sofa. He came after me. "Just one little kiss. Between you and me. Any friend of Sadie's is a friend of mine."

"You leave me alone, please!"

He grabbed me and pushed me down, pulling at my clothes. I reached for the nearest thing, which happened to be a bottle of J&B, and swung at him. It hit him on the chin. It stunned him long enough for me to get away. I stood up and was just straightening my clothes when the door opened and Sadie walked in.

"Sorry I took so long. There wasn't many stores opened on Sunday. How you two been getting along?"

Harry jumped up and grabbed her package. He kissed her on the cheek. "I'll take this into the kitchen for you."

"Ain't he the sweetest thing," Sadie said. "He's so good to me."

I looked around for my coat. "I just remembered. I got to get home. I promised my mother I'd call her at 4 PM." I lied. "She's expecting my call."

"When did she get a phone?" Sadie eyed me suspiciously.

"She don't have one. She's waiting for my call at Sam's grocery store. That's why I gotta go."

"What about dinner?   Girl, I slaved all morning long on it."

"I'm sorry.   I just remembered." I edged towards the door.

"Sarah, that's just like you. I shouldn't be surprised. You always had your head on backwards. Well, at least let me fix you a plate to carry with you."

I just wanted to get out of there. She fixed me a plate and walked me to the door.

"I'll let you go this time, but next time, I expect you to stay."

She called for Harry to say goodbye, but he had disappeared. I didn't remember the envelope until I was on the bus. It'll just have to wait until another time, I thought. Looking down at the paper bag with the food in it, I wondered if I should eat it. As soon as I got home, I dumped the food in the garbage and washed out the dish.

35

❧

Shanell

Shanell felt a wave of relief spread over her. Tricia had called the doctor and he told her Shanell wasn't pregnant, that she should see her regular doctor because her adrenal gland wasn't secreting enough hormones. Shanell didn't understand the rest of what Tricia said; she was too happy. Hugging her big sister, she couldn't think of anything to say other than, "I didn't want to be a mother yet. I wish I hadn't done it at all."

Tricia smiled at her. "How about going to see a movie with me tonight. There's a new Spike Lee picture playing at the Baldwin Theater."

"What about Ma'dear? Who's gonna look after her?"

"Momma said she'll be home early, after finals. Ma'dear'll be all right till then."

They peeked in on their grandmother and saw she was asleep.

"Are you sure?" Shanell hesitated. "You know Momma said not to leave Ma'dear alone."

"Don't worry. I called her at work and told her we were going to the movies. She said it would be okay. She should be home in a half hour."

They caught the bus over to the Baldwin Hills Plaza and got to the theater just in time for the 5:00 PM show. When the movie was over, it was still light outside. Tricia called home to tell Hazel where they were. "The mall will be open until 9 PM. There's a new dress shop I want to check out."

"Make sure you're home by 8 PM," Hazel said.

Shanell felt happy walking along with her big sister. It had been years since they spent any time together. And after her recent experience, she felt close to Tricia. They went from one dress shop to another, trying on dresses and modeling for each other. It was fun. Before they realized it, stores were closing, heavy metal blinds were being drawn down and lights were being turned out. Tricia looked at her watch. It was 8:45

"We'd better hurry before we get locked in." They hurried toward the main entrance. The security guard nodded to them as they rushed past.

"He sure is cute," Shanell grinned, glancing back over her shoulder.

"Sure is," Tricia agreed. "But right now we'd better catch the bus and get home. I didn't realize how late it was."

The bus was just pulling away from the curb as they approached the stop. They yelled and waved, but it was too late. At the now empty bus stop, they sat down to wait for the next bus. "May as well get comfortable. The next bus won't be here for another hour." She looked around for a phone booth. Seeing none, she hoped their mother wouldn't be too upset and worried. They forgot the time, she reasoned in her head. She'd take the blame.

"I had fun tonight," Shanell said.

"I did too," Tricia nodded. They giggled at nothing in particular. Shanell looked up at the star-filled sky. It was a warm night yet few people were in the street as it was a week- night.

A car drove by slowly. Shanell barely noticed it. Tricia chatted away about her career and about what she wanted to do after graduation. When the car passed again, it caught Shanell's eye. It was a late model black Chrysler with gold rims.

"Did you see that car?" She asked.

"What car?"

"That shiny black car with the gold rims that just went by."

Tricia looked, but by that time, it was gone.

Suddenly Shanell felt cold. "I wish the bus would come."

"It'll be here soon." Tricia said.

About 10 minutes later, Shanell looked up and saw the Chrysler parked across the street from them and the man inside staring at them. This time Tricia saw the car and the man. She didn't know why she felt uneasy.

"Come on, Shanell. Let's walk to the next bus stop." Tricia rose and started walking.

"Can we make it before the bus comes?" Shanell followed.

"I think so." They began to walk quickly to the next bus stop, two blocks away. However, before they reached it, the Chrysler pulled up alongside them.

"You girls want a lift?" The white man inside asked.

"No," Tricia said, grabbing Shanell's hand and pulling her along faster.

"Hop in. I'm going your way," he said.

"How do you know where we're going?" Shanell asked.

"Don't say anything to him," Tricia scolded.

"You're the Porter girls, aren't you? I'm a friend of your father."

This time Shanell stopped. "Our last name's not Porter. It's Johnson."

He stopped the car and stepped out. Despite the faint yellow haze cast by the street lamp, she was able to take a long look at this man who was dressed in a beige jacket with large strips, dark pants and fisherman's cap. He had a cigar gripped between his teeth, ashes trailed along his lapel. He was of medium height and his stomach protruded between the opening of his jacket. Beneath his cap, his long gray hair was pulled back into a ponytail.

Shanell caught a whiff of sweat and strong cologne. Stepping in front of them, he blocked their way. "I understand how you can't be too careful. Sorry if I scared you." He apologized. "You are Donald's children, aren't you?" His voice sounded husky as if he'd smoked a hundred packs of cigarettes.

"We don't know anybody by that name," Tricia said. "Now if you'll please step out of our way." She attempted to go around him.

"Who are you and why are you following us?" Shanell asked.

"My name's Foster. Leonard Foster." He reached out to shake hands with both girls; however, neither extended theirs, so he withdrew his. "Your mother has some property of mine, a black book. She was supposed to deliver it to me. Somehow we missed each other."

He reached into his breast pocket, pulled out a card and wrote down an address on it.

"Give your mother this and tell her to bring the property to me tonight around midnight. I'll be waiting. Tell her to come alone." He got back into his car and drove off.

"How did he know who we were?" Shanell asked. Tricia didn't answer. She turned the card over and read the address on the back.

"There's our bus," Shanell shouted as she took off running.

They ran the half block to the bus stop and made it just in time. It was almost 10:30 when they reached home. Their mother was waiting at the door; however, before she could scold them about coming back so late, Tricia told her what happened and gave her the card. Shanell described the man.

"I was so scared," she said.

"Momma, what's this all about? Is Donald in some kind of trouble?" Tricia asked.

Hazel took both their hands. "Donald's always in trouble."

"But are you gonna do what that man asked? Are you gonna give him back the black book tonight?" Shanell asked.

Hazel grunted. "I don't know. Don't worry. Go to bed. You've got school tomorrow."

Feeling very tired, Shanell ambled to her room. Peering intently into the mirror, she sighed. It had been an emotional day. First she found out she wasn't pregnant. Thank goodness, she thought. Next, she felt happy to have a big sister. Tricia had stood by her and she was grateful. She hadn't thrown "I told you so," in her face. And they saw a movie, tried on clothes together, and had a fun time. But when she thought of the man, Mr. Foster, she shuddered. After putting on her pajamas, she climbed into bed leaving the light on for Tricia who stayed up with Hazel. Before long, she drifted off to sleep.

36

❧

Tricia

"But Momma, You can't go there by yourself. I'm going with you!"

"No, Tricia. I don't want you to be involved in this. Besides, you've got school tomorrow."

Momma put the black book into her purse, slipped on her jacket, and started for the door. I grabbed my sweater and followed her. She didn't try to stop me as I jumped into the passenger seat. I could see she was grateful though she didn't say anything until we were on the freeway heading across town.

"Where're we going?" I asked as she got off the freeway on Hoover.

"It's the same building I went to earlier, where the answering service was," she said as she made a left turn into a small street, stopped in front this ugly old building and parked. The whole block was empty, no people, no other cars, and the streetlight hardly made a difference. My stomach was doing flip-flops. It was after midnight. I stood behind Momma as she tried the front door. It was locked

"Look," I said looking up at the windows on the top floor. "There's a light."

"Maybe there's a back entrance." Momma said, walking around to the alley. I followed close behind. I didn't want to be left by myself in the dark.

"Don't you think we should come back tomorrow during the day?" My voice sounded weak.

"Scared? I am, too. But if he said tonight, it's tonight. Besides I want to get this thing over with as soon as possible."

The back door to the building was unlocked. We went in. The hallway was deserted and looked gloomy. I followed Momma over to the elevator.

"The elevator's locked," she said when the gate wouldn't move. We searched for the stairs. "I'm glad you came with me."

We climbed up to the fourth floor. There was only one door at the end of the hall. Momma called out for Mr. Foster as she knocked. No answer. I remembered the time I went for the audition at that building downtown and how scared I was when I got to the office and nobody was there. I laughed nervously as I told Momma.

"He'd better be here. Getting me to come way down here at this time of night." She called out again as she turned the knob.

"Are you sure we should do this?" I touched Momma's arm.

We spotted a light on in the inner office. Momma went over to it and knocked on the door. When nobody answered, she opened the door. The next few minutes were a blur. All I remembered was seeing a man slumped over his desk. He looked like he was asleep. It took me a few minutes to recognize the red mat his head rested on was a pool of blood soaking the papers beneath his head. I started to scream. Momma put her hand over my mouth. She grabbed my arm and pulled me out of the office.

As we ran down the stairs, I heard voices. We kept running and didn't stop until we reached the car. Momma pushed me in and started the engine. I sank into the corner of the door trembling all over. Momma reached into her purse and pulled out a pack of cigarettes, lit one and passed it to me.

"Take a drag," she ordered. "It'll calm you."

I'd never smoked a cigarette before, but I took it and inhaled deeply. Immediately it felt like my lungs were on fire. I coughed.

"Yuk! How can you stand those things?" I handed it back to her. She took a long pull and blew the smoke out the window.

"Hope you never start," she said. We were speeding towards the freeway entrance, heading for home. As I grew calm, I felt my shoulders relax. I glanced down at my hands. They were shaking.

"Was he dead?" I asked Momma.

She nodded. "Was that the man who spoke to you earlier, who told you to give me the message?"

"I think so. It's hard to tell. All I saw was the blood. Momma, somebody murdered him!" I said, panic rising again. "Do you think it had anything to do with the book?

"I don't know."

"Maybe we should go to the police."

"And tell them what? That Donald gave us a black book and some money and told us to give the book to his partner? And what do you think they'll do about it? Assuming they believed me, they'd probably pick Donald up and arrest him. We don't know if he killed his partner. We don't know anything for that matter."

As we neared our block, Momma pulled over before we reached the building and killed the engine. "Look, don't say anything about this to Shanell or your grandmother. I don't want to upset them. Don't you worry either. I'll sort this thing out. And Tricia, thanks again for coming with me though I'm sorry you had to get involved." She hugged me. She started the engine, drove up to our building and parked. "Now you go upstairs. I'll be up in a minute."

I didn't want to leave her, but I did as she said. I climbed the stairs; opened the door quietly, so as not to wake anyone. After slipping into my pajamas, I went to the front window and looked out. Momma was still sitting in the car.

37

&

Hazel

Hazel awoke before her alarm went off. Outside her window, the early morning gray sky greeted her. She sat up, lit a cigarette, coughed, and leaned back against the headboard. Thoughts of last night seeped into her consciousness; a tremor ran through her body; her shoulders slumped, and her back ached. Wearily she got up and ambled to the bathroom. She didn't feel like going to work, but she knew she had to. She needed every penny knowing her days at the firm were numbered. Already they were cutting back on sick days and making it difficult to get any time off without being docked.

Standing in the shower, she wondered if she should call Kevin and tell him about her problem. Then she remembered, he was out of town and wouldn't be back for another week. When she told him about Donald, the money and the black book, he seemed annoyed. He told her to keep the money, get rid of Donald, and dump the book; a simple solution to a complex problem. When she told him about the break-in, he said she was being melodramatic. "Some kid looking for money to buy drugs." Another simple explanation. What would be his explanation for the dead body? That her imagination ran wild? No, she didn't need simple explanations. She needed solutions.

She toweled off, dressed, and went into the kitchen for her morning coffee. It was still early. She'd let the girls sleep a little longer especially after last night. One bright spot was that Tricia and Shanell had made up. She was grateful for that. And her mother seemed to be calmer though the improvements were just slight.

Seemingly unaware of her actions, Hazel reached up into the cupboard, retrieved the little book from the envelope, and began leafing through it. Could these be telephone numbers? They were written in such a way that they could be anything. She reached for the telephone, picked a number at random, and dialed. "I'm sorry, but your call cannot be completed as dialed." The mechanical voice of the operator got on her nerves. She opened the book again and picking another number at random, she dialed. The same message. Could they be license numbers? Social security numbers? bank account numbers? Who would list page after page of bank account numbers or license numbers? What does it mean?

"Hi Momma, Did you get any sleep last night?" Still in her pajamas, Tricia sat down opposite her. "I didn't get much. I'm too tired to go to school, but I suppose I'd better seeing as how we're near the end of the term." Tricia noticed the black book in her mother's hand.

"I'm trying to figure out what these numbers are?" Hazel said. Tricia took the book from her and studied the figures.

"Telephone numbers?"

"No, I've tried a couple of them."

"Maybe they're in other states," said Tricia.

"The area codes would have been written down too don't you think?"

"Could be post office box numbers."

"That's a possibility." Hazel responded. "But how would I find out?"

"What about Mr. Frazier? He used to work for the post office. He might know," Tricia suggested.

"I hate to bring Mr. Frazier into this. He'll tell Mrs. Frazier and before you know it, our business would be spread all over the neighborhood."

"But Momma, you don't have to tell him what it's for."

Hazel sighed, "I suppose I could try. Lord knows we need all the help we can get."

Both sat silent for a while, not realizing they were thinking the same thing until Tricia gave voice to it.

"Do you think we're in danger? From the police or from whoever killed that man?"

Hazel laughed nervously. "We didn't do anything and we don't know anything. Why would anybody want to bother with us?" She glanced down at the black book. "Except for this damn book!" She tossed it across the table.

"And the money," Tricia said. "Don't forget about the money."

"We'll worry about that later. Right now you'd better get ready for school. I'll stop by the Frazier's tonight." She got up quickly and started to her bedroom. "Wake Shanell and look in on Ma'dear, will you. I'm running behind."

The doorbell rang. Tricia let the nurse in. Nurse greeted her with a scowl, went in to Ma'dear's room. Tricia heard her greet her grandmother with in her usual booming voice, "AND HOW ARE WE TODAY?" as if her grandmother were hard of hearing. She shook her head and hurried to her room to wake Shanell.

It was almost 8 PM that evening when Hazel knocked on her neighbor's door. Mrs. Frazier let her in, a look of mild surprise on her face. Ready to gossip, Mrs. Frazier offered her a glass of lemonade, which Hazel refused, and sat down in her favorite chair. She picked up her knitting needles, and began telling Hazel about the latest neighborhood gossip. Hazel listened politely and then, before Mrs. Frazier could go on, told her that she'd come to see Mr. Frazier.

A look of suspicion crept across her neighbor's face.

"Mr. Frazier use to work for the post office, didn't he?" Hazel went on quickly. Mrs. Frazier smiled and leaned back in her chair.

"Yes, he retired two years ago. It hasn't been easy having him under foot all day. He tries to keep himself busy doing odd jobs. Is that what you want to see him for? Do you need help moving things around or fixing something? I'll call him for you." She rose from her chair and shambled to the door, her corpulent figure almost filling the doorframe.

"Jack," she yelled. "Mrs. Porter is here to see you." She ambled back to her chair and flopped back into it. "He'll be just a moment. He's in the bathroom." She peered over her glasses at Hazel. "You done something to your hair?"

"No, I just haven't had time to go to the beauty parlor." Hazel touched her hair self-consciously.

"Well, if I had hair like yours..." Mrs. Frazier patted her wig. Before she could continue, Mr. Frazier walked in. Laying down his newspaper, he plopped down in the recliner. "You wanted to see me? No more break-ins I hope. This neighborhood is getting to be something terrible. Too many young people with nothing better to do other than steal other folks' stuff."

Hazel looked first at Mrs. Frazier who had resumed her knitting, and then at Mr. Frazier. She wanted to speak to him alone. But there was no way she could avoid his wife hearing their conversation. She handed him a paper on which she'd copied the numbers from the book. "I thought you might have some idea as to whether these are post office box numbers."

"Where'd you get them?" Mrs. Frazier asked, looking over her husband's shoulder.

"She didn't come here to see you, Gertrude. She came to see me. Now mind your own business," he said peering down at the numbers and scratching his head. "Could be."

"Is there any way I can find out where the boxes are located?"

Stroking his chin, he thought for a while, "Tell you what I'll do. I still got some friends down at the station. I'll check around and let you know. How's that?"

Hazel smiled gratefully. "Thank you so much. I really appreciate that." She rose and moved towards the door. "I'm sorry to have disturbed you. Don't get up. I'll see myself out." She left quickly before they could ask any further questions and hurried up to her apartment.

38

✍

Ma'dear

About a week after my visit to Sadie's, who should show up at my door but her. It was after midnight. She had a black eye that she said she got when she bumped into a door, Harry, the door. She was a little drunk and I almost felt sorry for her. Then she asked if she could have that money Willie Joe left for her. I told her it was only $5.00. She said every little bit helps. Harry had accused her of stealing his money.

"That asshole hauled off and hit me." She laughed. "I picked up a bottle and smashed him across the head. When I left, he was laying on the floor moaning and trying to figure out what hit him. Child, you shoulda seen it. I laughed so hard I almost pee'd in my pants."

I made her a sandwich and a cup of coffee and let her sleep on my sofa. I told her I had to get up early for work in the morning. During the night, I decided that I really didn't have the heart for revenge. At first light I would take that tainted money and as dear as money is to me, I'd burn it up. To hell with spells. Then I went back to sleep.

She was snoring when I left for work. It wasn't until I was on my way home in the evening that I remembered what I'd planned to do. To my surprise the apartment was empty. Sadie had gone. Not only that but on the table was the envelope I had put the money in. It was torn open and empty. That wasn't the only thing that was gone. I discovered later that she had taken a necklace and earrings Willie Joe had given me. They was a birthday present he'd bought for me shortly after we was married. They weren't worth a lot, but they were from him and meant the world to me. At first I was angry. Then I remembered the money and I laughed out loud. Serves her right whatever happens. The more I thought about it, though, the more scared I got. What if something does happen to her? What if the spell worked and she died.

I tried calling her on the phone but didn't get no answer. The next day I took the bus over to her and Harry's place. The super said they had moved. "Snuck out during the night like rats. Stuck me for the rent."

It was six months before I heard any more about Sadie and Harry. One day I happened to be in the grocery store when I ran into my old friend Esther.

When she saw me, a strange look crossed her face. I caught it before she smiled and hugged me. She asked me had I heard what happened to Sadie. I told her about the last time I saw her. I didn't tell her about the money.

"I ran into her a few months back. She looked like a ghost, must not of weight more than 90 pounds," Esther said.

My stomach turned over. "What do you mean?"

"Your friend Sadie Brown is dead. Didn't you know?"

I felt tightness in my chest."Sadie...dead? When? How?"

"How you think? You know how Sadie loved to eat. Well, I heard she stopped eating and lost so much weight she died of starvation. She starved herself to death. Ain't that something?"

I didn't want to hear no more. I made some excuse to leave and went straight home. That night I couldn't eat. I tossed and turned and didn't get a bit of sleep. I kept seeing Sadie like she was the last time. And I cursed myself for not getting rid of the money. The next day I couldn't get out of bed. I didn't call in to work for a week. I wasn't surprised that I lost my job. Then I came close to losing my apartment. I couldn't think about anything else but that I had caused the death of another human being. If it wasn't for my mama and my son, I mighta taken my life. I was so miserable.

It took a while before I could pull myself together and scrape up enough money to go back home. I sold everything I could and when I had enough for a ticket, I hopped on the first bus going south.

39

෯

Tricia

"Tricia, phone," Momma called. As I took it from her, she gave me a dark look. "It's some man." She stood by with her hands on her hips. I covered the receiver and gave her a pleading look. After glaring at me, she went back into the kitchen, .

"Hello," I said, hoping it was Darien. I hadn't heard from him in a long while.

"Was that your mother? Is she as pretty as you?"

The last person I expected to hear from again was Hi C. His deep voice sent shivers up and down my spine.

"I was thinking about you. Have you been thinking about me? What are you doing this evening?"

I hated to tell him I was doing my homework. It sounded so juvenile. "Oh nothing. Just watching TV."

"I got somebody I want you to meet. I'd like him to hear you sing. Can you be ready in a half hour?"

"No problem," I said and gave him my address. I was so excited I didn't even think of Momma having any objections.

"Not on a week night, you're not. And not with a grown man I've never met," Momma said, putting her foot down firmly.

"Please. Just this once. It may be my one and only chance."

"When I say no, I mean no! Tricia, school comes first. Or it should. Now I don't want to hear any more about this. When this Mr. Hi C. comes to the door, I'll talk to him."

I went into my room and slammed the door. I couldn't believe it. She never stopped me before. Momma had always encouraged me to pursue my dreams. Now, all of a sudden, she pulls this! I was mad. "I'm going anyway," I told myself. "I'm almost eighteen. I can handle myself."

I dressed, slipped out the door and ran down the stairs. When Hi C pulled up in a beat-up T-Bird, I hopped in.

He let out a low whistle. "Whatachu know, Miss Jailbait?" he reached over and closed the door. Without saying another word, a lighted cigarette dangling between his lips, he pressed on the gas and we took off, racing across town to the 10 Freeway. I kept my eyes focused on the road, my right hand gripping the seat. In my mind's eye I could just see the headlines, "Teenager killed in a car crash. The driver must have been doing 90 when the car hit the center divider."

We got off on Central Ave in front of a club on 54th. I wondered if my legs would hold me as I reached for the door.

"Wait, lemme get that." Hi C jumped out and ran over to my side. "You can't open the door from inside."

Somehow I managed to stand up without falling. My knees were shaking as I walked beside him into the club. From behind a curtain separating the entrance from the main room, I heard music. I hesitated. "Will they let me in?"

He put an arm around my waist and gently pulled me along with him. "Don't worry. It's okay."

"I don't know. I'll have to think about it," I told Hi C as he drove me back home. It had been an unbelievable two hours. I had a chance to sing solo and be backed up by Hi C and his new band. I knew all the words to the songs they played. We started out with "Saving All My Love for You," my favorite by Whitney Houston. Then I sang Chaka Khan's, 'I'm Every Woman." With each song, my confidence grew so that by the time I sang Donna Summers, "Last Dance," the people got up and grooved to the music. The crowd was great. I mean, it was like my dreams had come true. I felt like I was on my way. I could see doors opening.

"We got a gig in San Diego next week. Can you get away?" Hi C asked.

I thought about graduation. I was so close. Next month I'd walk down that aisle, get that piece of paper, and be done with it.

"Yes. I will. I'll go with you."
"Good. I'll call you with the details," he said. He stopped the car in front of my building and came around to let me out. "If only you were a little older," he whispered in my ear. Squeezing me to him, he pecked me on the cheek, jumped back into his car and was gone before I could catch my breath.

"Tricia, is that you?" I turned around and standing a few feet away was Darien. I felt weak.

"What are you doing here?" I jumped. He moved closer.

"I was just walking by. On my way to see a friend who lives near here. What are you doing out this late? And who was that guy. You're dating older guys now?"

I started to tell him about my evening with Hi C. Then, I hesitated. It wasn't none of his business. "It's late and I gotta go in."

"Look, Tricia. It's been a long time. Can I call you?"

"If you want." I started up the steps. Unlocking the outer door, I glanced back and saw him halfway down the block. He turned to wave.

I couldn't believe it. What a night! I thought. I skipped up the stairs, almost reaching our apartment when I remembered. Momma will probably ground me for this. Then again, maybe she'll be happy for me when she hears the news. Yeah right, I opened the door as quietly as I could. Luckily the apartment was dark. Everybody was asleep, I hoped. I breathed a deep sigh and rushed to my room. I started to undress in the dark when suddenly the light came on.

"Where've you been? We've been looking all over for you." Shanell said, rubbing her eyes and stretching. "You're in trouble. Momma's 'bout to have a fit."

"You'll never believe it. Hi C took me over to a club across town and I sang. He wants me to go with them to San Diego. This could be the break I've been waiting for." I got into my pajamas and jumped into bed.

"San Diego? How you gonna get there? And what about school? Momma's not gonna let you go. You know that."

I didn't want to think about that. I was so filled up; I still hadn't come down. "Is Momma asleep?" I asked turning out the light.

"No. She got a call from Donald. He told her to meet him somewhere and she rushed out."

I bolted up. "From Donald? And she rushed out?" I felt my stomach turn over. "You shouldn't have let her go. This is bad. I leaped out of bed and started to put on my jeans and tee shirt. "What time did she leave? And where did she say she as going?"

"I don't know. She didn't say. There's nothing you can do. She told me to stay here and watch Ma'dear."

As I tied my sneakers, I suddenly realized I had no idea where Momma went.

"You're scaring me," said Shanell. "She don't have nothing to be afraid of from Donald, does she?"

"I don't know. I hope not." I sat back down on the bed, a helpless feeling washed over me.

40

❧

Hazel

Neon lights from The Blue Flame were the only illumination on the otherwise dark street. Hazel hurried toward the bar on the corner. The closest parking space was half a block away. A man and woman stood outside the door arguing. As Hazel approached she heard snatches of their conversation. "But Baby, I didn't know she was your sister..." "Like hell you didn't. If I ever catch you even so much as looking her way..."

The smoke hit Hazel in the face, thick and suffocating; the smell of stale alcohol assaulted her nostrils. She peered through the haze at her surroundings, searching for Donald. The bar had quite a few patrons considering it was a weeknight. Over in the corner Bobby Blue Bland sobbed from the jukebox muting the conversations.

"Oh Baby, Won't you come back home...."

At the end of the bar sat two men, their heads together in an animated exchange. Perched on a bar stool at the other end, a woman dressed in a tight fitting short dress gazed indifferently at Hazel as she blew a long stream of smoke into the air. Hazel drifted toward the back table where she saw a man hunched over his drink, his head bobbing to the music, his shoulders moving to the rhythm. He wore a hat pulled low over his brow. As she neared him, his head went up and he smiled at her, his mouth spreading into a gold toothy grin. She stopped midway.

"Hazel." she heard a voice near her whisper. "Over here." She turned and there, standing in the shadows beside a door marked "exit," stood Donald. Hazel could barely make him out, his head, a silhouette outlined by the red neon exit sign. He clutched her elbow and steered her to a small table beside the jukebox.

"Beer okay with you?" he asked. "Be right back."

She pulled a tissue from her purse and wiped the table where someone had spilled liquid and pushed aside the empty glasses. Taking out her cigarettes, she lit one and blew the smoke into the already smoke-filled air. The tightness in her stomach began to ease as she waited for Donald to return. He came back with two frosted tall glasses and two bottles of Guinness. He set them down and cleared the other empty glasses and bottles from the table, moving them to a vacant nearby one.

Hazel observed her ex husband, noticing how much thinner he looked than when she had seen him last. His jacket looked worn. She saw a stain on his shirt collar. His fingers were no longer encircled with flashy rings. His shoes were scuffed, and his face, usually smooth shaven, was covered with stubble. When he looked over at her, she noticed nervousness in his manner.

As he sat down beside her, an unwashed smell permeating his clothes made Hazel instinctively move back a fraction of an inch. She hoped he didn't notice.

"Did you bring the book?" He asked in a low voice.

"Yes," she patted her purse. "Listen Donald, I don't appreciate you involving me and the girls in whatever business you got going." She glanced around to see if anyone was near. "Did you have anything to do with your partner's murder?" she whispered.

"No. Believe me, I didn't."

"Well, what's this all about? If you don't tell me, I'm going to the police." As if she would. With disgust she thought about the article she'd seen in the newspaper. The article on the back page of the Times reported on the discovery of a body, "Leonard Foster, found stabbed to death in his office. Two black females seen fleeing the building are being sought in connection with the murder."

"Believe me, Baby. I'm more sorry than you'll ever know about getting you involved in this. When this thing straightens out, I'll do whatever it takes to make it up to you and the girls."

"When this thing is over, I hope I never see you again."

"I can't say as I blame you," he said. Suddenly he smiled at her and reached for her hand. For a minute, Hazel saw the old Donald emerging in his smooth, easy-going manner. She pulled her hand away.

"Tell me what's going on? Why are the cops after you? Where'd you get all that money? And what is this little black book?"

"Okay, I'll tell you. First, would you like another beer?"

She pushed over her empty glass. He looked around for the waitress and when he couldn't spot her, he picked up both bottles and rose. She watched him maneuver through the crowd to the bar and quickly return with two fresh bottles.

"I can't tell you the whole thing," he said sitting down. "It has to do with this business venture that Leonard and I had going. It didn't pan out. That's all."

"What didn't pan out? What was the business venture?"

He shrugged. "It's not important. It just didn't work out. I'm sorry about Leonard."

"Look, Donald. You haven't told me anything. You'd better start talking or I'm leaving." Hazel started to rise.

"Okay. I'll tell you."

He and Leonard had set up an escort service.' "It was going good for a while. But then, something happened. One of our clients was being investigated by the IRS, and we didn't know until they came sniffing around us. We closed down the business fast. I thought that was the end of it. What I didn't know was that Leonard got greedy and decided to blackmail the dude. You see, a little black book came into our possession. The book belonged to our client. One of our 'ladies' lifted it."

"There's nothing in the book but a lot of numbers."

"Yeah, I know. If the book falls in the hands of the IRS, this client would be in a lot of trouble."

"So why don't you just give the book back to the client?"

"It's not that simple. The problem is I know of the existence of the book, and that makes me a liability."

"Are you saying whether or not you give the book back, we're still in trouble? That our lives are in danger?"

"My life," he said. "I don't think they know about you. That's why I need the book, for leverage. I'm sure I can work out a deal."

"Yeah, and end up like Foster."

"No, Foster was stupid." He glanced at his watch and at the door, suddenly agitated again. "I gotta go. Give me the book."

This time Hazel reached across the table to touch his hand. "Donald, you don't look good. Where have you been staying?"

He reached into her pack of cigarettes and withdrew one. He lit it and inhaled deeply, not looking at her. "Here and there. I manage. Hey, I'm a survivor." He laughed. "You can't keep a good man down for long."

He gazed at her for a long moment. "Did I ever tell you, you were the best thing that ever walked into my life?"

Tearing her eyes from his face, Hazel felt her heart quicken. She reached into her shoulder bag for the book. "It's gone!" she said, frantically emptying the contents out on the table. "It's not here!"

"What do you mean, it's gone?" Donald leaned over the table to inspect her now empty bag. "Did you have it when you left home?"

"I thought I put it in here?"

His voice began to rise, "Well, did you or didn't you?"

"It must have fallen out."

"Dammit!" He stood up quickly knocking over the chair. "I stayed too long. Look, I'll call you."

Hazel saw him moving quickly to the door. He disappeared before she could rise. She glanced around the room at the bar patrons. No one even looked her way. Slowly she put her things back into her shoulder bag and started for the door.

"Miss," she heard the bartender call her. "You forgot to pay your bill." A beefy man with a cigar stuck in the corner of his mouth handed Hazel a slip of paper. "The dude you were with said you'd take care of it."

She peered down at the tab, took out her walled and handed him a $10.00 bill. He gave her the change.

"Leave it to Donald to stick me with the tab," she muttered to herself. Then, shaking her head, she went out into the night.

41

❧

Ma'dear

I had been living in Farmville for a little over six months and I was bored out of my mind. My only comfort was my little son, Melvin. He was growing so fast, it was all I could do to keep up with him. I had a piece of a job that I hated, working at the canning factory.

One Friday evening as we were getting off work, my friend Sug asked, "You ain't going straight home are you?"

Sug and me had become fast friends when I started working at the factory. A small woman who couldn't've weighed ninety pounds soaking wet, Sug was tough. I'd seen her pick up a ten-gallon can of tomatoes and throw it at the foreman because he complained about her being too slow. Luckily it missed his head or she woulda got arrested for assault. But I liked her. I couldn't tell her age but I figured she was a little older than me. We took to each other as soon as I started working there. I guess I looked completely lost and she felt sorry for me. Sug gave me advice, and cheered me up with her songs.

I was feeling particularly down that day as we walked towards the gate. She had a knack for reading people.

"What you need is a man," she said. "A man can stir up your juices, make you feel alive. A woman ain't meant to be alone."

I told her about Willie Joe and about my son Melvin. I didn't tell her about Sadie.

"I got just the man for you. He's my cousin once removed. 'come down from Detroit to visit for a while. I want you to come on over to my house this evening. We'll have dinner and I'll introduce you to Fred. You and him got something in common. Both of you can sit and talk about city life.

I tried to protest. I needed to take care of my son.

"What'chu got a mama for? One night out ain't gonna hurt."

That night I told Mama I was going to a friend's house.

"You need to get out once in a while," Mama said. "Don't worry about Melvin, I'll put him to bed."

I didn't really want to go, but once I got dressed and started on my way, I began to feel pretty good. That was the evening that changed my life and I don't mean for the better.

Fred was a big man, I mean big and husky, 250 lbs. and about 6'2. He was solid muscle. Said he worked on the docks from New York to Mississippi. He had a dark complexion with skin as smooth as velvet. He shaved his head but I could see that if he hadn't he woulda been bald anyway. He wasn't particularly good looking except when he smiled. He reminded me of Paul Robeson. His smile could light up the moon; and he liked to talk. He told me about his life, the jobs he'd worked, the fights he'd been in, the women he'd been with and what he liked in a woman. I was glad he didn't ask me about my life. Before the evening was over, I'd fallen hard for him.

Fred met me every day after work and carried me over to his room where we'd stay for hours. I wouldn't get home until well after 10 o'clock. Mama started complaining about how I wasn't spending any time with Melvin. I felt bad but there wasn't anything I could do. Fred had captured my heart and soul. Gone was my thoughts about Willie Joe and my nightmares about Sadie. I moved into Fred's little room and for three months all I did was work and come home to him.

Then I discovered I was pregnant. When I told him, he laughed. How could I let myself get pregnant, he asked. He didn't want to be a father. I thought in time, he'd change his mind. I thought he'd ask me to marry him.

"Marry you!" he laughed. "I can't marry you. I'm already married. You wouldn't want me to be a bigamist, would you?"

To say I was shocked would be mild. I almost went out of my mind. I started throwing things at him, pots, pans, the lamp, anything I could get my hands on. He just laughed and ducked out of the way. Then I collapsed on the floor in a heap of tears.

"Nobody told you to get your self pregnant. We was having fun, but I guess it's over."

After throwing my clothes into a shopping bag, I dragged myself back to my mama's. I didn't tell her I was carrying another baby. I knew she would put me out for sure. Mama was a churchgoing hardworking woman who minded her own business, took in laundry, raised her grandchild like he was her own, and now, here I come with another baby. I must have been out of my mind.

It didn't take long before she discovered my condition. She raised sand, but it wasn't her who put me out. It was my stepfather.

Isaac Johnson was a deacon in the local church. He also ran the only grocery store in a community of busybodies. He and I never got along. I did my best to stay out of his way.

When Mama told him I was going to have a baby, he said that was the last straw. He called me a whore. Said in their small community, their reputation would be ruined. It wasn't enough that they were raising my son; now I come back carrying another man's child. No. He wouldn't allow me to stay there any longer. I could see Mama was hurt, and I understood. I gathered Melvin's things and my own and started for the door. Mama stopped me.

"Sarah, you a grown woman, and I know we ain't got no right to tell you what to do. I apologize for the way Isaac talked to you, but you got to understand. He's a proud man. Leave Melvin with us. You gonna have enough trouble providing for that baby inside of you."

"As soon as things straighten out, I'll come back for him. I promise. And Mama, I'm so sorry."
I hated to leave my son, but I knew Mama was right. It would be hard for me with one child, let alone two. So, four months pregnant and alone, I kissed my son goodbye. He didn't understand what was going on. It broke my heart. I went quickly out the door, walked to

the Greyhound station and I caught the first bus to Philadelphia.

42

Hazel

Hazel walked quickly down the dark deserted street towards her car. Glancing at her watch she saw that it was 2 AM. Hearing footsteps behind her and thinking it was Donald, she turned. Two men hastened toward her. In a panic, she began to run, but they caught up with her before she could reach her car. The darkness hid their features; they seemed like apparitions in the night, yet they were real. One pushed her up against her car and held her there. The other grabbed her bag and rummaged through it. She tried to scream but the one holding her had a gloved hand over her mouth. He smelled of tobacco, stale beer, and sweat. She struggled to free herself, kicking out and connecting with her assailant's knee. He cried out, "Ow!" momentarily releasing his grip.

"Bitch," he whispered, grabbing her around the waist. "Hurry up," he said to his partner.

"Nothing here," the other man said, tossing her bag and its contents to the ground.

"Please, if this is a robbery, take my money. It's not much," she pleaded. The shorter of the two laughed. Hazel could see his mustache and goatee in the shadows. He was fat and held an unlit cigarette between his fingers. The taller one who held her had broad shoulders and a thick neck. He looked like a bouncer.

"We ain't looking for money. We want the book. Where is it? Did you give it to Porter?" His voice sounded hoarse like sandpaper.

"What book?" Hazel's mind raced, her breath short as if she had run a marathon. "I don't know anything about a book."

"Does Porter have it?" The short one repeated.

"I told you I don't know anything about a book."

"If you know what's good for you, you'll stay out of this," the tall one said pointing a thick finger in her face.

Released from a tight grip, Hazel watched as the men hopped into a blue Cadillac that was double parked beside hers, and pulled away with screeching tires. As they drove off, Hazel noticed the license plate, "LADELUK." She grabbed hold to the side of her car to keep from sinking to the ground.

It took several minutes before she could steady herself, to slow down her racing heart. Her breathing having returned to normal, she stooped to pick up her purse and its contents. She hadn't realized how scared she was until she reached for her lipstick, wallet and coins. Her hands were trembling so much she could hardly grasp her belongings. Managing to recover as much as she could see in the dim light, she scrambled to her car. Once inside, she locked the door, started the motor and drove as quickly as she could to Kevin's house.

She had to ring his buzzer several times before she heard his voice, heavy with sleep. He wore only a pajama bottoms, his chest and feet bare. Once in his apartment, all she could do was to lean against him. His arms held her tightly as he stroked her back.

"I've never seen you so glad to see me. I'm flattered," he said. "Maybe I need to leave town more often."

When she had calmed a bit, she recounted the evening, the meeting with Donald, and the subsequent encounter with the two men. She followed him into the kitchen where he brewed a pot of coffee. As she sat at the counter watching him, she felt completely drained.

"I told you not to get involved in this. It's Donald's mess. Let him handle it," he scolded.

"But I am involved. The girls are, too."

"How are the girls mixed up in this?"

She explained how Foster had accosted Tricia and Shanell in the street and the break-in. Kevin's jaw tightened as he listened. "Damn," he said. "First thing you gotta do is to make sure your kids and your mother are safe. Then you'd better go to the police."

"I can't go to the police. What am I gonna tell them? They're already looking for Donald, and they're looking for two women in connection with Foster's murder. I don't want to go to jail." Her voice rose in desperation. Tears began to flow. Kevin held her until she grew calm. He guided her toward his bedroom. Kicking off her shoes, she stretched out on his unmade bed. He lay down beside her, cradling her into his arms. Soon she was asleep, her breathing slowed, steady and deep.

When the darkness disappeared and the sky began to lighten, Hazel awoke suddenly. She glanced over at Kevin who was snoring soundly. The clock on his nightstand announced 5:30 AM. Throwing off the covers, she saw that she was wearing only her slip, bra, and panties. Realizing he must have removed her clothes, she saw them folded neatly on the chair. She dressed hurriedly trying not to wake him.

After scribbling a note, she placed it on the pillow, and then slipped quickly out the door. Once in her car, she drove home, barely noticing the night retreating hastily as dawn made her flashy entrance in orange, pale blue, and golden yellow, forecasting a warm day ahead.

Hoping the girls were asleep, Hazel turned the key and entered the apartment. There on the couch lay Tricia. Beside her, on the floor, wrapped in a comforter, lay Shanell. Deciding not to wake them, Hazel kissed them gently on the forehead, went to her room, put on her nightgown and slipped between the sheets for a few hours of sleep. However, sleep wouldn't come. In her mind she relived the encounter with Donald and the two men.

"I don't know what I'm gonna do," she said to herself. "But I know I gotta do something."

A few hours of sleep behind her, Hazel dodged the girls' questions about the previous evening as she gulped down her breakfast and set off to work.

"I'll explain it to you when I get home this evening."

"But Momma..." they protested. She hurried out the door and as she passed the Frazier's door, it opened. Mr. Frazier stuck his head out.

"I know you in a hurry, but what I been meaning to tell you," Mr. Frazier, dressed in his bathrobe and morning stubble, spoke slowly. Scratching his belly and removing the stocking cap covering his gray hair, he took a sip from his cup of coffee. "I got some information on that number you gave me."

Hazel's heart jumped. "Thank you, Mr. Frazier, but I gotta go. I mean, I'm late. I'll stop by on my way home this evening."

"Well, I thought you was in a hurry for the information." He turned to go back inside, disappointment written on his face.

"I'm sorry. Yes, I've got time. Go ahead. What did you find out?" If she was going to be late, she reasoned, did it matter whether it was a few minutes or thirty minutes. She followed him into his apartment.

"I had a friend check the numbers you give me against the post office boxes. Only one number matched." Mr. Frazier went over to his desk and started rummaging through the drawers.

Hazel sat on the edge of the sofa waiting.

Mrs. Frazier entered the room pulling her robe tightly around her stocky frame. "Good morning Mrs. Porter. My, isn't this a beautiful morning?" She walked over to the window and peered up at the sky;

then over at Hazel. "I see you're on your way to work. How are the girls? Would you like a cup of coffee?"

Before Hazel could respond, Mr. Frazier broke in, his voice laced with vexation. "Can't you see we're talking business! Just wait a minute."

"Thank you but I've already had breakfast," Hazel said feeling responsible for causing any animosity between the couple. Mrs. Frazier went back into the kitchen.

"Like I said, only one number matched. It's a post office box belonging to one of them big corporations located downtown," her neighbor said over his shoulder.

"Do you have a name?" asked Hazel.

"Let me see. I wrote it down on a piece of paper." Mr. Frazier searched the end table drawer. "I thought I put it in this drawer. Now, where's my glasses? Gertrude!" he called. "Have you seen my glasses?"

Mrs. Frazier came shuffling back, her house slippers making a flip flopping sound on the hardwood floor. "What are you looking for?" her tone matched his earlier harsh tone. She scolded him for making a mess. "Is this what you're looking for?" She strode over to the mantle where she picked up a tiny scrape of paper. Then she retrieved his glasses from on top of the newspaper where he'd laid it.

"You wouldn't be able to find your head if it wasn't screwed on!"

"Titus Corporation." He read the address and handed the paper to Hazel. Taking off his glasses, he smiled a smile of satisfaction.

"Thank you for your help," Hazel said rising and moving toward the door.

"If there's anything else you need, you know where we live," Mr. Frazier joked. Mrs. Frazier laughed.

Fifteen minutes late, Hazel thought as she glanced at her watch. What would be her excuse? The car wouldn't start? One of the girls was sick? No, she never liked to use that one in case one of them did get sick. Starting up the car, she reached for her purse and pulled out a cigarette. With one hand on the steering wheel, she used the other to search her pocketbook for her lighter. It wasn't there.

"Damn!" she thought. "I hope it isn't lost," she muttered aloud.

Kevin had given it to her, an expensive lighter with her name engraved on it. Giving up, she tossed the cigarette out the window as she swung into traffic and headed toward the Santa Monica Freeway. Pulling into the parking lot, she decided to make one more effort to find the lighter. Reaching her hand under the passenger seat, she felt something. A book.

She pulled it out and saw that it was the black book! 'How did it get there?' she wondered. It probably fell out of her jacket pocket when she went down to meet Donald. She hesitated before thrusting it deep into her bag. Remembering the incident with the men the night before, she shuddered. She shoved the book back under the car seat. It'd be safer there unless someone stole her car, she reasoned. Getting out, she locked the car door and hurried into the building.

43

୬

Tricia

When I got out of school today, who should be waiting at the curb but Darien. I was so surprised it took me almost a minute to get myself together. There he was leaning against the car looking fine. He wore a long sleeve gray shirt open to show a black tee underneath. The sleeves were rolled up to his strong forearms. He had on black jeans and black Nikes. His intoxicating smile lit up his whole face and almost made my heart stop. I caught my breath. Patrice, my girlfriend, flashed a flirtatious smile up at him; he gazed at me.

"Hi there, good looking. My name's Patrice. What's yours?"

"Patrice, this is Darien." I cut her off. Hoping she'd get the hint, I said, "I'll see you tomorrow."

She took her eyes off Darien and threw a grin at me. "See ya later, girl. See you Mr. Fine looking." She walked away switching her skinny behind like she had something to switch. Darien watched her go. When she reached the corner, she turned around and blew a kiss at him. He looked down at his feet, shoving his hands in his pocket.

"So, Darien," I asked. "What are you doing here? Aren't you supposed to be at work?"

"Naw. I got the day off so I thought I'd give you a ride home."

"All the time I been knowing you, you never did this before."

"There's always a first time. Get in." He opened the passenger side.

I climbed in and he headed across town. I wondered what he was thinking but I didn't say anything. When we got almost to my block, he turned off at the park and cut the engine.

"I got to be getting home. The nurse leaves and I got to tend to my grandmother," I said.

"I just want to talk to you. It won't take long." He turned towards me and took my hand. "Listen, Tricia. Let's forget about the past. I miss you. I want to see you again."

I didn't know what to say. On the one hand I missed him, too. But on the other hand, I had too much on my mind to want to add Darien to it. There was Hi C. He'd asked me to go to San Diego with him to introduce me to some important people who could help my career. Then there was the upcoming final exams. If I went to San Diego, I'd miss an important biology test and maybe not graduate. I couldn't let that happen. Mostly, though, was the trouble with Donald. I didn't want Momma to go through this thing alone. She was playing detective and I didn't like that. It was too dangerous. Now here comes Darien and with him I knew the question of sex would come up again. I wasn't ready for any more emotional trips.

Darien was watching me, waiting for my answer.

"Let me think about it," I said.

"What's there to think about? Either you want to get back together or you don't. Is it that old guy I saw you with the other night?"

I couldn't believe it! Darien was jealous. It's funny how guys never get jealous until they think they've lost you. I wasn't ready to play any games so I told him no. Then I told him I had to go.

He let go of my hand, started the engine, and drove me to my door. As I was getting out he said, "I'm not going to let you get away this time. I'll call you."

I stood on the steps watching his car until it disappeared around the corner, my heart doing flip-flops. I'm not getting involved again, I told myself. I don't need no complications! I turned and went upstairs.

Miss Nurse was waiting when I opened the door. "Bout time," she said as she got her things and left. I peeked in on Ma'dear. She was awake and watching TV. Beside her sat the tray of food the nurse had fixed for her - broth, toast, Jell-O, and apple juice. I sat down on the chair next to the bed and watched her eat. She seemed to be getting stronger each day. It had been almost three months since she came to live with us and I was starting to feel comfortable around her. Though I wished I could talk to her like I'd seen Shanell doing. I hadn't gotten to that point. I wanted to ask her advice about Darien, HiC, and my career. But I couldn't. I felt too uncomfortable. How can you talk to somebody who can't answer back? I could see she understood what people were saying by the look in her eyes.

After she had eaten, I took the tray into the kitchen; then I went into my room and began to study for my biology test on Monday, the same day I was suppose to be in San Diego to sing. I didn't have much time to think before the door opened and Shanell came banging into the room. She dropped her backpack on the floor, switched on the radio, and began to change her clothes. That put an end to my studying. I closed my book and went to the kitchen to start dinner.

Momma came home later that evening. She looked tired and worried. It seemed that some people at work were given pink slips and it was just a matter of time before she'd get hers.

"What's a pink slip?" Shanell asked.

"It means you're about to be let go," I said. I'd learned about it in my current events class. Shanell and I tried to cheer her up.

"Look Momma, you can get a job anywhere. You got plenty of skills. It shouldn't take long to find something else," Shanell said.

We fixed a special dinner for her and to celebrate my 18th birthday. "One day, when everything settles down, I'll take you on a shopping spree." Momma said, as she cut slices of cake for each of us. Shanell handed me a cute pair of earrings she said she'd been saving up for from her allowance. This was the first time we all ate together in Ma'dear's room.

That evening, as I lay in bed, I knew what I had to do. Hi C said if everything clicked, I could make big bucks. He said I had a lot of talent and that once things got started, there'd be no stopping me. Maybe if I went to San Diego and became a hit, I could make enough money to give to Momma so that she could open her own business like she always wanted. I would go with Hi C and be back in time to make the statewide exams. After all, exams were going on the whole week. I'd just miss one day. I decided I wouldn't tell Momma or Shanell. When I came back, I'd have a big surprise for them. That was my plan.

Monday morning, instead of going to school, I threw some things in Momma's overnight bag, a black tee strap dress I'd bought on layaway with the money I got from the gig with Big Jim Thornton, Momma's sequined pumps, (I knew she would probably have a fit but it was for a good cause); and makeup. I wrote a note explaining I would probably be late getting home, that I was studying at my friend Patrice's house, but at the last minute, I tore it up. Then I walked over to the park, sat down and waited.

Hi C told me to meet him in front of Fred's bar and Grill around noon. At eleven o'clock, I hopped on the bus that would take me across town. The bar wasn't open. It wouldn't matter. I wouldn't have gone inside anyway. I stood in the alcove and waited. A half hour passed, some people walking by didn't pay me no mind, but others stared at me and then at my overnight bag. I felt real uncomfortable like I was a streetwalker. One man even came over and asked me how much I charged. I moved away from the door when I saw a cop car drive by slowly as the cop took a long look at me.

Where was Hi C? I wondered. I made up my mind that if he didn't come in the next fifteen minutes, I'd go home. Just as I was about to leave, I saw his raggedy-ass yellow T-Bird. He swooped into an empty parking space nearby.

"I see you're ready to fly." He grabbed my bag and threw it onto the back seat, came around and kissed me on the cheek. His breath smelled like whisky and cigarette smoke. Usually he looked cool, together, like the world would just have to wait for him, but today he seemed up, I mean, like he had extra energy. I figured it must be the excitement of the gig. I was excited too. So much was riding on this trip.

As he drove the 405 to San Diego, weaving in and out of lanes, he searched the radio for a jazz station. Then he pulled out a cassette and stuck it into the slot. Every once in a while he glanced over at me and smiled, his cigarette dangling from his lips. Even though traffic was heavy, the car kept moving along wherever there was an open spot. He chattered away, something about the artist and the song; but I was so busy watching the road and holding on, I couldn't repeat what he was talking about to save my life. Then the traffic was behind us and I began to relax. Sinking back into the seat cushion, I got into the music.

The ocean looked so calm, the ride so smooth, the music hypnotic; I drifted off to sleep. Suddenly I was aware that the car had stopped. I opened my eyes and looking around I could see we were in the parking lot of Motel 8.

Hi C was coming out of the office.

"Why're we stopping here?" I asked. I knew San Diego wasn't that far away though I'd only been there once when we were kids and Momma took Shanell and me to the San Diego Zoo.

"I need to catch a few winks," Hi C said, opening my door. "I been up all night and if I'm gonna be at my best, I gotta take a nap. There's a diner across the street. We can go and get something to eat first."

That was fine with me. We left the car in the parking lot and walked over to the diner. I was so hungry. I hadn't realized that I hadn't had anything to eat since breakfast. I ordered spaghetti. Hi C ordered steak and potatoes. He joked as we ate about how once I got famous, I probably wouldn't know him.

"It's a shame you're underage. There're a lot of people I could introduce you to. I'd be your agent and we'd go places."

I told him my birthday was last week. "I'm eighteen. You can wish me happy birthday now. I don't usually make a big thing about my birthday. My mother said as soon as things calm down, we would have a big celebration." I told him about the problem with Donald, not telling him everything, just about some people looking for him. I don't think Hi C was even listening. He looked around for the waitress and when she came over, he asked for the check. I followed him back across the street to the motel.

"You can sit in the car if you want. I'll be out in about an hour or you can come in and watch TV while I sleep," he said.

I thought about it and decided time would pass quicker watching TV than sitting in his car in the parking lot of a seedy motel. Taking my overnight bag from the back seat thinking if I changed into what I'd planned to wear and put on my makeup, I'd save time. I followed him to his room.

It was a small ugly room with a full size bed taking up most of the space, a little oval table sitting up against the wall, a dresser with a nineteen inch TV set sitting on top of it. I flipped it on and sat down at the table. Hi C went into the bathroom. I made myself comfortable, put my feet up in the other chair, and settled down to wait, with a bag of Doritos and a can of Pepsi I bought from the vending machine in the hall. The only drawback was the TV had no remote. I'd have to get up to change the channels. Oh well, I thought, just for an hour.

Hi C came out of the bathroom wearing only his boxer shorts. That should've been my first clue. If he was just going to nap an hour, why did he need to take off his clothes? He pulled back the covers and hopped in.

"Why don't you join me? We gonna be up late tonight and you wanna be at your best."

"I'm fine," I said. "I got some sleep in the car so I'm not tired."

"How about a drink to relax you." He offered me a sip from the flask he carried and placed on the nightstand beside the bed.

"No, thank you. I don't drink."

"Com'on, baby. Loosen up. How you gonna perform tonight if you're so uptight.?

"Hi C, I thought you stopped here to take a nap."

"I did, but I want you to join me."

"Maybe I'd better wait for you in the car." I picked up my bag and started for the door.

Before I could get it open, he grabbed me around my waist and pulled me toward the bed.

"Don't!" I told him when he started pulling down my pants. He tried to pin my arms behind my back and started to kiss me as he pushed me down. When I bit his lip, he smacked me across face. I screamed. I kicked him in the balls and scratched his face.

"Bitch," he yelled, holding his groin. "Shut up, you stupid..."

He grabbed my arms and tried to pin them over my head as he reached down to pull off his shorts. Jerking my body to one side, I must have caught him off guard because he slid to the floor. This gave me just enough time to scramble off the bed. I ran into the bathroom and locked the door. He pounded on it a couple of times; then he stopped. I peeked through the keyhole and I saw him putting his pants on. Then I heard the outside door open and slam behind him. Even when I heard the car engine start, I couldn't move and I couldn't stop crying. I must've lay there a good hour or more. Outside it was growing dark, the only noise in the room was from the TV. Flickering light cast shadows against the wall.

Cautiously, I unlocked the bathroom door, crept back into the room and slid the dead bolt praying he wouldn't come back. Then I climbed into the shower, turned on the hot water full blast and let it wash away the shame I felt. I don't know how much time went by before the water turned cold. I picked up my clothes; my blouse was ripped. Glancing into the mirror, I saw that one side of my face was swollen. How could I go home looking like this? What would Momma say? In the back of my mind I knew I should report what HiC tried to do to me; but I knew I couldn't prove I hadn't come with him willingly. I was eighteen years old, no longer jailbait. I was in a motel room in or near San Diego. So many thoughts went round in my mind. Then it hit me. I was stranded. How was I gonna get home?

Swallowing my pride and humiliation, I walked up to the front desk and asked the manager if I could make a call. The manager, a chubby woman with short gray hair and bifocals, looked up from her plate, on which sat a half eaten pork chop. Dabbing her lips and wiping her hands on a napkin, she frowned. Then something in my face must've told her how desperate I was; she softened.

"It's against our policy, but there's a telephone on the corner, next to the diner. You got any money?"

I shook my head. I only had a dime. She handed me a dollar in change. "You young girls always getting yourselves in trouble. How old are you?"

Before I could answer, she went on. "I got a daughter your age. I hope if she gets into trouble, somebody'll help her out."

The clock on the wall behind the desk said 9 PM. Had I been there that long? As I walked to the corner telephone, I wondered who I could call. I didn't want to call Momma. I was so ashamed and I knew she'd be mad as hell. Besides, I'd rather deal with that when I felt better. Grace? Kanisha? No, Gracie had her number changed and I didn't have her new number since she got back from down south. The only other person I could think of was Darien. I dialed his number. After a few rings, he answered. I told him I was stranded and asked him if he could come and get me. He didn't ask no questions. Said he'd be here in about an hour. I went back to the room and waited. While I waited, I cried some more.

He was as good as his word. In exactly an hour, Darien came. I got into his car and we drove all the way back to L.A. in silence. It was only when we parked in front of my apartment that he asked if there was anything he could do. I told him how grateful I was that he'd come to my rescue.

"I can't explain anything to you now. But I will." I climbed out of the car and went upstairs.

Momma and Shanell met me at the door. Momma started yelling at me for being out late and not telling anybody where I was.

"Just because you're eighteen, and still living under my roof, you will obey my rules!"

Then she noticed my swollen face. "What happened? Who did this to you?" she asked. I broke down and cried. She put her arms around my shoulders. "Don't worry. You'll tell me when you want to."

"Damn! What happened to you?" Shanell asked. Momma threw her a look that shut her up.

I didn't say anything. I only wanted to go to bed. Shanell followed me to our room. Looking at me with eyes filled with sympathy. "How did the gig go?" I hadn't realized that she knew where I'd gone.

"How did you know?" I didn't remember telling her. "I didn't make it," I smiled weakly. "I'll tell you all about it someday." I undressed and hopped into bed. She hugged me.

44

&

Ma'dear

When I got to Philadelphia, I called my aunt. Mama had told her I was coming. I sat in the bus station for what seemed like hours until she came to pick me up. Then there was the long drive to her home. Her house was in a middle-class, respectable part of the city, a large Victorian-style house with plenty of small dark rooms filled with dark, oversized furniture that instantly made me depressed. Aunt Phoebe was a large woman. A few years older than Mama, she was as unlike her sister as night is to day. Where Mama was gentle and quiet, Aunt Phoebe was bold and had a lot of opinions that she didn't mind expressing. She was married to an undertaker. They had two grown children that didn't live at home. Mr. Booker, as she called him, ran the only Negro undertaking parlor in the city. You could say they didn't hurt for money.

Aunt Phoebe showed me to my room on the third floor. I was so tired from the long bus ride, I just fell on the bed and went to sleep. I must have slept a long time because when I woke up, it was dark outside. I heard Aunt Phoebe knocking at the door.

"Supper will be on the table in ten minutes. Get yourself washed up and come on down."

The bathroom was located on the second floor. I washed up, changed clothes and went downstairs to eat. The table was loaded with food, pork chops, green beans, mashed potatoes and cornbread. The smells made my stomach queasy. It was all I could do to keep from throwing up.

"I'm not very hungry," I said weakly. I just wanted to go back upstairs, be alone with my problems.

"Nonsense, you need to eat something," Aunt Phoebe said, dishing food into my plate and setting it down in front of me. My smile was thin as I looked down at the steaming food. After she finished filling up the plates, she asked Mr. Booker to say grace. He nodded.

"Let's bow our heads," he said in a deep voice. We did. As he said a long prayer, I peeked at the others. Besides Mr. Booker and Aunt Phoebe there was another man whom I hadn't met. When Mr. Booker finished, Aunt Phoebe introduced me to him.

"Sarah, this is Mr. Livingston. He rooms here with us." He nodded. "This is my niece Sarah. She'll be staying here for a while."

Mr. Livingston was a pleasant looking man, medium build, light complexion, high yellow, as we use to call people in them days. His face was covered with freckles. He grinned a toothy grin at me. That's about all I noticed about him except that he looked like my mother's age, his bald head glistened in the light from the chandelier as if he'd polished it up for the meal.

We ate in silence the only sounds were chewing and swallowing, and an occasional loud belch from Mr. Booker. I managed to eat a bit, enough to keep from insulting Aunt Phoebe. I made it through most of the meal and as soon as I felt it was the right time, I asked her if I could be excused.

"Don't you want dessert? I made apple pie especially for you," said Aunt Phoebe, clearing away the plates. She went into the kitchen and brought back a freshly baked pie and some dessert plates.

"Thank you, but I'm not feeling well. I'd like to go to my room and lie down."

She had a frown of disapproval on her face but she nodded. "You go right ahead. You're excused. Tomorrow, though, I expect you to help around the house."

"You're part of the family now," Mr. Booker said. "No free rides here." He laughed.

Though I was expecting in a few months, Aunt Phoebe managed to get me a job washing clothes for the white families across town. It was that or helping Mr. Booker at the mortuary. I'm not squeamish but I don't like being around dead bodies.

Both my aunt and Mr. Booker were active in their local church, United Methodist. Every evening or so they went to meetings at the church and occasionally I went with them to Bible Study. Mr. Livingston accompanied us on Sundays. He turned out to be a very nice man, one I could talk to easily. He told me about himself, his wife died five years ago from cancer. They had no children. When I told him about Willie Joe and my life in New York, he was genuinely sympathetic. He didn't ask about the father of the baby I was carrying. In time I found myself dependent upon his company and on our talks. He took it upon himself to look after me.

One evening after everybody had gone to bed, I crept down to the kitchen for a glass of milk. Milk helps me sleep. Mr. Livingston was at the kitchen table eating a piece of leftover chicken. He said he couldn't sleep either.

"Sarah, there's something I've been meaning to ask you. I know we haven't known each other but a few months, but I've grown real fond of you," he said reaching across the table for my hand. When he asked me to marry him, I was a little surprised. I told him I didn't love him. He reasoned that we should get married if only so that my child would be born legitimately, not with the stigma of being born out of wedlock. He said he would make a good home for me and would raise the child like his own.

I didn't answer him right away. I told him I had to sleep on it. He said he understood. I finished my glass of milk and hurried back upstairs to bed before he could get up. My head was spinning. The next day when I told Aunt Phoebe, she said it was a good idea.

"Mr. Livingston is a good man. I'm happy for the both of you."

Mr. John Livingston and me were married a week before Hazel was born. We went before the Justice of the Peace. As soon as I agreed to marry him, John, who worked as a porter on the railroad, went out and found us a little house across town. We moved into that place and for the next ten years that was our home. I was able to get Melvin from Mama, and with the four of us together, I felt blessed. John was a good father to my children up until the day he died. We had ten wonderful years together, and then he was gone.

When Hazel was eleven I took her and Melvin back to Farmville to visit Mama.   She was ill and not expected to live much longer. I hadn't been back but once since going down to pick up Melvin long ago. Every year, though, I sent him down to spend summer with her.

The house where I grew up looked the same except a little more run down. The garden Mama had planted was nothing but weeds.   A few chickens wandered around the yard scratching at the ground for whatever food they could find among the weeds. A rusted tractor stood beside the weather-beaten barn that looked like it was about to fall down.

My stepfather, Isaac, was nowhere to be seen. Instead there was a woman, who looked younger than me, traipsing around the house, dusting the furniture, straightening up, and fixing food for my mother. She looked familiar though I couldn't place her. A short busty woman, she wore a faded gingham housedress, and worn man's shoes with the backs folded under. Her hair was wrapped in a scarf, and she had a small mole above her lip. After greeting me she shooed Melvin and Hazel outside.

"Yall go play in the yard while your Mama visits your grandma."   She offered to bring me some lemonade, and before I could say yes, she disappeared *down the hall and into the kitchen. I went into the parlor.*

Mama sat in her rocker looking so thin and frail. She couldn't have weighed more than 90 pounds and when she tried to speak, she coughed. I kissed her forehead, pulled up a chair close to her and held her hand.

I couldn't hide the shock on my face at how sick she looked. Reaching into my purse, I pulled out a hanky and blew my nose, wiping away a tear that threatened to fall. I told her about my life, adding things to make her laugh, staying away from serious topics. We reminisced about when we all were together, Mama, Daddy, my sister and brothers.

The young woman came in bringing a tray on which sat a pitcher of lemonade, a glass filled with ice and a plate of cookies.

"She's already had her lunch," she said when I asked about a glass for Mama. When she left, I asked Mama, "Who's that?" My gaze followed the woman back down the hall.

"That's Edna Mae. Don't you remember her? She was your best friend Sadie's little sister. She came to help me out when Isaac left."

"Where is Isaac?"

"Old fool done run off with the pastor's wife. All I can say is good riddance." She laughed than started to

cough. I was just about to give her my glass of lemonade when Edna Mae came running in.

"She can't have that! She got sugar. Let me get her medicine." She rushed back into the kitchen and returned carrying a glass of water and a bottle of pills. She helped Mama with the pills and water. "There," she said. "She'll be alright."

I sat with Mama a while until she drifted off to sleep; then I took the tray back into the kitchen. Edna Mae was cutting up vegetables and putting them in a pot of boiling water.

"You don't remember me, do you?" she smiled. "You and Sadie ran off together when I was just a little girl. Couldn't have been much younger than your daughter.

A strange feeling came over me as I stood there listening to her talk about Sadie and how much her big sister had taught her. "I miss her so much."

She asked me about what Sadie and me did after we left.

"Sadie didn't write much. One letter she wrote she said she'd met a man and planned to get married. Willie Joe, I think she said his name was. She was so in love with that man."

My heart almost stopped. "Willie Joe?" I said.

"Yeah, Did you ever meet him? Anyways, later she wrote and said he'd gotten married. Next thing I heard was that he was dead. How you like that?"

"Did Sadie tell you how he died?" I could hardly get the words out. I sat down at the table to keep from falling.

"No Ma'am. She didn't say nothing about that. She was always promising to bring me up to New York to live with her. But that's Sadie. Always promising but never following through. Then I woulda got a chance to leave this old backwater town. Sure do miss her," she said again with a long sigh. She pulled a big cloth from her bosom, wiped the sweat from her face and stuck it back.

"Is it all folks say it is? You know, wall-to-wall people, bright lights, no body sleeps? Tell me what life is like in New York?"

"I don't live there no more," I said. I wanted to hear more about Sadie but I was afraid to ask. I watched her cut up some meat and toss it into the pot. Finally after a while I asked, "Did you hear anymore from her?"

"Who? Oh, my sister? Yeah, last time she called, she said she believed somebody put a spell on her."

I gasped. "A spell?"

"Yeah, you know, hoo doo. Sadie was always into something. I don't believe in none of that stuff, but she *did. She said she'd hadn't been able to eat, her appetite was gone."*

"What made her think somebody put a spell on her?"

"I don't know, a feeling, I guess. I use to be into that stuff, but not any more."

She went on and on, but I wasn't listening. All those dreadful memories came flooding back, Willie Joe and Sadie. Just then I heard Melvin and Hazel hollering at each other. Hazel came running into the kitchen. Her eyes filled with tears.

"Melvin hit me!"

I held her in my arms and wiped away her tears with my handkerchief. Then I went outside. "Melvin," I called looking around the dusty yard. I found him sitting behind the barn.

"Why'd you hit your sister? You too old for that and she's just a baby."

"She ain't no baby," he pouted. "I hit her because she was taunting me, calling me names and saying she was gonna turn me into a goat."

"Turn you into a goat? Where did that come from?"

"Tyreshia told her to do it."

"Tyreshia," I said. "Who's she?"

I looked around for Hazel and spotted her standing beside another girl I hadn't noticed before. About the same age as Hazel, but she was much thinner than my daughter, her complexion darker. She wore a faded yellow dress that looked too small and came up to the top of her thighs. She didn't have no shoes on and her hair looked like it hadn't been combed in quite a while. Both of them standing there reminded me of Sadie and myself when we were that age. As I drew closer to them, I stopped. Something about Tyreshia struck me, something in her eyes made me step back.

"Mama, this is Tyreshia, Miss Edna Mae's daughter," Hazel said.

I nodded to her, then turning my attention to Hazel, I stood between them. "Why were you taunting your brother? What's this about turning him into a goat?"

"We was only playing. He's so serious. He didn't have to hit me." She stuck her tongue out at Melvin.

"Sorry, Ma'am," Tyreshia said. "We was only playing. We won't do it again."

I barely glanced at her. I went back into the house and soon forgot all about what happened.

I didn't have to get back to work for another week and school was out for the summer, so me and the children stayed with Mama. Edna Mae was glad to get a vacation. I cooked, cleaned, and took care of Mama. Since Edna had shopped and the pantry was stocked with fruits and vegetables that Mama had canned before she got sick, I didn't need to go into town. Except for one day towards the end of our stay, I decided to take the children to the carnival. Melvin begged me so hard I had to give in. One of Mama's church members came over to look after her while we were gone.

It was a hot summer evening when we walked over to the carnival. Melvin and Hazel were getting along for a change. As we got closer to town, some friends Melvin knew joined us. Hazel walked beside me.

The carnival, in the field across from the canning factory, had transformed the place into a festive atmosphere. The Ferris wheel lit up the evening sky with its bright lights. There was bumper cars, a small roller coaster, all sorts of sideshows and stalls where you could eat your fill of hot dogs, cotton candy and Pepsi or lemonade. Melvin and his friends disappeared. Hazel's eyes were wide with amazement. They didn't have carnivals like this back in Philadelphia. This was her first carnival and I could feel her excitement. She wanted me to get on the Ferris wheel with her. Having a fear of heights, I wasn't too sure about that.

"I'll just sit here and watch you. Now you go on. I'll be right here when you get back." Disappointment showed on her face.

Suddenly, it seemed like out of nowhere, Tyreshia appeared. We hadn't seen her since the day Hazel and Melvin got into that argument. I assumed her mother had taken her with her on vacation. Hazel's face brightened as she ran over to her.

Grabbing her by the hand, Hazel pulled her over to where I sat.

"Tyreshia wants to go on the rides with me, but she don't have no money."

For a moment I didn't know what to say. I peered up at the girl who had on the same dirty dress she wore a week ago, hair uncombed, her skinny legs covered with dried mud and she was barefoot. I still couldn't believe she was Edna Mae's daughter and that her mother would let her go running around looking like that.

"Please," Hazel begged. "We won't go far."

"Well, go ahead." Feeling sorry for her, I gave them both a dime and off they ran. I watched them run over to the ticket booth, get tickets and head towards the Ferris wheel.

"Why it can't be. Is that you Sarah?" I turned around and there was Sug, looking just the same as when I saw her those many years ago at the factory, a little older and she'd put on some weight, otherwise she looked the same. I stood up and we hugged.

"Whatchu doing here, girl? I heard you was in town. Why haven't you come around to see me?"

I told her about my marriage and John's passing. "I'm just here to look after my mother. We're leaving on Monday."

I wanted to ask her about Fred, Hazel's father. But I didn't. She told me she was still working at the factory. She said the only thing changed was that some Civil Rights workers had come into town and were trying to get the Negroes to register and vote.

"This done stirred up the Klan. Some of them crackers been trying to scare us, riding through our neighborhood at night with their white sheets and burning crosses on people's lawns. But we fixed them. We showed them we wasn't scared. This is a new day."

Before she could finish, Hazel and Tyreshia came running back. I introduced my daughter to Sug.

"Nice to meet you, Ma'am" Hazel said politely, like I taught her. I gave her and Tyreshia another dime to ride the bumper cars. They took off skipping, holding hands and giggling.

"She sure is cute," Sug said after they'd gone. "Looks just like you. Got your nose and such a pretty smile. Her eyes, though, reminds me of somebody. I just can't think. And was that Tyreshia, Edna Mae's daughter with her? Girl, whatchu letting your baby hang around with her for? Don't you know?"

"Don't I know what?" I felt my stomach tighten.

"That girl's trouble. Takes after her aunt. The one that's dead, Sadie."

"What do you mean, takes after?'"

"You know... into all that strange stuff. The whole family's into it."

"Not Edna Mae?"

"No, I think she's the only sane one in the family. The rest of them is crazy. I wouldn't let my children around them."

Over Sug's shoulder, I watched Hazel and Tyreshia on the bumper cars. They were two eleven year olds having fun as they rode around the rink slamming into each other and others. Come Monday, we'll be gone, thank goodness, I thought.

I found myself watching Hazel closely after that. Watching to see what, I don't know. The weekend passed quickly and before long, it was time to go home. Mama had rallied a little. Edna Mae had come back and I had to be back at work on Tuesday. While I hated to leave Mama, especially knowing it might be the last time I'd see her alive, I was glad to be getting out of Farmville, away from painful memories, and most grateful to get Hazel away from Tyreshia and all that hoo doo nonsense.

45

✍

Hazel

Hazel sat at her desk shuffling through her papers but her mind was on the book and all she'd been through and what she'd learned. Mr. Frazier had told her that one of the numbers on the paper she'd given him was indeed a post office box number and that it belonged to the Titus Corporation. And she'd gotten the license plate number of the men who'd attacked her the night before. From a friend of Kevin's who worked for DMV, she found out the LADELUK belonged to a Manfield Jones who lived in Compton.

She reached for the telephone book to look up the address for the Titus Corporation. It was located in Century City, too far for her to go on her lunch hour. She'd have to wait until she got off. Hazel copied down the address and phone number and stuffed the paper into her purse. What she planned to do with the information, she didn't know.

"Hazel, Do you have that Strickland file ready?" Mr. Levine peered down at her. Startled, she almost jumped.

"Yes, it's nearly finished," she answered, glancing down at the pile of papers on her desk.

"Bring it into my office as soon as it's complete." He turned away.

She sighed as she searched through the disorganized pile for the Strickland account. When she found it, she began leafing through the file for the accounts payable page. As she tallied the figures, she was suddenly aware of Diane standing over her.

"You look like you could use some help. I could have one of the new temps take some of the load off your shoulders."

Hazel looked up and smiled. "Thanks, but I've got it together." Her eyes lingered on Diane as she watched her saunter down the aisle to another desk, peering over shoulders and issuing orders. Diane had moved up to supervisor and everyone knew how she got that position. Monica who had been there longer and knew more about the job than any of them had gotten her pink slip.

Even though Diane had been hired the same time as Hazel, she had secured her position and gone one better. If you can't beat them, join them, she'd said many times. She knew how to get what she wanted and more importantly, she knew the bosses. Despite the tinge of envy Hazel felt whenever she observed Diane, she liked her because she hadn't lost any of her down-to-earth qualities.

A good sense of humor, generous and a willingness to help, she didn't act like she was better than her peers.

After leaving Mr. Levine's office, Hazel passed Diane's desk. She hesitated. Deciding to take a chance, she sat down and waited for Diane to get off the phone.

"Have you ever heard of the Titus Corporation?" she asked.

"No, can't say that I have. Why?" Diane said.

"I came across their name and was wondering about the company, that's all."

"Hazel, you know you don't have to worry about getting laid off. I told you I'd look out for you." Diane took out her compact, smoothed her hair and refreshed her makeup.

"No, it's not that. I was just curious since I'd never heard of them before."

"I haven't either so I can't help you. It's almost lunchtime. Want to go out to lunch?" she asked.

"There's a new Greek restaurant on Grand that I've been dying to try but I don't want to go alone."

"Maybe next time," Hazel said. "I brought my lunch."

The phone rang and as Diane reached across to answer, Hazel returned to her desk.

The rest of the day went by as usual with no more thoughts of the Titus Corporation or the LADILUK license plate. Just as Hazel prepared to leave for the day, Diane came rushing over.

"I got so busy I almost forgot to give you this." She handed Hazel a stack of papers. "It's what I could find about the Titus Corporation. Hope it's what you're looking for. You missed a great meal. Next time you have nothing to do at lunch, I'll treat you. " She turned to go. "I got a hot date tonight with Joe McKinney. See you tomorrow."

"Joe McKinney. Isn't he the sales manager?"

Diane winked and headed for the door along with the first wave of departing employees. Hazel glanced through the material on the Titus Corporation her colleague had given her. Nothing unusual. But what did she know? She glanced at the names of the board members and their pictures. A collection of suits and smiles including a few women.

Hazel closed the report and gathered her things. Deciding to call it a day, she headed for the elevator.

In the parking lot, as she sat in her car, she reached under the seat and withdrew the black book. She leafed through the pages of numbers that meant nothing to her. As she turned on the freeway to head home, she passed her exit and kept going. When she realized it, she was near Century City. Titus Corporation Building was on the corner of Washington Blvd. and Sutter, a huge imposing structure surrounded by glass. Curiously, she pulled into the parking lot, got out of her car, and went into the lobby suddenly feeling the urge to use the restroom. "I should have gone before I left work," she chided herself.

Most of the flow of human traffic in the lobby was heading for the exit door. It was after five. Glancing around the huge lobby, she saw a uniformed man sitting at a circular desk at the far end. As she hurried toward him, another man dressed in a business suit and carrying a briefcase stopped by the desk and said something to the security guard, which made him laugh. As Hazel approached them she heard them engaged in an animated conversation about baseball. "Bet you two tickets to the game if the Dodgers win tonight," the man in the suit said.

Hazel stood beside the desk and waited for them to notice her.

"You're on. And if they lose, what will I get?" the security guard responded.

Hazel could wait no longer. Interrupting their banter, she asked where the restrooms were. The security guard glanced at her and pointed to the elevators at the other end.

"Just beyond that bank of elevators, turn right and you can't miss it." He turned back to the man in the suit.

She walked quickly towards the elevators, following his directions; however, just as she located the doors marked "Women's Restroom," her eyes fell upon a man coming towards her. He was pushing a large trashcan. Every few feet, he stopped to empty the receptacles lining the hall. Instantly she recognized him. It was one of the men who attacked her. Though it had been dark, his bulky frame, thick neck and broad shoulders were imprinted on her memory. What confirmed it was the way he moved; slightly rocking from side to side on bowed legs. She was sure he'd recognize her if he saw her.

She dashed into the nearest door, which happened to be a small service closet. Cracking the door, she watched him pass. Despite her bursting bladder, she followed him. Fortunately the flow of people in the lobby had ebbed somewhat yet it was still possible to tail him without being spotted. He stopped to speak to the security guard; then he went down another corridor and through a door marked "Employees Only."

Hazel hesitated. After counting to twenty-five she eased the door open and saw a flight of stairs. Cautiously making her way down the steps, she listened for sounds. Facing her were several doors. She listened at each one. Behind the door marked "Locker Room" she heard voices and laughter. She waited, her heart beating fast, her bladder nearly bursting.

"See you folks tomorrow," she heard someone say and then the sound of a time clock being punched.

"Don't come in with another hangover, Manny."

"Fuck you," she heard him reply.

The door opened and out walked the man Hazel was following. Quickly she ducked into a niche, hugging the wall and praying he didn't see her. Now dressed in street clothes, plaid shirt, brown pants, he took the steps two at a time, reaching the top before Hazel could pull herself together to follow.

By the time she got to the door, she saw him through the plate glass window, striding towards the parking lot.

"Can I help you, Miss? The building will be closing in fifteen minutes." She whirled around and saw the guard who had directed her to the restroom earlier. Unable to ignore her bladder any longer, she said, "Excuse me, I forgot something," and before he could reply, she dashed off to the restroom. Giving up on being able to continue her sleuthing for the day, she drove home. There's always tomorrow, she thought.

46

&

Ma'dear

Mama didn't live more than a few weeks after we got home. I was able to get two days off from my job and leaving the children with a neighbor, I went down to the funeral. Life began to return to normal and for a while, my spirits picked up and I began to believe everything would be all right. No more thoughts of Sadie, Farmville, or the past. The year went by too quickly. Then one day, I got a call from Edna saying she was in Philly for a few days and wanted to drop by. I really didn't want her to but I couldn't say no. Still, when she showed up at my door a few hours later, I was happy to see her smiling face until I saw stepping out from behind her, Tyreshia, her daughter.

"Give your aunt a hug, Tyreshia," Edna said.

Seeing the surprised look on my face, she explained. "You don't mind if she calls you aunt?"

Tyreshia, looking a lot cleaner than the last time I saw her, hugged me and kissed me on the cheek. She'd grown a bit, her body filled out in the gingham dress she wore. Her hair parted down the center with two braids pinned to the top of her head. She looked almost innocent except when you looked into her eyes. There was something devilish there. I stepped back.

"How's the children?" Edna asked.

"Melvin went to the movies. Hazel's at her friend's house."

"I was hoping to see them while we was here."

When I heard Edna was coming, I sent Hazel to play at her friend's house hoping she'd be away until she left.

"Child, you got a nice looking place here," Edna said, walking around the room, peering into the kitchen. "You got an eye for decorating. I can tell." She settled down on the sofa. Tyreshia sat down near the window.

"I know you wondering why I'm here. I got a cousin who don't live too far from here and we had some time to kill before the bus leaves and I wanted to bring this to you. It's a letter from Sadie. Don't make no sense to me but since she mentions you, I thought you might understand it."

She handed me an envelope that looked like it had been stuffed somewhere for a long time. It was *crumbled, stained, and tore open roughly.   It was addressed to Edna and postmarked some fifteen years earlier. My hand shook as I opened it.*

"My dear sister," it read in Sadie's neat scrawl. I had always admired how she wrote, how the letters slanted just right and she had a way of making her "g's" and "y's" stand out in a fancy way. As I read through the three pages, I was struck by the affection Sadie had for her little sister. Then I got to the part about me. I held my breath as I read,

> "When you get to New York, look up my old friend Sarah. You remember I told you about her. 'bout how she and me ran away from home together. We both fell for the same man, but she got him. Willie Joe. I couldn't stay mad.   Well, when Willie Joe died, I think Sarah blamed me. I don't know why, but she did. But you know what I always say, "no need to cry over spilt milk." Too much living to do. Look her up. She's good people."

I finished the letter and handed it back to her.
"So, here I am. Funny, one day she was living it up and the next, she's at death's door."

I spoke before I could think. "Do you know what she died of?"

Edna laughed, "Maybe somebody put the evil eye on her."

A chill passed through my body. I glanced over at Tyreshia. She was busy looking out the window. "I'm just kidding. I don't believe in that stuff. Last time I spoke with Sadie she'd been to the doctor and the doctor said she had cirrhosis of the liver. Everybody told her to lay off the booze. But you know Sadie. She always was a heavy drinker."

Just at that moment, I heard the door open. Hazel burst in. "Tyreshia," she shouted. The girls ran toward each other and hugged.

"Hazel, didn't I teach you better than that. Say hello to Miss Edna."

Edna hugged her. "You're getting so pretty," she said.

"Come on, Tyreshia. Let me show you my room." Before I could say anything, the girls were gone.

"What I really came to ask you was could Tyreshia stay with you a few days?" Edna said, sitting back down on the sofa. "I'm looking for a job and a place to stay and seeing as how I don't know nobody else in the city. When I ran across Sadie's letter, I thought I'd just look up her old friend."

I held my breath as she went on. "I been wanting to get out of that hick town and make a fresh start with my little girl. You know how it is."

I started to ask about the cousin she said who lived nearby and about the bus she had to catch. Why tell me all that when what she really wanted was for Tyreshia to stay with me while she looked for a job? Was she really here to look for a job? I felt ashamed at my suspicions. Then I remembered all she'd done for my mother.

"She can stay until you get yourself straight," I said. "Hazel would enjoy the company."

"I knew I could count on you. Tyreshia," she called. She got to her feet as her daughter came back followed by Hazel. "Now I'm only gonna be gone a few days. You mind Aunt Sarah. No backtalk. You be good." She turned to me. "I'm going now. I'll be in touch in a few days."

She kissed Tyreshia and Hazel on the cheek. "God bless you," she squeezed my hand.

As she was leaving, she set down a small cardboard suitcase I hadn't noticed. It all happened so fast, I didn't have time to think. Hazel was so happy to have her friend with her, I soon forgot my misgivings about the girl, at least for a while.

Tyreshia stayed with us a week. At times during the week, I would find myself watching her, searching for what? I couldn't say. She was a normal twelve year-old as far as I could see. At the end of the week, Edna came back and they left. I don't know if she'd found a place, got a job or anything and I didn't ask. I gave her a bag of Hazel's old clothes and even though they were a little small, Tyreshia loved them.

A few months went by, then one day, as I was cleaning the apartment, I decided to sweep under Hazel's bed. Lord knows, even the cleanest child seldom sweeps under her bed and Hazel was not the neatest. I pushed the bed out so that I could clear out whatever was under it. That's when I saw the box. What's this? I said to myself. Curious, I picked it up and examined it. It was flat with a strange design on it. I tilted it and out dropped a playing board. It looked like a checker board only it wasn't. It had the word "OUIJA" in big letters on it and other symbols. It slipped right through my fingers and on to the bed. I tried to remember where I'd heard that word before. Then it came to me. One time, long ago when Willie Joe and me use to play cards with Esther and her husband Herman, she mentioned a board where you could receive messages from spirits. I think she called it a "Ouija" board. I put the board back in the box, sat down on the bed and waited until Hazel came home from school.

As soon as she hit the door, I lit into her. "I don't want no black magic in this house, you hear!" I yelled.

She looked startled. Then she saw the box in my hand.

"Whatchu doing in my room messing with my stuff?" She tried to grab it from me.

"Where'd you get this thing from? Who gave it to you?" I stood over her.

"A friend," she said.

"Who, Tyreshia?"

"What if she did!" She looked at me defiantly. I swore she had that same look I'd seen on Tyreshia's face long ago in the yard at Mama's. That did it. I slammed the board down so hard, it broke in two. Then I whipped Hazel's behind so hard my arm hurt and sent her to bed without supper. For months after that the only person she spoke to was Melvin.

From time to time, whenever I picked up the mail, if a letter came to her from Tyreshia, I'd tear it up without opening it and throw it in the trash. I didn't want no communication between that evil girl and my daughter. Eventually, though, as everything does, our relationship got better though we never got as close as we once was.

47

❧

Hazel

Just as Hazel was getting into her Toyota, she spotted Manfield standing beside his car smoking a cigarette and talking with another man. Having to use the restroom, she'd thought she'd lost him. But there he was; a few rows from where she'd parked. She slid behind the wheel, and glancing into her rear view mirror, she watched the two men in what seemed to be a friendly conversation. Jones threw back his head, laughing at something the other man said. Then he opened his car door, slid behind the wheel, and waved as he maneuvered the 1954 blue Cadillac down the aisle towards the exit. Hazel followed, not too close behind. With all the traffic, she could stay behind him and not be spotted. He made a right onto the 10 Freeway, joining the line of cars heading east. Driving

40 mph, he leaped frog from one lane to the other, wherever there was an opening. This made it difficult for Hazel to keep up; however, she managed to see his car just as he swung off at La Brea. She dived headlong into the far right lane to the consternation of the other drivers who sounded their horns in disgust. Manfield's car loomed in the distance, going north on La Brea to Olympic where he turned right. Praying she wouldn't be caught by a red light, Hazel increased her speed to keep him in sight. When she got to Olympic, she didn't see his car anywhere. It had disappeared. She glanced up and down the boulevard. Disappointed, she pulled into a strip mall and idled the engine.

Feeling defeated, she thought, this is crazy. What would I do if I caught up with him? He could kill me. Glancing down at her watch she saw that it was almost seven p.m.

'I'd better call the girls so they won't be worried.' She turned off the engine, stepped from the car and searched for a phone booth. Spotting one on the other side of the busy street, she cautiously crossed the boulevard against the light. Once in the graffiti ravaged booth, she picked up the sticky receiver only to discover the insides had been torn out. Frustrated, her shoulders slumped.

In the growing darkness, the neon lights from a Budweiser sign outlined in red and blue caught her eye. The bar sat between a mini-mart and a hardware store. The hardware store was closed. Through the window of the bar, Hazel saw a pay phone on the wall. She entered the almost empty bar and walked over to the phone and dialed her home.

"Where are you, are you all right?" Tricia's voice sounded anxious.

"I decided to stop off at a friend's house but I'll be along soon," Hazel said not wanting to increase their worry. "Don't wait on me for dinner, and be sure you and Shanell do your homework. Clean up the kitchen and look in on Ma'dear."

"Yes, mother," Tricia said patiently, and added something about knowing what to do before she hung up.

Hazel smiled. As she turned to leave, she noticed sitting at a booth in the back was Manfield Jones. Two middle-aged white men in dark suits walked in and sat down across from him. One was tall and had broad shoulders. The shorter one was built like a wrestler. Despite his expensive looking suit, his jacket barely contained his bulging muscles. Both wore hats pulled down so she couldn't make out their features.

Seeing the booth near them unoccupied, she slid in and hoping to make herself invisible, huddled in the corner, her back to the occupants in the next booth.

"What'll you have, Miss?" The waitress stood beside her notepad at the ready. A bored expression on her face, the woman patted her foot impatiently.

Startled, Hazel said quickly, "Wine, I'll have a glass of wine."

"White or red?"

"Red," she said, in almost a whisper.

The waitress sauntered off, wiping tables and straightening chairs as she went back to the bar. Hazel leaned her head against the vinyl upholstery. She lit a cigarette and tried to catch the conversation in the next booth.

"Well, you've been paid but you haven't delivered. What are you gonna do?" she heard one of the men ask. It didn't sound like Manfield Jones. It was harsh and grating as if the man's throat had been swabbed with sandpaper.

"Look fellows. I did my best. I didn't know what was involved. I can't think of nothing else to do." Hazel identified Manfield's voice.

"So, what do you want us to do? You said you could handle the job, you've been paid, now you'd better deliver," The other voice said. "Or else." His voice was soft but with a menacing quality that sent shivers up Hazel's spine.

"Lenny," said the first man. "Why are we wasting our time on this two-bit bum. I told you I didn't trust him."

"I'm sorry," Manfield said. "I'll try again."

"You better come up with something or you'll be wishing you'd never met us." the second man said as both men slid out of the booth. Hazel tried to get a look at them as they passed her on their way to the exit. All she noted was that their suits looked of high quality, their shoes were polished and one wore a brand of cologne Kevin used.

"Here's your wine. That'll be $5.00." The waitress set the glass on the table. Hazel dropped a $10 dollar bill on the tray. "I'll be back with your change," the waitress said as she moved on.

Before reaching the door, one of them glanced back at Manfield. Hazel shifted hoping they hadn't noticed her. Then they were gone.

The waitress returned shortly placing five singles on the table and stood for a moment until Hazel placed $1.00 on the tray. Hips swinging, gum cracking in her mouth, she strolled off to the next booth where Manfield Jones sat.

"You look down in the mouth, Manny? Want some company?" the waitress asked.

"Bring me another scotch and soda, Doll, and some matches."

Hazel sipped her glass of wine slowly wondering what to do next. Deep in thought, she was suddenly aware of someone leaning over her. "Excuse me, Miss. You got a light?" Manfield stood before her.

"Sure, here." She handed him her lighter.

"Thanks." he handed it back to her as he took a long drag on his cigarette. He returned to his seat.

"You mind if I join you?" Hazel said sliding into the seat next to him. "I hate drinking alone." Operating on autopilot, she didn't know where she was going. When opportunity knocks.... she thought. She took a chance that he wouldn't recognize her.

"Naw," he shook his head and drained his glass just as the waitress set another one before him.

"Here're your matches." She looked over at Hazel. "You work fast," she said, a frown on her face.

"Bring her whatever she's drinking and put it on my tab, and bring me another, make it a double." Manny drained his glass again.

"Whoa, slow down. You're putting it away too fast," Darlene, the waitress said.

"Just bring me another one. I know my limit."

Darlene shrugged and went over to the bar.

Manny stared at Hazel for a couple of minutes.

"Haven't I seen you somewhere before?" he said exhaling a cloud of smoke. "I never forget a face."

"Everybody's always telling me I look like somebody else," Hazel laughed as she picked up her glass. What do I do now? She wondered unnecessarily, because soon Manny had reached the talkative stage. Good thing he wasn't one of those ugly drunks, Hazel thought as his tongue began to loosen.

"I just came in for a drink after work, and I noticed you sitting with your friends. I'm glad they left because it gave me a chance to meet you," she said. She could see he was eating that up. He smiled. Then he stared down at his glass.

"What's the matter?" said Hazel. "You look like you've lost your best friend."

"Like them white boys scare me. Shit...I'll wipe up the floor with them." His words slurred.

"Your business partners?" she asked.

"Are you kidding? I don't do no business with them. Well, we got a business deal going." He spilled half his drink but managed to get the rest down. His head started toward the table. "Get me another drink. Hey," he shouted towards the bar. "Bring me another double."

"Naw, baby," Darlene rushed over. "You've had enough." She turned to Hazel. "Lookahere Lady. He can't have no more. You gotta get him outta here

before Joe throws him out." She gestured over to the
bar

"Isn't he a friend of yours?" Hazel asked.

"He's a regular, if that's what you mean. Names
Manny something or other. Nice guy when he don't
drink too much."

"Do you know where he lives?" Hazel asked.

"Look in his wallet," Darlene said. "I gotta get
back to work or I'd help you. Joe don't like drunks in
here. He'd beat him up as look at him."

Hazel shook him enough to wake him; then as she
guided him towards the door, the waitress stuck the
bill in her hand. Hazel handed over her last twenty.

Now what am I gonna do with him? She
whispered to herself as she maneuvered him to her
car and shoved him in. His head dropped back against
the car seat and in less than a minute, he was snoring.
Gently she searched his pockets for his wallet. She
found it in his pants pocket and opened it. On his
license she noted his address, 43rd near Central Ave.
"Damn," she said aloud. "That's all the way across
town." Why couldn't she have shoved him into his
Cadillac and left him?

Forty-five minutes later, she pulled up in front of
the address, a small house surrounded by a chain-
linked fence. The place had seen better days. The
house was sorely in need of a paint job and the yard

needed weeding, but other than that, it was cute from what Hazel could see. The porch light was on and few people were on the street. A thought hit Hazel. What if he's married? What would his wife think me bringing him home like this?

I'll just have to take my chances, she told herself.

Coming around to his side of the car, she shook him until he was half awake. Managing to get him on his feet, she helped him stumble to the door. Finding his key in his jacket pocket, she opened the door, switched on the light, and spying a couch nearby, she half pulled him over to it and let go. He sprawled across it. Turning over into a fetal position, he went back to sleep and within minutes began snoring.

Fortunately, the house was empty. Hazel went through the place quickly. A tiny kitchen, one bedroom, and a living room, all sparsely furnished. Paying close attention to the snores coming from the sofa, she returned to the bedroom and began examining his dresser but found nothing that told her much about him except a few photographs of him and different ladies, the kind of photos you take at a photo vending machine; bills, and racing forms. She had just about given up when she spotted a folded slip of paper in an ashtray on the nightstand near the telephone. She picked it up and read it. Along with her address, she saw Donald's name and another name and address she didn't recognize. Just as she slipped it into her pocket, she heard a loud cough and the sound of a toilet being flushed. She hurried back to the living room and sat down before Manny came out of the bathroom.

"Who are you?" he growled. "And what are you doing here?"

Her heart racing, she answered as casually as her voice would allow her, "Don't you remember? I brought you home from the Silver Spoon. You were too drunk to drive."

"Oh, yeah," he said. "Thanks. I need a beer. Everything's spinning."

He staggered past her to the kitchen and pulled out a can from his bare refrigerator, bare except for a six-pack of Coors.

"Could I make you some coffee?" she asked.

"If you can find some. I'll stick with the beer." He popped open the can and guzzled down the contents quickly. "What did you say your name was?" He eyed her as she peered into his cabinets for a jar of instant coffee.

"H..hu, Harriet. Harriet Emerson. You forgot that you invited me for a drink." Having found the coffee and whatever else she needed, she put water in the teakettle and set it on the stove.

He lit a cigarette and got another beer. "I don't remember much when I drink." He gazed at her through a haze of smoke. She turned her head away, glancing around his tiny kitchen. A roach crawled up the wall. Her eyes followed it as it meandered towards the cabinets and then down towards the sink.

He rose quickly and knocked it to the floor with his hand and crushed it beneath his feet.

"Hate them things! Hate this place! Hate L.A.!" He began to curse but quickly apologized. "Soon as I get enough money, I'm outta here. Going back home, buy me some land, and..."

The piercing whistle from the kettle drowned out his words. Hazel leaped up and shut off the stove. As she measured out the coffee and poured water into two cups, she responded, "I hate L.A. too. I'd love to live in the country," she lied. Manny went on about his dream house. After a while, she brought the conversation back to the present.

"Tonight, at the Silver Spoon, you seemed upset about something."

He lit another cigarette and stared at his cup. "Got mixed up in something I wish I hadn't." He shook his head. "But I can handle it." Changing the subject, he returned to his dream house. Hazel tried unsuccessfully to bring the conversation back to the Silver Spoon.

Suddenly he said, "I know you from somewhere." He stared at her like an artist preparing to paint her portrait.

"I do that sometimes myself. I see a face and think I know that person," she laughed nervously. "Turns out we all have doubles or so I've heard." She noticed he no longer looked drunk. And the longer he stared, the more uncomfortable she felt.

"I never forget a face." He seemed to be trying hard to place her. Time for me to go before he remembers, she thought.

After draining his cup, he rose. "I gotta take a leak. Be right back." He got up with a bit more energy than he had before. As soon as she heard him reliving himself, she made for the door, slipped out and hurried to her car. Glancing at her watch, she saw that it was after 2 A.M. As she headed for the freeway she said aloud, "A wasted evening." She plunged her hand into her purse in search of her pack of cigarettes and instead, pulled out the slip of paper she'd taken from Manny's dresser. Maybe not completely wasted, she thought as she scanned it.

48

Tricia

Momma got in real late. I heard the door open, but I didn't feel like getting up. She didn't turn on any lights, just went to bed. The next morning she told us about her evening.

"You coulda been killed," Shanell said.

"Momma, you're always telling us to be careful and you just followed this man and went to his house." I shook my head. I was mad. "If anything had happened to you..."

"Well, it didn't." Momma said. "I shouldn't have told you."

"So what do we do now?" Shanell asked.

"You two don't do anything except go to school and get your education. The term's almost over,

Tricia's about to graduate. You let me worry about this. Now run along to school before you're late."

School, yeah. Only a two weeks to go and with luck, I'll be walking down the aisle to get my diploma. It didn't seem real yet that I'd be graduating soon. I'd managed to pull up my grades and with final exams coming, I needed to spend all my spare time studying. But I was worried about Momma and this thing with Donald.

Me and Shanell had dinner ready by the time Momma got home.

"How's Ma'dear?" she asked as soon as she settled down.

Each day Ma'dear seemed a little better. She was staying awake longer and even putting together a few words. The nurse says she's even got Ma'dear to take a few steps. Once school is out, Momma said we have to let the nurse go because she can't afford her much longer. I guess we'll have to take care of her during the summer until Momma can figure something else out.

I hadn't told anybody not even Shanell about that time with Hi C though I hadn't forgotten about it. At first it felt like everybody was looking at me. Then I realized nobody could tell that I'd almost been raped. I never got up enough nerve to tell Darien about that night, and he never asked. He'd call and we'd talk on the phone, but for some reason, every time he asked me out, I'd make up some excuse not to go. I'd tell him I had to study or Momma wanted me to do something, or I'd have to take care of Ma'dear. He said he understood and didn't press me. I wondered how long I could keep making excuses. One day I'd have to tell him.

As far as my singing career went, I'd put that in the back of my mind. Whenever I'd think about it, Hi C would pop into my head like a sour note.

"What's this?" Mama said, spreading the newspaper out on the table. "MAN FOUND DEAD IN THE PARKING LOT OF THE SILVER SPOON." She held her breath.

"They're always finding people dead somewhere," Shanell said. She reached over and tried to take the newspaper from Momma. "Can I read my horoscope?"

"Who?" I asked noticing the shocked look on Momma's face.

"Manfield Jones found dead in his car at the Silver Spoon, shot three times in the head..." Momma read.

"Did you know him?" Shanell asked.

"He's the man Momma told us about. I'm getting scared." I felt my heart pounding.

"Me, too," Shanell echoed.

"You all don't have anything to worry about." Momma tried to reassure us, but I could tell she wasn't feeling too comfortable about it either.

"The last thing he said was that he just wanted to go back South and buy some land."

"Shouldn't we go to the police?" I asked.

"It's not a "we" problem. You and Shanell are not involved. It's Donald's problem. He dragged us into it. Now I've got to get us out of it. Go to the police? What would I tell them? That Manfield Jones tried to steal my purse and then I drove him home after he'd had too much to drink? They'd think I'd lost my mind or worse; that I had something to do with his death. Don't forget, they're still looking for two women in connection with Foster's death. No, I can't go to the police."

"But Momma," I said. "Suppose one of those men in the Silver Spoon comes looking for you."

"You let me worry about that."

When I suggested she tell Kevin, she said she didn't want him involved. I could see she had her mind made up. There wasn't anything me and Shanell could do.

A week went by and one evening Momma came home from work and told us she'd been laid off.

"I'm glad it's finally happened. Having it hang over my head like a brick waiting to fall hasn't been easy. At least now I can get on with other things. Maybe I can finish school quicker and take the paralegal exam.

"I'll be out of school soon and I can look for a job and help with the bills," I said. She smiled and went in to see how Ma'dear was. We sat down that night and Momma discussed ways we could manage our finances. Along with a cut in our allowances, and no more buying lunch at school, the nurse would have to be let go sooner than she'd planned.

"Since I'm going to be home, until I can find another job, I'll take care of Ma'dear."

One thing we never talked about since Ma'dear came to live with us, but something I noticed and that was Momma's relationship with her mother. It seemed like even though she looked in on Ma'dear every evening when she came home, she never spent any time with her like Shanell and me. I asked her once why she never talked to Ma'dear like Shanell and I did. She said something like she had nothing to say. It'd all been said years ago. I suspect that whatever happened between them must have been heavy. So when she said she'd be taking care of Ma'dear, I was surprised.

Staying home every day seemed to be wearing on Momma; actually, on all of us. At first it was great because every morning she'd have our lunch made to take to school and when we got home she'd cooked a fancy meal. We didn't have chores to do because Momma took care of them. The apartment was sparkling.

Every day she'd take Ma'dear to the park. And sometimes when I got in from school, Ma'dear would be sitting in the living room. Sometimes I'd even hear her and Momma having a conversation together. I didn't know what they were saying, but at least they were talking.

Soon though, Momma seemed to be getting restless. She said her unemployment check hadn't started yet, and her savings were getting low, she needed to start going out to look for a job. It had been a while since she mentioned Donald, Mr. Foster, or Manfield Jones. I was glad. I didn't want any distractions. Studying all the time was paying off for me. Final exams were next week.

49

❦

Ma'dear

"*How could you do this to me, Mama!*" *Hazel waved a letter in my face. "How could you take my mail and rip it up. You got no right!"*

"Don't you tell me what I can and can't do. Just who do you think you're talking to, Miss Sassy? Just because you're eighteen you think you're too grown to be slapped. Now just get out of my face."

I turned away and went back to frying chicken knowing full well she was right. I heard the door slam. Probably gone down to her friend Benita's house like she always do whenever she's mad. My thoughts went back to the letter. How could I have missed that one? I was the only one with the mailbox key. At first chance, I checked for it in my purse. It was still there on the key ring with all the other keys.

I went to Hazel's room and there was the letter on her dresser. I picked it up and knowing I was in the wrong, I read it. "It was so good hearing from you after all these years. I wondered why you never answered my letters." So, that was how Hazel knew. Then I remembered. The other day she asked if she could pick up the mail. I don't know where my mind was but I told her to get the keys from my purse.

After that day with the letter, Hazel became a different person. We were drifting even further apart. Not long after, when I came in from work, I found a note saying that she had run away. I called Melvin. He had joined the Air Force and was stationed in North Carolina.

"Well, Ma. She's eighteen, which means she's grown. There's nothing the police can do."

I didn't tell him the real reason she'd run away. I didn't tell him that it was because of the fight we had over Tyreshia. We had a terrible battle. She even accused me of being responsible for Sadie's death. She said Tyreshia found out that I had something to do with my best friend's death. Said she hated me and didn't care if she never saw me again. The next day, she was gone.

I had a dream one night about Willie Joe and Sadie. I dreamed about the good times in Harlem, the house rent parties, and the dances at Rockland Palace and the

Savoy. I remember the times we went to the Apollo Theatre to see Buck and Bubbles and Moms Mabley. Those were happy times. When I woke up, I knew I had to find Hazel and explain.

The people I worked for, Dr. and Mrs. Winters, were going on vacation soon and I knew if I asked Mrs. Winters, she'd let me go for a few days. They'd be closing down the house anyway until they came back.

A few days later, I boarded the Greyhound bus to Baltimore and armed with an address Edna had given me, I took a taxi there. The taxi stopped in front of an old run down looking rooming house. I stood for a moment looking up at the three-story building. It seemed like every one of them large windows was open and people had their heads stuck out. It was the noisiest place I'd been to in a long while. Children playing out in the street, running every whichaway, cars honking and zipping up and down the street, music blaring.

I walked up the stairs and knocked on the first door I came to. I heard a baby crying. After a few minutes, somebody yelled, "Who is it!" A young girl about seven years old opened and peeked up at me, her face stained with dirt. I asked for Edna's room.

"Don't nobody named Edna live here." She slammed the door in my face. I knocked on another door and another until finally, an old lady in a wheel chair told me that a woman named Edna with a strange acting daughter use to live there but had moved.

"Don't know where."

I had run into a blank wall. Disappointed, not knowing where to turn, I took the bus back home. My baby was gone and I didn't know where to look. Yes, she was eighteen, but that didn't make no difference. She was still my child.

The feeling of hopelessness gradually went away. As they say, "Time heals all wounds," and even though I missed her, I had to go on with my life. Somehow I knew she was all right and that she'd come home when she needed me.

Little did I know how true that statement was. Eight months later, when I got home from work one evening, so tired I could hardly drag myself up the steps, who should be sitting outside my door but a very pregnant Hazel.

"Mama, I'm sorry," was all she said. She didn't have to say any more. I was so happy to see her; my tiredness seemed to disappear. I didn't ask her about her pregnancy or where she'd been. It wasn't important. We didn't say anything about Tyreshia either.

It didn't matter. My baby was back and she needed me. We needed each other. A month later, Tricia was born.

50

❧

Shanell

Shanell was feeling out of sorts. She'd stayed home from school on the pretense of being sick. Actually, she hadn't been able to sleep and had been awake most of the night. At first Hazel had insisted she go, with school ending soon. Then she relented especially since she had job-hunting to do and Shanell could watch Ma'dear while she was out.

The sun was bright, the weather mild, little smog, and generally a very pleasant day. Shanell got up around eleven o'clock and tiptoed into her grandmother's room. Hazel had made breakfast so there was little for Shanell to do except remove the dishes and tend to any needs Ma'dear might have.

Ma'dear was awake. She smiled at Shanell when she walked into the room and patted the bed for the girl to sit.

Anna Christian

"How you doing this morning, Ma'dear?" She kissed her grandmother on the cheek, climbed on the bed and curled up beside her.

"What'chu doing home? Saturday?" Ma'dear said, her voice barely above a whisper. Each day she seemed to be getting stronger. The doctor was pleased with her progress. Though she hadn't fully regained her speech, she could get out enough words to be understood.

"Nobody's home but me. I didn't feel well. Would you like to go to the park?" Shanell asked. "It's a beautiful day? I'll get dressed; then I'll ask our neighbor, Mr. Frazier, to help me take you downstairs and we'll have a picnic in the park. Okay?"

Shanell took a quick shower, dressed, made sandwiches, packed them in a bag, and went in to help her grandmother. For a month now, Ma'dear had been able to move around by herself. She had regained enough strength to go to the bathroom by herself and with some difficulty, washed herself. However, because it took so much effort, she tired easily and therefore, seldom ventured far from the bedroom. On rare occasions, the girls and sometimes Hazel, would help her into the living room to sit and watch TV together.

This morning, sitting on the side of her bed, she tried to put on her dress but it was hung up around her neck. Shanell helped her get into the dress and into the wheel chair. She pushed her to the door and then went down to the Fraziers. Mr. Frazier followed her back up to her apartment and carried Ma'dear down to the street.

"She's looking much better. How's she feeling?" Mr. Frazier asked Shanell. Turning to Ma'dear, he shouted, "HOW ARE YOU FEELING, MRS. WASHINGTON?" Shanell sighed. Why do people act like she can't hear, she thought. Ma'dear shook her head and smiled.

"YOU TAKING HER TO THE PARK? IT'S A NICE DAY FOR IT. I WISH I WAS GOING THERE MYSELF," He laughed as he caught himself. "Now when you come back, be sure to call me. I'm happy to be of service to a pretty little girl like yourself." He ambled back up the steps and went inside.

"Let's see if we can't find a good place for a picnic," said Shanell as she wheeled her grandmother down the block and across the street to the park entrance. She passed several cement tables. Though they were empty, they were dotted with pigeon waste. Some were covered with graffiti. Others had broken benches, while still others were heavily stained.

"Looks like we'll have to have our picnic over here." She stopped at a bench near the sandbox and swings. Unwrapping one peanut butter sandwich, she handed it to her grandmother. She ate the other one as they sat and watched the children play. Suddenly, she saw one child she recognized.

"Tommy, stop kicking sand on that girl!" she heard someone yell from some distance away. Then she saw the young woman coming over to the child. It was Gloria, the girl she had met several months ago. Shanell considered calling out to her. She stopped herself remembering how Gloria had left her with her two children at her apartment and didn't get back until late. Gloria grabbed Tommy around the waist, dangling him precariously on her hip, his head bumping against her, she hauled him over to the stroller where his sister Chemise sat howling. Shanell watched Gloria as she spanked Tommy on the behind and jammed a pacifier in Chemise's mouth. Holding Tommy securely by the arm, she propelled the stroller down the path towards Shanell. As they drew closer, Shanell stood up to say hello, but Gloria didn't glance her way. "Just wait until I get your ass home." She pulled Tommy along as they walked past.

"She didn't even remember me," Shanell mumbled once they were out of earshot. Another thing Shanell noticed with surprise - Gloria's swollen belly. She was expecting her third child!

"I knew her once," She explained to Ma'dear. "I babysat for her. She went out to the store and was supposed to come right back but she didn't. Not until late and I got in trouble with Momma.

I use to wonder why Momma was so strict with Tricia and me. Now I see. She didn't want us to end up like Gloria."

"Your Momma's strict on you both, because I was with her," Ma'dear said in a hoarse whisper.

"You mean you watched over her every move? Didn't want her to go out with boys until she was grown?"

Ma'dear smiled. "Mothers want best for children. Hard because don't want make same mistakes." Shanell had to lean close to Ma'dear. Her speech was slow and halting. It took a lot of effort.

"You didn't get into no trouble when you was growing up, did you? You grew up in the South. There wasn't no way you could get into trouble down on the farm. Not like now with drugs and gangs and teenagers having babies. Things are much worse now."

"Times changed but same. No drugs or gangs but girls having babies. Not accepted, sent away. Worse, no opportunity. Had to know your place."

Shanell knew what she meant. She'd studied about the Civil Rights Movement in school.

"I'm glad I didn't live back then."

"Left South when little older than you. Ran off New York."

"You did? I didn't know that. Did you go alone?"

Ma'dear's eyes misted. Her voice dropped even lower. "No, with friend Sadie." She laughed. "Sadie, more energy than wild horses. Talked loud always telling jokes."

In her halting way, Ma'dear told Shanell about coming North and having no skills, getting her first job working in service. Getting married.

"To Grandpa Washington?"

"No, first husband name Willie Joe Harris. Died suddenly, Melvin's father."

"What happened to your friend Sadie?"

Ma'dear coughed. "Thirsty." Shanell looked into the bag she'd packed with lunch. All that remained was a warm can of Ginger ale. She carefully opened it and held it up for Ma'dear to take a sip.

"Tired," Ma'dear whispered.

Shanell waited in silence for her grandmother to continue. They sat a little longer and she noticed Ma'dear had fallen asleep. The sun beat down on them. She felt a bead of sweat roll down her cheek.

"Guess we'd better be getting home." She tossed the empty paper bag, used napkins and empty soda can into the trash bin and started for home pushing Ma'dear slowly so as not to wake her.

Once she got her grandmother home, and in bed, Shanell turned to go, but Ma'dear held her hand. Once again she patted the space on the bed to indicate she wanted her granddaughter to sit beside her for a while. Shanell noticed tears in the corner of her grandmother's eyes as she tried to speak, slowly at first; as she went on, her voice grew stronger. She told Shanell about her life in New York with Willie Joe and Sadie. After Melvin was born, she sent him to live with her mother. She spoke about meeting and marrying Grandpa Washington and Hazel's birth.

Shanell realized that Ma'dear wasn't talking to her; it was as if she needed to relieve herself of a weight she'd been carrying so long. Finally, when she stopped, after a long moment of silence, Shanell asked, "How did your first husband die? Was he killed in a car accident or lynched or something?"

"No, he just got sick and died."

"Tell me more about Sadie. What happened to her?"

Ma'dear didn't answer. She turned over on her side, away from her granddaughter. Shanell took that as a sign her grandmother wanted to sleep, so she turned off the TV and tiptoed from the room.

That evening as the family sat down to dinner, Shanell related her afternoon to her mother and sister. "Ma'dear and me was talking about the time when she was young. She told me about her first husband. I didn't know she'd been married before. Did you, Momma?"

Hazel seemed preoccupied. She'd been out all day, trying to find another job without much luck.

"Yes, I think I remember something about it. Melvin told me."

"She said her husband got sick and died. He wasn't that old, was he?" asked Shanell, as she sprinkled a generous amount of salt over everything on her plate.

Hazel frowned, "No, I don't think so." She picked up the saltshaker and moved it to the far side of the table out of her daughter's reach.

"Ma'dear told me about her friend Sadie, too. She didn't say much though."

"Why are you so curious? Sound like a detective or something," Tricia said. Hazel didn't respond.

"Did you know Sadie, Momma?" asked Tricia, reaching over for a slice of bread.

"I heard your grandmother speak of her at one time," said Hazel.

"Wasn't she your friend Tyreshia's aunt?" continued Tricia.

"Now who's being nosey?" Shanell said.

Looking up from her plate, she glared at Tricia. "How do you know about Tyreshia?" Hazel asked in a harsh voice.

"I remember when I was about ten, this woman came to the house," responded Tricia, seeming not to notice her mother's sudden tenseness.

"It's a long story and it's not important," Hazel answered hoping to close the matter. They ate in silence when suddenly the phone rang, startling everyone. Shanell jumped up to answer it.

"It's for you, Momma," she said handing the phone to her mother. "It's the police."

The old fear that had gripped them when they were involved with Donald and his troubles came back hovering over the family like a time bomb. Each had believed or hoped that the matter had been resolved, though Hazel knew better. As she spoke into the receiver, Shanell and Tricia strained to listen.

"They want me to come down to the station tonight," she said as she hung up the telephone.

"You're not going, are you?" Shanell asked. "Why do they want to see you? What for?"

Tricia jumped up. "I'm going with you."

Hazel tried to dissuade her but her daughter insisted.

"Can I come too?" Shanell asked.

"No, you stay home and look after Ma'dear." Hazel gathered her things as she and Tricia started for the door, "And clean up the kitchen," she called before going out.

Once they had gone, Shanell felt dissatisfied. So many unanswered questions. Ma'dear was asleep, the apartment was quiet, and TV was a wasteland. She didn't feel like calling her friend Babe, and after she finished washing and putting away the dishes, pots and pans, she felt restless. Reluctantly, she decided to finish the boring book she needed to write a report on for her English class.

Trying to remember where she'd laid it, she looked around the living room and the bedroom she and Tricia shared. Then she remembered. She'd left it in Ma'dear's room. Quietly slipping into the room, she looked around. Ma'dear's gentle snoring comforted her somewhat. Searching quickly for the book she spotted it on the floor beside Ma'dear's suitcase. The suitcase was open and an old notebook was sticking out. Curiosity got the best of Shanell. She slid the notebook from beneath her grandmother's winter clothes that Hazel had promised to pack away one day. Shanell recognized it as a journal written in her Ma'dear's distinct handwriting. She glanced over at her sleeping grandmother and then at the notebook.

Sliding silently to the floor, her back resting against the closet, she opened the notebook and started reading.

"I remember when I was a little girl..." Before long, Shanell sank deep into the yellowed pages. When she heard her grandmother's deep sigh, she jumped. Pushing off feelings of guilt, she stashed the notebook beneath her tee shirt and quietly made her way from the room. Once in her and Tricia's bedroom, she propped herself on the bed and continued to read.

Two hours later she heard the front door open and knew that her mother and Tricia were back. She greeted them, not even asking details about their adventure at the police station. Once her sister and mother had gone to sleep, she slipped backed into her grandmother's room and put the notebook back where she found it. Tomorrow she'd continue where she left off. In those hours of reading her grandmother's journal, what she'd learned about Willie Joe and Sadie whetted her appetite for more.

51

❧

Tricia

When Momma and I walked into the police station, I was more than a little nervous. This was the first time I'd been in a place like that. I had expected it to look like those places I'd seen in those old movies set in a big city, a grimy old building with a tall ceiling, dingy walls and huge wooden desks where a mean sergeant peered down on everybody, and sweaty cops hauled in suspects; noisy with a lot of shouting.

I was surprised to see how the place looked like a regular office with cubicles, like where Momma worked. It was neat, quiet and except for the men in uniforms, I wouldn't have believed this was a police station. Don't get me wrong, it didn't look all that innocent but it wasn't a bit like I had expected.

While Momma went up to speak to an officer at the desk, I sat down and waited. On the walls I saw photos of all the past police chiefs. There was only one other person who seemed to be waiting, a small man who looked like he'd seen better days. He smelled bad, like he needed a bath, his head kept dropping to his chest, as if he was trying not to fall asleep but couldn't help himself. I slid to the other end of the bench as far away from him as I could.

As I sat there waiting, a tune started playing in my head, not a complete song, just a melody that had been bugging me off and on. You know how you get a jingle in your head and can't let go. I started to put words to it. It'd been a good month since I'd even thought about singing. That time with Hi C just knocked the desire right out of me. When I think about that time, I start to shake. Now, all of a sudden, I was feeling the urge to write down the words. And it's strange because I never before thought about writing a song. I never even thought I could write. That was what Kanisha did. Gracie and I just sang. Maybe it was seeing Darien again. No, I wasn't ready to deal with that.

I looked around for something to write on. Somebody had left a stack of flyers on the table next to me. I glanced at the announcement telling people about scams. "Don't be a Victim!" I didn't think anybody would miss a few pieces of paper so I took a couple and started writing on the back. I wrote down the lines in my head. I got so caught up in writing, I didn't see Momma when she came out and stood in front of me.

"Let's get out of here," she said as she headed for the door.

I shoved the paper in my pocket. "What happened inside? What did they want?" I hurried to keep up with her.

Momma stopped to light a cigarette before unlocking the car door. "I'm so sick of this mess. I wish I'd never heard of Donald Porter." She seemed to be talking to herself.

"What did they want?" I asked again.

"They found my name and address in Manfield Jones's apartment and they wanted to know if I knew him."

"What did you tell them?"

"What could I tell them? That he and his friend assaulted me, and that I picked him up at a bar and drove him home? No, I told them I didn't. I said I don't know how he got my name and address. Then one of the detectives that came to the house remembered seeing me and asked if I'd heard from Donald. I think they know there's some connection, but they haven't figured it out yet. Another thing they asked me that almost scared the life out of me. They asked about Foster. I said I never heard of him. I don't think they believed me."

She was speeding down the freeway, clutching the steering wheel. I could see she was scared and it was scaring me. But by the time we reached home, she was calm.

She smiled and said, "You go on upstairs. I'm going to see Kevin for a little while. I'll be back soon. Look in on 'Nell and your grandmother. I'm sorry I laid this all on you."

"That's alright, Momma. We're a team, right? We'll get through this thing together." I tried to smile back. "Don't worry. Are you sure you're alright?"

She pulled me over and hugged me. "You're growing up to be a beautiful young lady. You and 'Nell make me proud." She kissed me on the cheek.

I got out of the car and started up the steps. I stopped halfway up and watched the car as it disappeared down the street. As I reached in my pocket for the door key, my hand touched a scrap of paper. I pulled it out. On it was written a telephone number. Then it came back to me.

Earlier that day I had run into Kanisha. I was coming out of the grocery store and who should be on her way in but Kanisha. I hadn't seen or spoken to her in months. I use to avoid her whenever I spotted her before she saw me. We didn't like each other, I suppose. It wasn't that I didn't like her. I was uncomfortable around her. When she was high, she seemed to be mad all the time, always yelling or cursing somebody out. This time, though she had a big smile on her face when she saw me.

"Tricia, what have you been up to, girl?" She hugged me.

"Nothing much. Just trying to finish school." Pulling away carefully, I tried to hide my surprise.

"I miss you. Never heard from Gracie again. Guess she's still down south or wherever the hell she went. I guess she's planning to stay. Anyway, I wrote some new songs, got me a new manager, and a guy I met down at the studio is looking for a lead vocalist. I thought about you. You've got a fantastic voice. You got a piece of paper? I'll give you his number."

She tore off a corner of the paper bag I was carrying and wrote down a name and number.

"Now, you be sure to call him."

I told her I would, though I wasn't sure I wanted to.

"Gotta go," she said. "Good seeing you." She grabbed a shopping cart and walked into the store.

I waited until she was out of sight. Then caught the bus home

52

❧

Hazel

Hazel was more shaken than she wished to admit. The police had questioned her and warned her about withholding evidence. She'd hoped that since she hadn't heard from Donald or anybody else, it had all blown over, leaving her to concentrate on finding another job. But no, the problem was still there, waiting. Damn! She thought. When will it end?

Glancing down at her watch, she debated whether to disturb Kevin. It was 1:30 AM and he was probably asleep. Yet she needed to talk to someone; she needed him. After ringing his bell several times with no answer, she remembered he was out of town on business and wouldn't be back until next week. She sat down on his steps and let the tears that she'd been holding in flow. The frustration of having lost her job; the fear of her being arrested for something she had no control over; the danger she'd put her family in because she let Donald use her home as a mail drop. Feeling completely alone and overwhelmed, she cried until she felt weak and extremely tired. When the tears finally stopped, she pulled herself up from the steps and went back to her car and drove home.

The next morning, Hazel was awakened by the telephone ringing.

"Mrs. Porter?" the voice on the other end asked.

"Yes." Hazel's voice sounded hoarse to her ears. Covering the mouthpiece, she cleared her throat.

"You don't know me but I know you and you have something that belongs to me."

Hazel sat up, her heart beat rapidly.

"Are you still there?" A man's voice asked.

"Yes, I'm still here."

"As I was saying, you have something that belongs to me and I'd like to have it back." His voice was cold and detached, like someone planning a funeral. She felt shivers run down her spine.

"You know what I'm speaking of?" he continued.

She nodded then mumbled, "Yes."

"Would you prefer I sent someone to pick it up or will you bring it to me? I'd rather not disturb your mother and your daughters if I don't have to."

"I'll bring it to you," she said, holding the receiver with both hands, aware of the trembling fear she felt.

"Good. This is what I want you to do." He waited while she got a pencil and paper to write down the directions.

"One last thing, If I were you, I wouldn't tell anyone else about this. Don't you agree?"

She nodded, catching herself. "Yes."

It was 10:15 AM. He gave her an hour. Hazel leaped out of bed, hopped in the shower, dressed, and after looking in on her mother who was asleep, she picked up the tray holding the empty breakfast dishes, and quietly closed the door. Tricia must have given her breakfast before going to school. Grateful, Hazel made herself a cup of coffee, stuffed the black book into her purse and started on her way.

Traffic was heavy driving out to the Marina. Finding a place to park was not easy. By the time Hazel reached the restaurant where she was supposed to hand over the book, it was almost 11:20. Though lunchtime was forty minutes away, Fishermen's Haven was already crowded—Middle-aged men, a few dressed in suits, others dressed casually in polo shirts and slacks, women in floral sun dresses, skirts, and some in shorts, most wearing expensive looking necklaces, earrings and bracelets.

Hazel stood for a moment in the foyer behind two couples waiting. Surveying the crowd she didn't know whom she was supposed to meet. The man on the phone had given her the address and only told her to be there in an hour.

Suddenly she felt a hand on her arm and being pulled roughly to the side. Stifling a scream, she slapped her hand over her mouth when she saw who it was.

"Donald! What are you doing here?"

"Quick, come with me. Don't look back!" He dragged her out to the parking lot and over to his car.

"Get in! Hurry!"

She scrambled in and closed the door.

He jumped behind the wheel, backed out and headed for the exit.

"What's this all about? What are you doing here?" she asked.

It was all she could do to get her seat belt fastened as he drove recklessly down the busy highway.

"Did you bring the book?" he glanced over at her.

"Who was it on the phone this morning?"

"I'll explain it all later. Did you bring the black book?"

She reached into her purse and pulled it out.

"What's going on? There's been two murders, I've been threatened, my family has been threatened, my house ransacked. I'm scared out of my wits, Donald. How could you do this to us?"

"I'm sorry I got you involved. Really I am. It's almost over."

"The restaurant. I was supposed to turn this book over to some man at Fishermen's Haven. Who is he?"

"He owns the book. If you'd given it back, you would be just as dead as Foster and Jones. You know too much."

"But I don't know anything, that's the problem. I haven't a clue about what's going on."

Just then, Donald glanced in the rear view mirror.

"A car is following us. Hold on!" He pressed the accelerator to the floor. The car shot forward doing almost 90 mph. The Mercedes behind kept up.

'Look, I'm not going to be able to outrun whoever's following. There's a place just up ahead. I'm going to pull in and let you out. Don't worry; it's always packed. You'll get lost in the crowd. Give me the book and take this." He handed her a thick envelope. "This will explain everything." He exited the freeway and made a right into the parking lot of the Malibu Colony Plaza.

"Hazel, I've always loved you. Wish I hadn't let you get away. What's that thing they say, 'you never miss the water...'"

She scrambled out of his car and dashed into the nearest souvenir store. As she watched him pull out, she saw the silver Mercedes come up, maneuvering slowly between the hordes of people climbing down from a tour bus. Donald managed to put distance between him and the Mercedes, turning left and speeding back the way they had come.

Finally getting free from the mass of people, the Mercedes reached the exit, turned left and continued on its pursuit.

"May I help you?" A smiling young lady greeted Hazel.

"No, thank you," Hazel responded. "Where's the ladies room?"

Once safely in the stall, Hazel felt her heartbeat slow. She took a deep breath, pulled out the papers Donald had given her and began to read.

"So that's what this is all about," she muttered. With trembling hands, she tucked the papers back into her purse.

That evening, as the family watched the news on TV, with all the usual disasters - police standoffs, kidnapping, freeway chases, - one story in particular caught Hazel's attention. It was about a car crash on PCH.

"Earlier today," the announcer read, "there was a horrendous accident on Pacific Coast Highway. A 1975 red Datsun tumbled down the cliff, hitting the rocks below and falling into the ocean. Witnesses say the car was traveling at over 100 mph when it hit the guardrail and plunged over the side, probably killing the driver instantly."

"Donald!" Hazel drew in her breath. She felt as if she'd been punched in the stomach.

"What did you say, Momma?" Shanell asked.

"Nothing." It's over she whispered to herself as she said a silent prayer for him. Tomorrow, I'll take this envelope to the police and tell them everything I know.

53

❧

Tricia - Graduation Day

I can't believe it! It's finally over. I mean over. This is the beginning and ending of something. What I mean to say is I'm done with high school - that's the ending. It's also the beginning. I called that number Kanisha gave me. I auditioned for a record producer and would you believe, I get to make a demo next week? I've decided that even if I do make it in the music business, I'm seriously thinking about going to college in the fall. Maybe I'll major in fashion design. It's just a thought. And Darien; He's out there sitting with Momma, her boyfriend Kevin, Shanell and Ma'dear. He wants to take me out after the program.

Ma'dear's gotten a lot better; well enough to come to my graduation. Uncle Melvin and his wife bought a house and want Ma'dear to come and stay with them.

Momma told them Ma'dear's staying with us. Whatever the problem was between them, it was resolved. Would you believe Shanell had a hand in it? It seems that Nell read Ma'dear's diary and showed it to Momma. At first Momma was angry at her for reading Ma'dear's diary, but then she said she felt relieved and ashamed for all she'd put her mother through. When I asked her about it, she just said she'd tell me one day. I guess I'll never learn the details.

Oh yes, that business with Donald is over. We thought he'd been killed in a car crash, but about a week later, after Momma had gone to the police with the papers he'd given her, the senator was arrested for murder. Momma got this long distance collect call from Ghana and who should it be but Donald. He said he'd faked the crash to get the senator off his back. As far as everyone is concerned, he's dead and he wants it to stay that way. He's off on another hair brain scheme—this time in Africa. He told Momma she could keep the money. Thank goodness because she'll need it until she finds another job.

As far as that black book is concerned, Momma told us the book contained names of prominent business men and politicians, dates and phone numbers, and money paid to call girls. All in code. Sounds like a bad B movie. Anyway, Donald's partner Mr. Foster had set up an escort service and when it fell through, he started blackmailing some of the clients. Somehow the book disappeared along with $10,000. Donald stole it from his partner, of course. Before anyone could pay him off, Mr. Foster was murdered and Donald, the jerk, disappeared leaving Momma holding the bag. And then...

"Tricia, stop daydreaming, you're on."
"Now for a special treat. One of our most talented students, Tricia Porter, will sing a song she wrote for the graduating class."

Anna Christian was born in New York but has spent most of her adult life in California. A retired high school and college instructor, her first book, *Meet it, Greet it, an Defeat it, The Biography of Frances E. Williams, Actress/Activist,* was published in 1999. It was Mrs. Williams' inspiring life and her motto "Just Do It!" which motivated the author to keep this unsung hero's memory alive. She has since written and published four more books, *Daniel's Wife*, fiction/contemporary women; *Mrs. Griffin is Missing and Other Stories*, and *The Newcomer*, Bobby and Sonny Mystery Series for preteens; *The Big Table*, a children's picture book; *Then Sings My Soul* is her latest novel. Christian is the recipient of the 1999 Research and Status of Black Women in the Arts award from the Southern California Conference Branch, Women's Missionary society of the AME Church.

Contact Information:
> Anna Christian
> P.O. Box 1266
> Moreno Valley, Ca. 92556-1266
>   email: anadoodlin@yahoo.com
> Websites: www.anachristian.com
> www.francesplace.org

www.ingramcontent.com/pod-product-compliance
Lightning Source LLC
Chambersburg PA
CBHW071305200626
46813CB00015B/41